Jessie's Way
The Last Word

Jan Womble

PUBLISH AMERICA

PublishAmerica
Baltimore

ISBN: 1-4241-1163-3
PUBLISHED BY PUBLISHAMERICA, LLLP
www.publishamerica.com
Baltimore

Printed in the United States of America

Jessie's Way

The Last Word

Jan Womble

Chapter 1

Warily eyeing his client, Mark Sanders sat across from her at his desk. She was definitely not happy with him, but he didn't think he had done anything so terrible.

"Do you mean to tell me that you had me come all the way to New York just for a phone conference that I don't even want to have?" Jessica Martin demanded of her erstwhile agent.

Mark calmly attempted to explain his position on the business matter at hand. "Look, Jessie. This is a great offer, and as your representative, I needed to talk with you in person before the conference. I don't think this is something we can refuse to consider. Besides, you know that I wouldn't get you up here for no good reason," he said, trying to mollify her.

Jessie had to admit that in the past Mark had always been considerate of her wish not to be dragged away from her Mississippi home any more than absolutely necessary. But here she was in New York, as much a fish out of water as ever.

"I have to give you that one. You *have* been very good about that, so what am I doing here now?"

Mark studied her for a few moments before answering her question. At thirty-one, she was not a physically attractive woman. At least fifty pounds over weight, she wore ill-fitting, nondescript slacks and shirt. Her long blonde hair was pulled into its usual tight little knot at the back of her head, which only served to accentuate her rather large nose. Nor was her appearance enhanced in the slightest by the horn-rimmed glasses, which obscured her hazel green eyes.

On the other hand, she had a very engaging personality, which endeared her to all who met her.

Mark had found her to be the kindest, most caring, and most completely honest person with whom he had ever worked, *and* she had a great sense of humor. He knew that she was a Christian, which was what had influenced her to be the kind of person she was. However, she had never tried to shove her Christianity down his throat the way some people had. He knew that she simply cared about him as a human being and conducted business with the highest level of integrity. He had certainly hit the jackpot when he'd agreed to represent her after she'd written her first novel almost seven years ago. Ever since that time, she'd written nothing but best sellers, the last one having been a monumental success.

"Raymond Hanson wants to purchase the rights to your last novel," Mark reminded her.

"That much I know. What I don't know is who Raymond Hanson is and why he would want rights to anything I had written," she came back.

"You're kidding! Right?" He sounded incredulous.

"I assure you that I am not kidding. Who is he, anyhow?"

"He's that famous actor who formed his own production company. He does the directing as well, and he's had a couple of mildly successful hits. He wants to make a movie of your novel because he can smell an Oscar," he informed her. Then, hoping to persuade her, he continued, "You realize this could be a very lucrative venture for you. Plus it could get your name out there even more."

"Mark, you know that I don't care about the money and fame. I'm just not sure about selling the rights to any of my work. I have doubts about how it could be presented," she confessed with a concerned expression on her face.

"That's why Mr. Hanson wanted to talk with you on the phone. He wants to try to explain the situation to you," he said.

"Why couldn't he have just called me at home?" she wondered out loud.

Mark was beginning to lose patience. "I have never given out a client's phone number, with or without permission. I have too much respect for your privacy and confidence in me to ever do that. This is why I needed for you to come here."

Jessie could see the logic of his position and greatly appreciated his looking out for her welfare. She told him as much.

Mark acknowledged her appreciation with a smile and inquired, "Will you talk with him then? He's waiting for the call."

Jessie hesitated before answering him. She still didn't know who Raymond Hanson was. She hadn't been to a movie in years. Though she had been quite a fan of the older programs, the only television she watched these days was the local newscast. But she supposed she owed it to Mark to at least give Mr. Hanson a chance to explain.

"All right," she conceded, albeit a little reluctantly.

"Great. It'll be fine. You wait and see," he replied as he reached for the phone.

Mark dialed the number, and after several rings, someone apparently answered because he responded, "Hello. Mr. Hanson? This is Mark Sanders." A pause. "Yes, she's here with me now. I'll put you on speaker." He pushed a button on the phone's control panel and asked, "There. How's that?"

"Fine. Miss Martin, I'd like to introduce myself to you and get you to hear me out on a proposal for your last novel," he began, his voice strong and confident, yet low and soothing—almost like velvet.

"Mr. Hanson, Mark has given me a few of the details about your proposal, but to save you any more time and effort, I have to tell you that I just don't think that I'm interested in a movie deal," she jumped in, hoping that would be the end of it. She totally ignored the face that Mark was making at her.

"Please, call me Ray," he offered, evidently unfazed by her words.

"Ray, then. You can call me Jessie. Did you hear what I said?" she asked, in an effort to keep on point.

"I heard *you*, but I don't think *I'm* getting a fair hearing," he lamented.

"Mr. Hanson…" she began, but he interrupted.

"Ray," he reminded her quietly.

"Ray, I just don't have a good feeling about this." She was at a loss as to how to explain her reluctance.

"Look. I see now that this phone conference is not working. I can deal better with people in person. Will you allow me to meet with you at your convenience?" His tone was extremely persuasive.

"I'm going back home tomorrow," she told him. After only one day in New York, she was homesick for Mississippi.

He was silent for a few seconds and then, "May I come there to talk with you, Jessie?"

Using her first name at that particular moment was a smart move on his part. Jessie was completely disarmed. Such was the effect of his voice on her. Imagine what he must be like in person!

"Please," he reinforced his request.

Still hesitant, she glanced at Mark for a sign as to what she should do. Signaling that the decision was hers, he just shrugged his shoulders.

Jessie was more reluctant than ever to have someone at her home trying to do a hard sell on her.

"Jessie, hello," Ray prompted from the other end of the line.

She sighed heavily and came to a sudden decision. "Okay. You can come, but I warn you. If I begin to suspect your motives, I'll toss you out on your rear!"

He chuckled at her reaction. "I assure you that my only motive is to acquire rights to a work that I firmly believe has Oscar potential."

"We'll see," was her only response.

"May I get directions to your home and your telephone number, in case something comes up? I'm sure Mr. Sanders can give you my number." At her inquiring glance, Mark nodded affirmation.

She rattled off her home number and then began giving him directions to her house. "You'll fly in to Memphis International Airport and then…" She stopped and thought for a few moments. "There's really no easy way to tell you how to get to my place, so I'll just meet you at the airport. Okay?" she offered helpfully.

"I really appreciate that. I'd hate to get lost out in the sticks somewhere."

Jessie didn't know whether or not he was trying to be insulting, but she took offense anyway.

"I know that the Mid-South may not be as cosmopolitan as Hollywood, but I don't think you'd be in the same danger as Ned Beatty in 'Deliverance,' you know," she replied in an accusing tone.

"I didn't mean to imply that I would. I'm sorry if I offended you." He seemed sincere.

Jessie tried to get control of herself. She didn't know why she was being so waspish with the man. She didn't even know him, so she apologized, "No. I'm sorry. I shouldn't be so sensitive. Anyway, when do you plan to come?"

"How does next Monday work for you?" he suggested.

That was fine with her. "Good. I'll call soon and give you the specifics. I look forward to seeing you then. Anything else? Mr. Sanders?" he asked.

"No. That's all. Goodbye." And Mark broke the connection.

Jessie looked at Mark and shook her head. "I don't know what I've gotten myself in to! You think it's too late to cancel?" she said only half joking.

"Don't worry. Mr. Hanson's a nice guy. It'll be okay," Mark said in an attempt to reassure her.

After a restless night, Jessie tried to get some sleep on her flight to Memphis, but she was too keyed up to rest. Flying always did that to her, especially these days. So she just let her mind wander to events that had led to the impending visit of Raymond Hanson.

Her life had certainly changed in the past few years. First her mother had developed severe heart problems, which had required that she have constant care. Jessie's father had taken on the task of caring for her fulltime, with Jessie, an only child, pitching in as much as she could

9

despite her teaching job in Memphis. Then her beloved dad had been killed in an accident on an icy road on his way home from the pharmacy.

Heartbroken over the loss of her father, Jessie couldn't bear the thought of putting her mother in a nursing home, so she quit her job and stayed home to care for her. Sometimes the tedium of caring for someone who was so ill would weigh heavily upon Jessie. She would sit by her mother's bedside for hours with nothing to do, until she finally decided to try her hand at writing. It was something that she'd never considered before, but, as it turned out, it proved to be something for which she had a natural talent.

When she'd finished her first novel, her mother had been so proud of her and had urged her to find an agent to help her get published. She came across an agent named Mark Sanders, and the rest, as they say, was history. Mrs. Martin had lived long enough to see her daughter become a famous author. Her writing had gone so well that after her mother's death Jessie had not gone back to her teaching job, opting for a writing career instead.

Jessie couldn't bring herself to live alone in her parents' house, so with some of the money that she'd earned from her novels, she had built the house that she'd always dreamed of owning. Located in a wooded area at the front of her parents' property, her dream home was constructed of yellow pine logs and ledgestone. Since she knew that this was a one-time opportunity, she had spared no expense and had gotten exactly what she wanted. So far, she had been very happy there. That was why she always dreaded the trips that took her away from her home, even though she was alone there a good bit of the time and would likely remain that way.

Most of her life, Jessie had loved working with children and, until her late teens, had cherished the thought of being a mother some day. However, her doctor had discovered a serious uterine problem and had advised her and her parents that at the tender age of seventeen she would need to have a hysterectomy. For some time afterward, the fact that she could never have children had colored her outlook on life. She had gone through a brief period of depression, but the love and support of her parents and her faith in God had gotten her through those dark days. Though the depression was gone, she still had trouble developing relationships with men, most of whom would naturally want a wife who could bear children. Consequently, she didn't date at all and pursued her writing career and overeating instead.

Jessie was brought out of her reverie by the announcement to fasten seatbelts. Soon she would be home and would begin the task of preparing for her guest, a prospect that caused her more than a little consternation. Normally she loved having company, but she still had misgivings about this visit.

Chapter 2

On Monday, her stomach knotted with nervous tension, Jessie awaited the 1:00 PM arrival of Raymond Hanson's flight. She wasn't sure why she was putting herself through this ordeal, but she'd given her word and couldn't back out now.

Since the flight was on schedule, Jessie tried to get as close to the gates as security would allow. Mr. Hanson had assured her that he would be able to recognize her from the photo on her novel, but she had thought it prudent not to tell him that she wouldn't know him from Adam's housecat. Not knowing if he was vain, she didn't want to risk this meeting's starting off on the wrong foot.

Suddenly the doors opened and passengers began filing down the long concourse to the gates. Trying to guess which passenger was the right one, Jessie studied each man carefully. She didn't want to make an embarrassing mistake and pick the wrong one, so she just sort of hung back and watched.

When she first saw him, she somehow knew that he was the one. He was tall, dark, poised, and self-assured, *and* he was also the best-looking man that she'd ever seen. Jessie's heart gave a strange little leap into her throat, and her palms felt clammy. Either she was having a heart attack, or she was falling in love. Jessie thought that the former might prove less painful in the long run.

Before he reached her, she fought to regain control of herself and wiped her hands on her seat. As he approached, his face broke out into a smile of recognition that was intended to charm, which, in fact, it did. "Jessie! It's so good to finally meet you!" he enthused, as he took her outstretched hand.

She called upon every ounce of dignity and grace that she could muster and returned his greeting with her usual friendly smile and, "It's nice to meet you, too, Ray."

She noticed the bag he was carrying and inquired, "Is that your only luggage?"

"Yes. I usually travel light," he replied.

"So I see. Ready to go?"

"You're the boss."

"Let's go then. We have quite a trek to the parking lot." And she led the way out of the terminal.

In an attempt to make polite conversation, she asked, "How was your flight?"

He responded, "Not bad. This is my first time flying in to Memphis, or anywhere in the South, for that matter. So it's been different – a lot more laid-back than flying in to LaGuardia or O'Hare, for instance."

Jessie smiled at him. "Oh, I know what you mean. Even with 9/11 security in effect, the pace is a lot more relaxed here than y'all have in the big cities."

She noticed that Ray was having difficulty trying to hide a grin and inquired suspiciously, "What's so funny?"

"I'm sorry. I'm not laughing at you. It's just that I'm not used to being around Southerners, and I find myself completely fascinated by the expression *y'all*," he confessed. Then he continued, "You have to admit that it's really a very colorful way of talking."

Jessie conceded, "I suppose it could seem that way, but I've never really noticed. It's what I'm used to. It's just natural."

By this time, they'd reached the parking lot, and Jessie led the way to her car, a Dodge Durango. After unlocking the doors and stowing Ray's bag, they were ready to leave the airport.

Before she cranked the car, Jessie looked at him and asked, "It'll take a good hour to get to my house. Are you hungry now? Or can you wait till then?"

"I'm still on Pacific time, so I'm not hungry yet. How about you?" He smiled at her again.

Jessie took a moment to wonder if he knew the effect that his smile and warm brown eyes had on her or any other woman, for that matter, and then responded calmly, "No. I'm fine. I prefer eating at home anyhow. I can rustle up something for us there."

She started the car and headed for the exit. When she stopped at the booth to pay for parking, Ray pulled out his wallet.

"Don't be silly. I've got it covered. Besides, you're my guest," she insisted.

He tried arguing with her, "But I invited myself."

"I could have said no," she reminded him.

He shook his head at her and chuckled. "Are you always going to have the last word in our association?"

As she threaded her way toward Highway 78, she gave his question more serious consideration than it warranted and then replied, "Only in important matters."

"I can see that I'm out of my league here, *and* you have the home advantage," he opined, only half serious.

"I promise that I'll take it easy on you. I'll be fair."

"And I promise to remind you of your promise before I leave."

As she turned the car on to Highway 78, she shot him a quizzical look and started to respond.

Ray interrupted her, "Let's not argue, Jessie. It's too much of a distraction, and I want to see as much of this countryside as I can. If we can come to an agreement on your novel, it's quite possible that I would want to film the project here."

"Really? In the sticks?" She couldn't resist that little jab at him.

He sighed and glared at her in frustration. "That last word, Jessie?"

"Okay. I'm sorry. I'll behave," she promised like a recalcitrant child.

"That's better," he remarked, a broad grin splitting his face. Mark

Sanders had warned him about her personality, and he was proving to be quite accurate. Ray found himself enjoying her quick wit.

Jessie opened her mouth to make a retort, but she thought better of it. Then Ray turned to study the passing scenery.

"Exactly where are we now?" he wanted to know.

"We're now entering Marshall County, Mississippi," she answered, sounding like a tour guide.

In a few minutes, she exited the four-lane and drove east for several miles on a winding, tree-lined country road. Finally, after a couple more turns on to more narrow roads, she arrived at her gated driveway. She reached for the remote that would open the automatic gate.

"Whew! I'm certainly grateful that you didn't leave me to my own devices in trying to find your house. I would have been lost from the airport on," he admitted ruefully.

When the gate had opened, Jessie drove the car through, closed the gate from the other side, and nodded, "Yes, I know. I've lived in this neighborhood all my life and naturally have no problems finding places here, but I've discovered that giving directions to my house is almost impossible. In fact, I usually just tell people that you can't get here from there and then meet them somewhere easier to find."

As the house came into view, Ray gave a long, low whistle of appreciation of what he saw. It was a sprawling, yellow pine log home, nestled among the trees. A wraparound, covered porch flanked the front and sides of the house. The green metal roof glistened in the early afternoon, January sun. The lawn in close proximity to the house consisted mostly of the stamped concrete drive and parking area and flowerbeds filled with a variety of colorful shrubbery.

"Wow! I never expected anything like this!" He looked at her and admitted, "Somehow I never pictured you as the log home type."

"Oh, yeah? What type *did* you see me as, if I might be so bold?" she asked, her curiosity getting the better of her.

"I guess the Victorian that you described in *The Sixth Commandment*," he replied.

As she pulled up to the garage door and opened it with another remote, she confessed, "That's my parents' house."

"If I may, I'd like to see it before I leave, but first I want a tour of this house. It's fascinating!"

"Thanks. Why don't we start the tour with the garage?" she asked, tongue-in-cheek. Suddenly, a thought struck her. "By the way, I just assumed that it would be okay with you if I put you up here in the guest suite on the back of the house. You'll have all kinds of privacy there, and it is a very long drive to the nearest lodging."

"That sounds great. You're being very accommodating about this whole visit. It must be that Southern hospitality that I've always heard about," Ray added gratefully.

"I hope you'll remember those kind words when we begin to talk business," Jessie came back.

"Hmm. I'll try," he qualified.

Jessie closed the garage door, and they got out of the car, Ray retrieving his bag from the back seat.

"May I ask you a personal question?" he queried.

"I'll probably ask *you* some later, so sure. Fire away."

Ray hesitated. He wasn't certain that he liked the sound of that, but he asked his question, nonetheless. "Why did you build a house this big?"

Jessie felt relieved that his question was so easy to answer. "Simple. I have a lot of friends and aunts, uncles, and cousins who like to come visit.

"In that case, it makes perfect sense," he acknowledged.

She led him through the garage entry into the laundry room and, grabbing a set of keys from a hook, informed him, "I'll show you the guest suite first." Jessie headed toward a French door opening out onto a screened porch. Across the porch was another French door leading into a bedroom with a private bath, a bar with a small sink, microwave, and refrigerator, and a built-in desk equipped with a computer.

Jessie explained about the computer. "Sometimes when I have a lot of company *and* work to do, I come out here where I can get away from the noise."

As he let his appreciative gaze wander around the rustic luxury of the suite, Ray placed his bag on the floor. The walls were logs with white chinking, and the ceiling was tongue-and-groove yellow pine. There was a queen-sized log bed with a homemade quilt spread over it. In front of the bed, was a ledgestone fireplace with a gas log insert. An old-fashioned wardrobe that had been converted into a TV cabinet, an antique dresser with mirror, a washstand serving as a night table, and a few rustic accessories completed the furnishings of the room.

Jessie pointed toward a door and told him, "The bathroom is through there. I think you'll find everything you need. Just let me know if you need anything else. Now. Do you want the fifty-cent tour, or do you need to freshen up or eat or what?"

He fished two quarters out of his pocket and, handing them to her, said, "I'm ready for the tour."

Jessie laughed and told him, "It was only an expression, you know."

"I know, but I wanted the last word just this once," he joked.

She smiled, shook her head at him, and led him from the guest suite. From there, she crossed the screened porch out onto a deck from which one could enjoy the view of a grassy slope that led down to a grove of trees surrounding a large pond.

Then they went back inside to see the rest of the house. After she had shown him the kitchen with an island, pine cabinets, granite countertops, and large dining area, she moved on to the great room, which adjoined the kitchen. It had a cathedral ceiling, and the outside wall was almost all glass, which allowed in lots of sunlight. Also there was a large gas fireplace along one wall.

The tour continued down a hallway that led to the master suite across from the study, which included a bathroom. Then she showed him two other bedrooms with a connecting bathroom between them, which were located on the other side of the great room. At the front of the house, was a sunroom.

"I have to tell you that I'm really impressed. It's a terrific house," Ray enthused. "Who designed it?"

"Thanks. An architect friend and I collaborated on it," she explained.

With the tour complete, Ray went to freshen up while Jessie began preparing a light lunch of green salad with chunks of grilled chicken.

When he returned, he sat on a stool at the island and chatted with his hostess. For a while, they enjoyed an amiable discussion as they ate, but then she asked him if he had a family.

At first, he was reluctant to speak about his family. He seemed to be considering her question and then answered, "I have three daughters and a son."

"What about your wife?"

Ray stared at her for a moment and then shrugged his shoulders as if it didn't matter and responded, "My wife Helen and I are separated."

For some reason, Jessie was disappointed with his answer. She supposed she had somehow expected more from him.

"Why?" she dared to ask him.

"Don't you think that's a little too personal?" he hedged.

"I warned you earlier that I might ask you some personal questions," she reminded him. "So why are y'all separated?"

He smiled at her *y'all* and sighed. Then he replied in a low tone, "We've drifted apart. I just don't love her anymore."

"I see." Jessie gritted her teeth and nodded as if she understood more than he was telling. "What's her name?"

"I *told* you. Her name is Helen," he said a bit testily.

"I'm talking about the woman for whom you're about to leave your wife," she responded candidly.

Ray glared at her. Mark Sanders had warned him about her directness and integrity. He wanted to stay on good terms with this woman, but he felt she had just crossed the line. "Now just a minute! You don't have any right…"

Jessie interrupted with, "Yes, I do! If you're cheating on your wife, then I won't be able to trust you. And if I can't trust you, I can't do business with you!"

He clamped his mouth shut and continued to glare at her as she glared back at him. He glanced away for a few seconds and then back. "Alissa. Her name is Alissa," he admitted huskily. "But I'm not having an affair with her, if that's what you're thinking."

"Yet," Jessie stipulated.

"Look! I admit that I'm considering leaving my wife for her, but as long as I'm married to Helen, I won't be with Alissa. I would never hurt my children that way. Will you at least trust me on that?"

"I believe that you don't *intend* to hurt your children, but can't you see that they'll be hurt anyway?" Jessie didn't know why it was so important to her to try to make him see her point.

"I've never understood how a person can love someone enough to get married and then fall out of love," she complained.

"Spoken like someone who has never been married," Ray shot at her, extremely irritated with her at that moment.

She ignored his remark and continued, "How did you treat your wife when you first fell in love with her?"

"What do you mean by that?" He was not used to being given the third degree about his personal life, and he didn't like it at all.

Jessie was leading up to a vital point, so she patiently clarified for him, "Did you send her flowers and love letters, whisper sweet nothings in her ear, hang on her every word, want to spend all your time with her? That sort of thing."

Ray considered her question. "I suppose that pretty well describes our courtship and early marriage," he admitted. "Why?"

"What do you think would happen if you started treating her that way again, acting as if you were in love with her, as if she was the most important person in your life?" Jessie proposed.

Ray's temper was about to erupt. To avoid an explosion, he said, "I've had it! I'm getting out of here!" And he strode from the room in the direction of the guest suite.

Jessie was deeply disappointed—in Ray, in the whole situation. She could see that they had no hope of working together now that he was so angry with her, and that was the biggest disappointment of all.

Ray strode into the guest suite and slammed the door shut, causing the glass panes to rattle in protest. He closed the wood blinds covering the door and threw himself face up on the bed. Still fuming, he covered his aching forehead with the back of his hand. Jessie's meddling had given him a headache, and he was frustrated because he could see that

Oscar slipping out of his grasp. There was no way that she was going to sell him the rights to her novel after all this.

He breathed deeply in an attempt to calm himself down. No one had ever before presumed to ask him such personal questions. Who did she think she was, anyhow?

Face it, Ray. She's the one holding all the cards, he thought miserably.

Unable to stop himself, he lay there thinking about what Jessie had asked him. When *was* the last time he'd done those things for Helen? He tried, but he couldn't remember! It had been *that* long! Rather selfishly, he had blamed the demise of their marriage on Helen's coolness toward him, her preoccupation with the children, and his resentment at not being her top priority all the time. But could she possibly be the way she was because of his neglect? The thought had never occurred to him in over seventeen years of marriage.

He groaned and considered the possibilities. What if Jessie was right and he could reverse the trend that his marriage had taken? Was he so taken with the idea of being with someone new and exciting that he couldn't stop now? Or would he want to try again with Helen—for the kids' sakes—for all their sakes?

He sat up straight on the bed. He was astounded to realize that he wanted his family back! He missed them – all of them, including his wife! He missed her vivacity and warmth, both of which he had probably quenched, if he was honest with himself. He missed talking with her and holding her and making love to her.

He got up off the bed and began pacing. Where had all this come from? All it had taken to get him thinking about the viability of his shaky marriage had been a few simple but direct questions from someone who was practically a stranger to him.

All of a sudden, he felt a desperate need to talk to his wife. He retrieved his bag from the floor and got out his cell phone, but the signal was too weak that far out.

Great! Now what was he going to do? He supposed that he would have to humble himself and go apologize to Jessie and beg to use her phone. The very idea galled him!

He stopped short. What was wrong with him? Couldn't he see that Jessie had spoken only out of concern for him and his family? She wasn't trying to be nosey. That was another thing that Mark had told him about her. She had a genuine concern for people, especially children.

Ray left the guest suite to go in search of Jessie. He found her where he had left her. With her arms resting on the cold granite surface of the island, she appeared to be in an attitude of prayer. When he opened the door, she raised her head and immediately began to apologize with tears welling up in her eyes.

"Ray, I'm so sorry that I interfered in your private life. It wasn't my place to say those things to you. Can you forgive me?" she pleaded.

Her apology had taken him by surprise. Most people wouldn't be so quick to take responsibility for an argument or misunderstanding. But here was that directness, that innate integrity manifesting itself again. Ray couldn't remember having met anyone like her before. The fact that she would be completely trustworthy, albeit irritating, was all the more reason to want to work with her.

However, he just had to ask, "Simply out of curiosity, why do you care anyway?"

Trying to gather her thoughts to make a reasonable reply, she hesitated for a few seconds. "I think it's because I'm so fond of children and I never like the thought of their being hurt," was her honest response.

"Then why don't you have your own children and leave mine alone?" The second that the words had left his mouth, Ray wished that he could call them back. When he saw the stricken expression that crossed her face, he felt even worse.

After the way she had cross-examined him earlier, Jessie supposed that she deserved to have the tables turned. She took a steadying breath and explained in a subdued voice, "Because of a uterine condition that developed during my teens, I had to have a hysterectomy. I can't have children."

Ray could see that this was something that still caused her pain. He apologized, "Jessie, I'm sorry. I shouldn't have said that. Anyway, I didn't come in here to fight with you. I thought about the things you said to me, and I've decided to give your suggestion a try right now. I want to call Helen, but we're too far out here for my cell phone to work."

Jessie practically beamed at him. "Oh, Ray! I'm so glad that you want to talk to your wife! Please, feel free to use my phone for as long as it takes! Did you notice the phone in the guest suite?"

"Yes, thanks. I'll make the call in there."

As he turned to leave, Jessie called after him, "I'll be praying for you two."

Ray stopped. As far as he knew, no one had ever prayed for him before. He studied her expression for a few seconds to judge the sincerity of her words and could see that she was totally sincere. Deeply moved, he replied softly, "Thanks. We'll need it."

Ray glanced at his wrist. He hadn't run his watch forward to Central time. It was one thirty in California, which meant that it was naptime for their youngest daughter, four-year-old Maggie. In that case, Helen should be at home.

For a few minutes, he thought about what he wanted to say to her. Then gathering his courage, he dialed his home phone number. After three rings, someone picked up on the other end.

"Hello." He recognized Helen's voice. She sounded tired and a little dispirited.

Regret mixed with guilt stabbed at Ray's heart before he spoke to her. "Helen, it's Ray."

"Ray! Where are you? Still in Mississippi?"

"Yes. Still here." Before leaving California, he had left word with Helen of his destination in case of an emergency.

"What do you want, Ray?" she asked tersely.

How should I begin? he wondered. Then he recalled Jessie's question about how he had treated Helen when they first fell in love.

"I miss you," he replied huskily.

"You *miss* me? Really?" There was a wistful quality to her voice.

"Really." Then he continued, "When I get back to California, can I come home?" he asked like a homesick schoolboy who had been away at camp.

"If you want to," she replied breathlessly.

"I want to. Helen?" he whispered.

"What?"

"I love you."

"I love you, too, Ray," she choked.

"Bye."

"Goodbye." And then the phone went dead.

Ray hung up the phone and sat thinking about the words he and his wife had just exchanged. He realized that he had meant every word, and he could tell that Helen had been deeply affected by his admissions. At least, it was a beginning.

He went in search of Jessie again and found her as he had before—praying.

He came over to the island and sat down beside her. He could tell that she was extremely curious about his conversation with his wife, but, keeping in mind her earlier apology, she refrained from asking any personal questions.

He had a question for her. "Were you ever a psychologist?"

"No. Why do you ask?"

"Because I took your advice about treating my wife the way I did when we first fell in love and it worked!"

"Oh, I'm so glad!" she said, her expression one of relief.

"What I want to know now is where does a person who is not a psychologist and has never been married get advice like you gave me?" he asked, waiting expectantly for a brilliant answer.

Grinning, she responded, "Easy. From Dr. Laura."

"Dr. Laura? You're not referring to that conservative radio talk show, are you?" He sounded horrified.

"Yes! That's the one! Dr. Laura Schlessinger! I just love her!" she confessed, taking a great deal of enjoyment from the look on his face.

"I don't believe it! I just took advice from a radio talk show! And what's even more amazing is how well it worked! When I get back to

California, I'm going home to my family!" Ray put his arm around Jessie and gave her a kiss on the cheek.

That little gesture caught Jessie completely off guard and caused her cheeks to flame a brilliant red.

"I don't care if it was Dr. Laura or Freud. The important thing is it worked! Now. Does Dr. Laura have any advice on how to deal with you?" Ray wanted to know.

She touched her cheek where he had kissed her and laughingly assured him, "Oh, I think you're doing fine without her right now."

"Maybe so, but I think I need to rest up before I tackle the job of doing business with you," Ray admitted ruefully. "Can we talk later this evening?"

"Certainly."

"I'll see you then."

As he left the room, Jessie wondered about the havoc he was wreaking with her emotions. This man seemed to have a profound effect on her, and she'd only just met him. She'd have to be very careful and get herself under control, or she might end up making a complete fool of herself over a married man. That was something she was not going to allow.

Chapter 3

After dinner that evening, Jessie and Ray finally got down to a serious discussion about his offer.

They sat in the great room as he explained to her why he felt that *The Sixth Commandment* had Oscar potential. Then he outlined his plans for developing a viable screenplay. In concluding his selling points, he named what appeared to Jessie to be an overly generous price for the rights to her novel, not that she had any experience with such matters.

She had listened carefully while he made his spiel. He had spoken very eloquently and persuasively, but Jessie was still not sold on the idea.

"I understand and appreciate everything you've said. I'm just worried about how my work will be represented on film. Some people would want to leave out completely any references to Jesus and God. If I sell you the rights, do I have any say in how it's portrayed? What about casting? What if I don't like the actors you choose to play my characters?" she queried, her brow furrowed with concern.

"These are legitimate concerns. To be perfectly honest, we would consider your preferences in these areas, but when it came down to brass tacks, I would have the final say," he admitted candidly.

"That's what I thought. Another thing—this figure that you've named seems more than generous to me. I have to admit that I have no knowledge about such things."

"What kind of business woman are you to confess something like that right in the middle of negotiations?" he asked with a wry smile.

"Not a very good one, I suppose, but money's not that important to me. What happens to you if, God forbid, the film were not as successful as you hope? Your company would be out all that money?"

Ray was amazed again by her concern for other people! How many authors would be concerned about the success of a production company? "There's always a risk, but it's one I'm willing to take." Ray sounded confident and sure of himself. Jessie envied the air of confidence he possessed.

"Why can't I just waive the money to begin with and make payment contingent upon the success of the film and thus retain some rights to my book?" she suggested thoughtfully.

"That's not the way we do things in Hollywood, Jessie."

"Hello, Ray! This isn't Hollywood, in case you haven't noticed."

"Very funny. You knew what I meant though," he averred.

"I know. But why do we have to do it the Hollywood way? Why can't we just trust each other?"

Ray wondered if she was really as naïve as she sounded or if she was just being difficult. He was beginning to become exasperated with her.

"We have to have legal contracts to protect all parties. That's just good business, Jessie."

"Can't we modify the contracts to suit this particular case," she wanted to know.

Ray sighed in frustration, which was something he did a lot in dealing with her. "I don't know. I'd have to check with our lawyers."

"Could you do that, please?" Jessie queried sweetly.

Losing patience with her, he asked, somewhat peevishly, "Is this the only way that I'm going to get to produce this film?"

Giving his question due consideration, she paused for a moment before answering, "I think *so*."

"You know that you're making me crazy, don't you? Are you getting some kind of perverse pleasure out of being an obstructionist?

Is that why you're being so stubborn?" he vented.

Jessie bridled at that. "I resent that estimation of my character! I am not trying to obstruct anything! I'm just being protective of something that means a lot to me! If you call that being stubborn, then I guess I am!" She got up out of her chair and stormed from the room.

"Jessie! Wait!" he called after her.

She stopped, and he went over to her. Shaking his head, he whined, "You really know how to push my buttons."

When she made to continue on her way, he put his hand on her arm and apologized, "I'm sorry. We just don't seem to be able to get along much of the time, do we?" He sighed again and conceded. "All right. We'll try it your way." He glanced at his watch. It was still early. "I'll go call the lawyers now if that's okay with you."

"Fine," she replied shortly.

"Jessie, please. I said I was sorry, and I meant it," he coaxed.

She took a deep breath and gave him a weak smile. "I guess I'm not the only one who knows how to push buttons. At any rate, I accept your apology."

"Good." He seemed genuinely glad that she had forgiven him. "I'll go make that call now."

"Use the phone in the study. It's closer," she offered practically.

"Thanks."

She opened the door, turned on the light, and left him to it. Returning to the great room, she plopped down into a chair and sighed heavily. What was wrong with her? Normally she was even-tempered and worked well with others, but something about this man put her hackles up.

When Ray came back twenty minutes later, Jessie was completely lost in thought. She gave a slight start when he came and sat in the chair opposite her.

As he sat there with his elbows resting on the arms of the chair and both hands pressed together in front of him, he studied her for a few moments before speaking.

"I located my attorney, and he's confident that he can come up with a contract that will accommodate both of us. He'll try to get that completed by tomorrow and will email it to us if you'll provide him your address," he qualified for her.

"No problem." She smiled her relief that they had ostensibly worked out their differences.

"Yes, I know you're happy now that you've had the last word again," he grimaced.

In a good mood now, Jessie chuckled and reminded him, "I told you only in important matters, and to me, this is vitally important."

Ray resigned himself to the inevitable and held up his hands in surrender. Rising from his chair, he said, "I give up. I'm bushed, so if you'll excuse me, I think I'll turn in."

From her chair, Jessie looked up at him and replied, "Goodnight. Let me know if you need anything."

"Thanks." And he turned to leave the room. Then he stopped, a thought occurring to him. "By the way, do you think that we could scout the area tomorrow? I'm still interested in filming here, *if* that's okay with you."

She ignored that little dig and offered helpfully, "I can take you any place you want to go. What time would you like to get started?"

"I'm an early riser. How does eight o'clock work for you?"

"That's fine. I'm a morning person myself. After breakfast then."

"Great. Goodnight." Then he went to the French door and left the room.

———————

When they'd finished breakfast, Ray helped Jessie load the dishwasher. Promptly at eight o'clock, they left for their tour.

"Any ideas about where you'd like to start?" she asked as they got into the car.

"I'd like to see your parents' house first, please. Will they be up by now?"

"They're both deceased," she answered quietly as she headed the car toward her parents' driveway.

"I'm sorry. When did that happen?" he inquired gently, noting the pain that momentarily crossed her face.

"My dad was killed in an auto accident almost eight years ago, and my mom died about five years ago from a heart condition that had left her incapacitated for years." She went on to explain, "It was while I was taking care of her that I began writing. I might never have tried my hand at it, otherwise. God has a wonderful way of working things out. He took my parents, but he gave me writing to fill my heart."

Ray was silent. There was no bitterness in Jessie about her parents, only gratitude. It must feel good to have so much faith in something or someone. He wouldn't know.

"What about your parents, Ray? Are they still alive?"

"No. They were killed in a plane crash when I was a sophomore at USC," he told her. "It was quick, and, at least, they were together."

She nodded. "Sometimes that can be a blessing," she commiserated with him.

He smiled wryly and said, "I guess." That had been almost twenty years ago. By now, he'd come to terms with it.

As Jessie turned the car in to her parents' gravel driveway, Ray noticed that the old Victorian seemed to be well tended and asked, "So who lives here now?"

"No one. I couldn't bring myself to live here without my parents, nor could I bear to rent it out, much less sell it. So, for now at least, I just pay someone to keep the place up. I know that I'll probably have to let go of it soon though," she admitted.

Jessie stopped the car at the front of the house and taking the keys from the ignition, got out. She led the way up the steps and unlocked the front door. With a wave of her hand, she indicated that Ray should precede her.

He entered the foyer, which despite its emptiness did not seem musty or neglected. It actually gave Ray the sense that the house had been waiting for a moment such as this one to receive guests. He remarked on this sensation to Jessie.

"I know what you mean. This house deserves to have a family living in it. That's why I have to do something soon."

She showed him the entire house and then the grounds, including the old canning shed. It hadn't been used for that purpose in over fifty years, but it had been maintained for storage.

Ray seemed preoccupied and pensive. Then he shook his head and turned to look at her and say, "I feel as if I've been here before. It's exactly as you described in the novel."

"I told you so," she reminded him.

"So you did. Where to now?"

Jessie showed him other scenery that she had described so convincingly in her book. When she felt that they had seen just about everything that there was to see, she headed back to her house. Ray suggested that they needed to send her email address to his attorney.

With that accomplished, they sat down in the great room. Ray had a question and came straight to the point. "If I'm able to film this project the way I want—I mean here in Mississippi—will you let me use your parents' house as the main setting?"

As far as his using the house was concerned, she had no problem at all and told him as much.

"But…" He could tell that one was coming.

"*But* won't that mean leaving your wife and children again and, at the very least, commuting back and forth on the weekends?"

"It can't be helped. Sometimes sacrifices have to be made if the prize is worth the effort. And, in this case, I believe an Oscar *is* worth it." Here she was, worried about him and his family again! Ray didn't know what to make of her at all.

Jessie had a sudden inspiration. "Why not bring them with you?" She warmed up to her theme.

"Y'all could stay here. I have plenty of room. Your girls could share the two bedrooms. Your son could sleep in the study, where there's a Murphy bed. You and your wife could have my room, and I'd move into the guest suite."

"Absolutely not! That would be too much of an imposition," he declared emphatically.

"I say it wouldn't, and who would know better than I?" she insisted.

"Besides, the kids are in a private school in California. I just can't see them settling too well into schools here."

"So home school them for a few months."

He shook his head. "Helen has no teaching experience. It would never work."

"I have. I was a teacher before I was a writer, and I'd be glad to help," she proposed.

Ray was temporarily dumbstruck. "Why are you doing this, Jessie?" he asked in wonder.

She didn't even have to consider her answer. She knew why she had made the offer. "You've just made the first effort to pull your marriage back together. Don't you think an absence of this duration would put a strain on it, no matter how hard you tried? And that would hurt your kids."

Ray found himself actually considering her amazing offer. She was correct in her assumption about how difficult it would be to sustain his shaky marriage under those difficult conditions, but he was still hesitant. He had one more excuse. "We have a dog, too. It would be cruel to board him for several months, and the kids would never leave him."

"I like dogs, though I haven't had one since I was a teenager. What kind is he?"

"A three-year-old golden retriever named Sanson," he told her.

"Sanson Hanson?" Jessie laughed.

"Yes, I know. It was my son's idea of a little joke," he admitted ruefully.

She sobered up and looked at him with an earnest expression on her face. "Don't you see that this will work best for all the Hansons, including the dog, and I promise you that it won't place an undue burden on me. I'm used to having a houseful of company for long periods of time, and I can do what I always do. I just shut myself off in the guest suite."

"I don't know what to say, Jessie. It's a very generous offer, and I know it would be the best solution for my family, but I don't know."

"Why don't you talk it over with Helen when you get home and then let me know what you decide?" she prompted.

He sighed and nodded agreement, "Thanks. I'll do that then."

Later that day, Ray's attorney emailed the contract to Jessie's address. She printed a hard copy, and after both had carefully read it, they signed it, made a copy for Ray, and faxed a copy to his lawyer.

"Well I guess I've done all that I can do on this end for now, so tomorrow I'll be heading back home," he informed her. He got up from his chair and came and stood over her. "I can honestly say that I have never met anyone quite like you before, Jessie Martin. At times, you've been a real pain-you-know-where, but I've learned a lot, especially about myself, in my dealings with you. In case I don't get another opportunity, thanks for everything."

She smiled up at him in response, "As one pain-you-know-where to another, you're welcome. It was my pleasure."

He grinned at her and then said goodnight.

Since Ray's flight was at 11:15 AM, they had to get an early start to Memphis. Insisting that he would be fine, he had her drop him off in front of the terminal. "I've taken up enough of your time." Then he patted her hand resting on the steering wheel, and after thanking her again and saying goodbye, he grabbed his bag from the back seat and got out of the car.

"I'll be in touch." Then with a wave of his hand, he turned and entered the terminal.

Jessie didn't have time to sit there and think about how she felt. People were already getting impatient with her, so she pulled back into traffic and headed toward home.

When Ray got back to his house that afternoon, he was expecting a good bit of awkwardness between his wife and him, but Helen greeted him affectionately, as if he had only been gone a couple of days. Keeping in mind the advice Jessie had given, he took his wife into his arms and gave her a passionate kiss on the lips. Then he held her while he told her how glad he was to see her and be back home again.

"Oh, Ray!" she cried. "I've missed you so much!"

He kissed her again and found that he was enjoying the experience *and* getting excited.

Ending the kiss, he lowered his head to nuzzle the softness of her neck while his hands rubbed her back in a circular motion.

"Mmm. This feels so good, Ray."

"I know," he whispered huskily. And then he bent and picked her up to carry her up to their bedroom. He half expected she might protest that the children would hear or need her or something, but all she did was wrap her arms around his neck and look adoringly into his eyes.

"Don't you have anything to say about the kids?" he said smiling down at her.

"They're having dinner out with my mother. They won't be home until eight," she answered, a knowing little smile playing about her lips.

He entered the bedroom and kicked the door shut.

Much later when they were sitting at the kitchen table and holding hands, Helen asked Ray about his trip to Mississippi. "Did you get what you went for?"

He appeared to consider her question for a moment. Then he replied, "Yes, I suppose I did if my purpose was to be able to film this project."

"And wasn't it?"

"Well, I would have preferred a clean contract to purchase the rights to *The Sixth Commandment*, but Jessica Martin wasn't having it," he informed her.

"What's she like?" Helen wanted to know.

"Have you read the novel?"

Helen admitted that she hadn't read it.

"Just a minute." And he got up and left the room.

When he came back, he carried a hardcover book in his hand. It was a copy of Jessie's novel. Turning to the inside back cover, he showed her Jessie's photo.

She saw a plump, fairly young woman with blonde hair pinned back into a bun of sorts. She wore horn-rimmed glasses perched on her unattractively large nose.

"That's not a very flattering picture, is it?" Helen observed.

He studied it for a moment and confirmed that it wasn't. "She looks pretty much like the picture, but a picture can't give many clues to her personality. Her agent had warned me about her and had given me some ideas about what to expect, but I was still pretty much caught off guard."

"What do you mean?"

"I mean that she's the most opinionated, obstinate, interfering person that I've ever met. On the other hand, she is the kindest, most caring, most giving, and funniest person—present company excluded—with whom I have ever worked. She *can* be a royal pain in the butt."

"But you liked her," Helen guessed.

"Yes, I suppose I did," he admitted.

He went on to explain to her about his plan to film in Mississippi. Noting the dread that crept into her eyes, he stopped and said, "I know what you're thinking."

"You do?"

"Yes, I do. You're thinking that we're just now trying to put our marriage back together and that this will place more of a strain on it. You're thinking about how it will affect the kids. Right?"

"How'd you know?" she wondered.

He decided to tell her everything that Jessie had suggested about how to treat his wife and save his marriage. Then he told her about Jessie's suggestions about bringing his family with him.

"What do you think?"

"I think that I can't wait to meet this woman for myself! She sounds priceless!" She was very enthusiastic, except for one thing. "You know how Becca is going to react to all this. She won't be happy about leaving her friends, even if it's only for a few months." She referred to their fifteen-year-old daughter, who was going through a rebellious stage.

"You think we ought to take Jessie up on her offer then?" He watched her as if he was hanging on her every word, as if she was the most important person in the world to him. He realized, for the first time in a long time, that was exactly what she was.

"Yes. We can handle Becca. After all, we're the adults. I just think Jessie's offered us the perfect solution," she explained her position. "How do you feel about it?"

Ray had been watching Helen intently. He'd sensed the relief that had washed over her as the offer had unfolded. He reached out and brushed her auburn hair away from her forehead. "I can see how important this is to you. To *us*. So I think I ought to call Jessie and accept her offer once I get a few other details worked out."

He pulled her into his arms to kiss her again. It was at that precise moment that their children—fifteen-year-old Becca, eight-year-old Bret, six-year-old Mara, and four-year-old Maggie—came running into the house. When they saw their parents together, they squealed with delight and swarmed them like a litter of squirming puppies.

"Daddy! You're home!" they cried in unison as Ray tried to hug the four of them.

He knew they had a lot to talk about, but most of it would have to wait until tomorrow. By the time they had calmed down, it was bedtime.

Chapter 4

Unsure of what her true feelings were, Jessie sat by the phone after Ray's call. He'd called to accept her offer to have him and his family as her guests during filming. Consequently, in less than four months her house would be teeming with activity. She would have to work double time to finish her latest work-in-progress before then.

In addition, Ray had asked if she would have the local power company put up extra utility poles at her parents' house. He also asked if she would have gravel brought onto the open field beside the house. He wanted plenty of parking for the number of vehicles, trailers, and equipment that would be necessary for the actors and crew without having to tear up the lawn. He gave her his home address so that the bills could be sent to him.

During the two days since Ray had left, she had come to the disturbing realization that she had fallen for him. How could she have let that happen? (As if she'd had a choice in the matter.) Her entire adult life, Jessie had avoided relationships, and here she was now mushy over a man who was completely unavailable to her and out of her league anyway. She was glad that she wouldn't have to be alone with him anymore. Perhaps with his wife and children around, she'd find that it was just some sort of adolescent crush on a movie star, and she'd be able to keep her emotions in check before she humiliated herself.

In the weeks that followed, Jessie worked feverishly getting her manuscript ready for her publisher. She'd advised Mark Sanders that she would probably not get that much work done after her guests arrived and filming began, so with the completion of this novel, he could consider her on hiatus.

In the meantime, she had several calls from Ray about the progress being made on both ends. His planned arrival date was some time after Easter. She'd even met Helen over the phone. Jessie had gotten some information about home schooling and had wanted to discuss it with her. She had found Helen to be intelligent, witty, and friendly and more than open to suggestions about teaching her children. It seemed as if they could work well together.

With only a few days to spare, Jessie had emailed the final revisions of her novel to her publisher. She spent the last few days before her guests arrived in a frenzy of cleaning, moving her belongings to the guest suite, and baking.

Ray called one last time to tell her that he would be arriving a day early with the crew and that he'd be meeting his family at the airport the following day.

"I know you'll be extremely busy setting up. If you like, I can collect Helen, the kids, *and* the dog for you," she offered.

Ray hesitated before he spoke. "Jessie, you're already doing so much. I hate to impose any further."

"I don't mind. Honestly."

"To tell you the truth, it would be a big help," he confessed.

"Consider it done then. Just tell me the day and time."

"I'd better do that now because I probably won't have a chance to talk to you much until they're already there. I'll be staying on site until we're completely set up." He gave her the flight information and then said, "Thanks again, Jessie. You're a real lifesaver."

"You're welcome. Any other instructions?"

"I can't think of anything. I'm just so keyed up. Jessie, it's finally going to happen!"

She smiled to herself. He sounded so excited, just like a kid let loose in a toy store. "I'm happy for you, Ray. I hope that it's everything you want it to be," she told him sincerely.

"Thanks. I know you mean that. Well, I'd better go now. We'll see you in a couple of days. Goodbye, Jessie."

"Bye, Ray."

She hung up. Well, that had gone okay. This time as she talked with him, she'd managed to make her heart behave in a relatively normal way. She hoped and prayed that it would get easier.

Ray and his filming crew, together with tons of equipment, had arrived the day before, and even though he had stopped by to get the keys to her parents' house and drop off some of his family's luggage, Jessie didn't get a chance to say more than a quick hello and advise him that she'd had phone service returned to the house. When she had seen Ray again after so many weeks, her heart had given that same strange little leap as the first time. Otherwise, she had been fairly calm.

If someone should be able to read her chaotic thoughts, that person might find it a bit odd that she was going to such pains to protect the marriage of the man responsible for the chaos. Jessie wondered about that herself sometimes, but deep down she knew the real reason behind her actions. She had to be honest with herself. Even if Ray didn't love his wife and even if he weren't married, he would never be interested in someone like Jessie Martin. However, more important was the fact that the best thing for him was to be in love with and married to the mother of his children. Anything less would shatter all their lives, and Jessie was too tenderhearted to allow that to happen when she had the power to do something about it.

The flight arrived on schedule. Jessie waited nervously near the gate as she watched for a woman with four children, who she didn't think would be too difficult to recognize. She was right. Before too many passengers had streamed through the gate, she noticed a teenage girl and a young boy followed closely by a tall, slender, and very attractive, auburn-haired woman with two little girls, each clutching her mother's hand.

Jessie smiled and waved at Helen, who recognized her immediately and returned the smile as she approached.

"Jessie, hi! I'm Helen Hanson." She loosened her right hand from her daughter's grasp and extended it to take Jessie's hand in a firm, warm grip.

"Helen, it's great to finally meet you in person!" Jessie greeted her.

Then Helen introduced her children. "This is Maggie." Maggie gave her a wide grin and, holding up four fingers, said, "I'm four years old."

Jessie squatted down in front of the little girl, who had her mother's brown eyes and auburn hair. "Oh, really? I would have guessed you were much older than that." Maggie just continued to grin at her as Helen went on to introduce the other little girl.

"This is Mara."

"Hi, Mara. And how old are you?" she asked the little girl, who, but for her size, could have passed for Maggie's twin.

"Six and a half," she smiled shyly.

"Oh," Jessie replied and nodded as if she were greatly impressed by her answer.

"This is my son Bret."

He said, "Hi. I'm eight." And he politely shook hands with Jessie.

"Hi, Bret," she greeted him, trying to keep her expression solemn. All three younger children favored their mom.

"And last, but not least, this unsmiling teenager is Becca. You might not be able to tell by her demeanor, but she's not happy about being separated from her friends," Helen explained sarcastically.

Jessie turned to the sullen Becca, who was a carbon copy of her father with his coloring and apparently his personality.

"Hi, Becca. I'm pleased to meet you," she responded warmly in spite of the coolness emanating from the hostile young woman.

"Whatever," she responded in a deliberate attempt to be rude.

"Rebecca Hanson! You mind your manners!" her mother commanded her.

Becca's face turned red, and she mumbled an insincere, "Nice to meet you, too."

What fun! Several months with a resentful, rebellious teenager! On the other hand, Jessie could kind of understand why she was upset, since she had gone through a similar period herself years ago. She would just have to work harder to win over Becca.

Jessie suggested that they go claim their bags and the dog. With that job completed, Jessie went to get her car and bring it to the loading area. Packing the car carefully to make room for seven passengers, including a full-grown golden retriever, she finally had everyone and everything safely in the car. Bret sat on the third seat with Sanson and some luggage. Helen and the two little girls sat on the second seat, while Becca sat beside Jessie in the front.

Jessie pulled away from the loading area as quickly as possible and inquired, "Now before we get started to my house, who needs to go to the restroom? Is anybody hungry? Thirsty? What?"

Helen laughed and told her, "I imagine it's all the above."

"What kind of food does everybody want?" Jessie prompted.

"I want a Big Mac," Bret chimed in.

"Me, too," both little girls seconded.

Jessie glanced at Becca to see if she had a preference, but all she said was, "Whatever."

She stole a look at Helen in the rearview mirror and saw her rolling her eyes at her eldest child.

"What about it, Mom?" she deferred to Helen's maternal instincts.

"If it's not out of your way, that would be fine," she agreed.

"Oh, no problem. There's a MacDonald's right on the way home."

In a few minutes, she pulled into a parking space, and everyone got out. Bret took the dog for a little walk and got him some water, and Jessie insisted that she would stay and watch them while Helen took the others to the restroom.

Since it was a cool March day, they left the dog in the car while they ate their meal. Helen would not allow Jessie to buy lunch.

"But y'all are my guests!" she declared.

"You're already doing too much. I'm buying," she informed her, her voice brooking no argument.

Rather than continue the disagreement, Jessie gave in gracefully and accepted Helen's offer.

When lunch was finished and everyone was comfortable, they continued on their way to Jessie's house. If possible, it seemed that Becca grew more and more sullen the farther they drove.

Finally, she complained, "My gosh! It's out in the sticks!"

Jessie bit her lip to keep from bursting out laughing. The likeness to her father was amazing!

"Yes, I am a long way from town, but I've lived here all my life. I actually prefer the quiet and solitude of having no neighbors within half a mile of me," she informed her as she turned the car into her driveway and opened the gate.

Becca groaned as if she had been punched. She probably wondered if things could get much worse. Jessie *almost* felt sorry for her.

When the house came into view, Helen and the younger children voiced their appreciation of her home. Even Becca's expression showed a softening of her dislike of the rural setting, though she appeared determined not to give any sign of approval.

After she'd pulled into the garage and closed the door, everybody piled out of the car.

"Can we see our room now, Jessie?" Maggie wanted to know.

"Yes, Sweetheart. Let's go," she said as she unlocked the entry and led the way to the girls' rooms.

"Oh, this is neat!" remarked Bret. "It's just like a cabin in the woods!"

"Some cabin!" Helen piped in, as she glanced into the great room on the way to the bedrooms.

Jessie had added some little girl touches to the room that Mara and Maggie would be sharing: antique dolls and dresses and a small table with a tea set just waiting for a party. Other than that, the typical rustic décor together with the log walls, log bed, and wooden floor, covered with a hook rug, finished out the room. Their mother and they were delighted with her efforts.

Then they all trailed through the bathroom to see where Becca would be staying. Jessie had asked some teenagers exactly what would please a teenage girl these days, so she had kept Becca's room simple but feminine. She hoped the TV and CD player would meet a teenager's standards. Though silent, the child seemed to be pleased with her room as well.

Next she took them to the study, where Bret, and presumably Sanson, would sleep. The boy was happy about having his own bathroom, but he was completely fascinated by the Murphy bed. Jessie had always wondered if it was possible for someone to be closed up accidentally in the bed, but so far it hadn't happened. She had Bret promise that he wouldn't try to find out.

"I promise that I won't do that."

"Right," his mother put in. "I guess if he or the dog comes up missing, we can look in there first," she teased her son.

"Aw, Mom," he moaned in protest.

Jessie giggled and then took them to the master suite, which was decorated much the same as the other rooms with rustic simplicity but on a grander scale. Because of the size of the room and the vaulted ceiling, the furniture included a king size log bed, two night tables, dresser, chest of drawers and antique TV armoire. Over by the bay window through which sunlight streamed at the moment, was a sitting area. Jessie had brought in another chair to accommodate both Helen and Ray. A huge ledgestone gas fireplace lined the wall beside the sitting area. In the middle of the floor, was the pile of luggage that Ray had left the day before. The master bath was equipped with a whirlpool tub, a large shower, and two lavatories. There were also a private toilet and two walk-in closets.

"This is where you and Ray will sleep," she informed Helen.

"Jessie, this is simply fabulous! But we can't run you out of your room. Not with all you're doing for us. I won't hear of it."

"It's all settled. This will work better for everyone. You'll be closer to the children, and I'll be farther away. It's perfect. You'll see," she assured her.

Helen sighed. "If you're sure, then."

"I'm sure. Let me show y'all the rest of the house."

When the tour was complete, Jessie suggested that her guests might want to rest awhile. She had no idea when Ray might come in. She thought that Helen might have a better knowledge of that than she did.

"There's really no telling, but maybe when we've rested we could go over and visit the location if we won't get in his way too much," she proposed.

"Again, I have no knowledge of such things, so I defer to you. However, I would be happy to take y'all over there whenever you like."

Helen grinned at her and gushed, "I just love the *y'alls*! Ray warned me about them, but they're so unlike anything I'm used to."

"I aim to please...y'all," she threw in for good measure.

Helen laughed outright. "Ray also warned me about your sense of humor. I see that he was most perceptive, in this case."

Jessie could already see that she was going to like Helen and that they would probably become friends.

"I'm going to go to my room to complete something that I was working on out there. Let me know if you need anything."

"Thanks, Jessie. We'll be fine."

Jessie went out to the guest suite and turned on the computer. Her publisher had found one more revision that he needed right away, and she wanted to get that finished before she attempted anything else. Then she could email it to him and be done with it—she hoped.

Working for over an hour without interruption, she was able to complete her revision and get it sent without any complications. This done, she went back into the house to see if anyone was stirring. She could detect no signs of anyone's being awake, so she decided to just sit in the great room and relax awhile in her favorite easy chair. She promptly fell asleep.

About twenty minutes later, a noise awoke her. There it went again. It was the buzzer at the gate. One long buzz meant that someone wanted in, and two short ones meant that the remote had been used.

Jessie jumped up to look at the monitor. She saw that it was Ray, so she pushed the button that would open the gate and allow him entrance and then closed it when he had pulled through. Since she had several extra remotes for the gate as well as the garage, she was going to have to remember to give him one of each plus a house key. It would be more convenient for everyone. She decided to search those out before she forgot.

By the time he rang the front doorbell, Jessie had located the key and the remotes and laid them on the island, where she could remember them. Then she went to open the door.

"Hi, Ray," she greeted him.

"Hi, Jessie." He looked around and asked, "Where have you hidden my family?"

She grinned at his attempt at humor. "I believe they're all resting at the moment." She walked to the island and told him, "Before I forget, I want to give you these. Put them in your vehicle, and you won't have to depend on someone inside the house to get in."

"Thanks. I believe I'll do that right now so that I won't forget." And he quickly went out to the SUV that he was driving, clipped the remotes to the sun visor, and put the key on his key ring.

When he returned, he thanked her again and said, "I've got to get back to the set, but I wanted to see how everyone was doing. I'm going to see if Helen is awake."

Jessie remarked, "I'm sure she would prefer your waking her to missing you altogether."

Ray nodded, "Maybe you're right." Then he went to the master suite and entered, closing the door behind him.

Jessie felt a pang of something she didn't recognize. Jealousy? She hoped not. They were husband and wife, and they *should* want to be together. She would have to get a tighter grip on herself or else be awkward around Ray and Helen for the next few months.

In a few minutes, they emerged from the master suite. Ray knocked on the study door and went in to greet his son, while Helen came through to wake her daughters so that they could see their daddy before he had to get back.

The little girls came running out and threw themselves on Ray as he entered the great room.

"Daddy! We're so glad to see you! We've had so much fun today!" Maggie enthused.

Ray bent to pick up his youngest child, "Have you, Sweetie? I'm glad."

Mara told him, "Our room is *beautiful*, Daddy! It even has a tea set!"

"That's great, Pumpkin. Can I get an invitation to the first tea party?" he requested with a serious expression on his face.

"Oh sure, Daddy," she answered, equally serious.

Becca finally dragged into the room and went over to hug her father. "Hi, Daddy."

"Hi, Becca Honey. How are you holding up? Do you know yet if you're going to survive?" On the surface he appeared to be very solicitous.

"Very funny," she replied, obviously still not in a good mood.

"Now, Ray! Don't egg her on!" Helen admonished him.

"Sorry," he grinned, evidently not sorry at all.

His wife reminded him, "You only do that because you two are so much alike."

Jessie laughed out loud at that because she had been thinking the same thing.

Ray turned to look at her and, smiling broadly, warned, "That'll be enough out of you, Jessie Martin!" Then he left, telling them that he had to get back to the set and that he'd be back by dark.

After Helen had unpacked and supervised her children's unpacking, she insisted on helping Jessie cook supper. It seemed that all of the Hansons would eat just about anything, so Jessie decided to start them off with a typical Southern meal of fried chicken, mashed potatoes and gravy, black eyed peas, and cornbread.

As they worked, the two women chatted about their home schooling plans. Jessie had decided that the sunroom would make a good schoolroom, so she had found four antique school desks and an old chalkboard to put in there to give it the proper atmosphere. Helen seemed very excited about the prospect of actually teaching her children.

"It won't be too much different from what you've probably always done with them. I mean that you probably help them with their homework and encourage them. The only difference is now you'll be assigning the homework," Jessie smiled at her.

"You make it sound so easy," Helen told her. "I hope you're right."

Since the next day would be Friday, they decided to treat it as a holiday and start class bright and early Monday morning.

Ray came in and announced that the setting up process was complete with all the actors and equipment in place and that filming would begin the following morning at first light. The meal then became a twofold celebration – their first day in Mississippi and the start of filming. Ray proposed a toast with his glass of ice water. "May this be just the beginning of a very special friendship and an unforgettable film."

Chapter 5

Jessie didn't get any takers on her invitation to attend church, but she went anyway, leaving the others to their own devices. When she returned, Helen had taken care of the breakfast dishes and begun preparing Sunday lunch with the help of two little girls.

When Jessie protested, she remarked, "You told us to make ourselves at home, so that's what I did."

Jessie shook her head, "That's not what I meant."

Ray had reluctantly allowed his actors and crew to have the weekend off, but it was obvious that he was anxious for Monday to come so that he could resume work.

On Monday, the pattern of the days and weeks to follow was set in motion. Ray was up and out on location before dawn and would not return to the house before dark, except on rare occasions.

Jessie, Helen, and the children would start school promptly at eight AM and would work until the day's lessons were complete. Both women supervised the four children, who were all on different levels. Once they got a schedule worked out and a rhythm going, it worked quite well.

On one occasion, Jessie had put Becca to work on the computer and was patiently trying to explain to her how the program worked. She could tell that Becca was extremely bored with the whole thing, so she suggested in exasperation, "If you would just realize how very blessed you are, you would take advantage of every learning opportunity that presents itself to you." It was *teacher speak*, she knew.

Becca looked at Jessie and responded insultingly, "You are such a dork!"

"Becca!" Helen scolded from the door. "Go to your room this instant! And you wait there until I decide what to do with you!"

Becca, red faced, got up and ran from the room.

"Oh, Jessie, I have to apologize for my ill-mannered daughter! I'm so sorry! She *will* be punished. When her father finds out what she said..." she trailed off.

Helen looked so mortified that Jessie had to stop her.

"Don't worry about it, Helen. That wasn't so bad. Besides, I've been called worse," she said, trying to cheer her up. "And I wish you wouldn't punish her. I'd ask you to just let Becca and me work out our own problems. Obviously, she blames me for having to come here and leave her friends, so if you punish her on my behalf, it will just make things worse."

Helen disagreed, "She simply cannot be allowed to get away with a breach like this, Jessie."

Jessie smiled at her and continued, "Now I'm going to quote Dr. Laura to you. 'Is this the hill you want to die on?' Or would you like to live to fight another day?"

Helen shrugged her shoulders and said with obvious confusion, "I don't get it."

"In this case, it means that in the battle of wills that goes on between parents and their children, is this one that you *have* to win, no matter the cost, or is it one on which you can cut Becca some slack?"

"I don't know, Jessie," she hesitated.

"Please, let Becca and me work it out," she prompted.

Helen sighed heavily and relented. "All right, but I'm still going to have to tell Ray about this."

"As long as you keep him out of it. Deal?" Jessie put out her hand.

She hesitated again. Finally she took Jessie's hand. "Deal."

"Now I'm going to talk to that daughter of yours." Squaring her shoulders, she left the room.

———————————

That night in bed, Helen told Ray about the morning's incident. Ray almost blew a fuse. "My daughter did *what*?"

Helen repeated it for him, and he started to get out of bed. "Wait! I promised Jessie I'd keep you out of it."

"Now why did you do that?" Helen could tell that he was quite angry.

"Jessie wants a chance to work things out with Becca. She feels that if we get into it with her that it will just make things worse. She even quoted Dr. Laura to me," Helen explained with a chuckle.

"Not again!" Ray moaned. "What pearls of wisdom did the good doctor have to offer this time?" he inquired snidely.

"Okay. Here goes." She tried to remember the gist of what Jessie had told her. "She asked if this was the hill we wanted to die on—meaning were we willing to fight this battle to the death or would we be willing to cut Becca some slack and let Jessie handle the situation."

Ray mulled that over for a few moments and reluctantly admitted, "Actually, I like it. That makes a lot of sense. I have to hand it to Jessie, although I'm beginning to wonder about her role models. Who else does she like to quote?"

"Nobody, so far, but, Ray, you have to admit that it's kind of sweet. And, so far, Dr. Laura and Jessie have been right on."

"I admit nothing except the fact that I'm tired of talking." Then he turned out the light and took his wife into his arms.

———————————

From that day on until the end of the semester, Becca's attitude did a complete turn-around. She was polite, even friendly, to Jessie. Though Helen tried to find out what had transpired between the two, neither of them was talking. Jessie informed her that she had promised Becca that their discussion would remain between the two of them.

There were a few times when Ray had asked Jessie to come to the set and Becca had stepped in to help her mom with the younger kids. Helen was greatly impressed with her daughter and openly expressed her appreciation for her assistance.

The first time that Ray had requested her presence, Jessie had been awed by the transformation that had taken place at her parents' house. There were cameras, lights, and glamorous people everywhere. It all seemed so very *Hollywood* to her.

She remarked to Ray, "I feel just like Lucy, Ricky, and the Mertzes must have felt when they went to Hollywood."

Ray gave her a look and said, "You're not going to start quoting Lucy to me now, are you?"

She smiled at him and acknowledged, "Lucy or Walker, Texas Ranger. He's my favorite."

He laughed and then explained that they were having trouble with a scene and needed the author's input to work out the problem. She studied the situation for a while and then made a suggestion based on her rapport with and knowledge of the characters. After considering her suggestion for a few moments, Ray and his assistant director, decided that she was right. Problem solved.

"Thanks, Jessie. You want to hang around and watch filming?" he offered.

"No thanks. I might get in your way. Besides, I should get back to school. I'll see you at home." With that, she left.

As time passed, great strides were made both in filming *and* home schooling. However, Helen remarked to Jessie that Ray seemed to be under too much stress.

"I'm afraid that he's pinned all of his hopes on this movie and is having trouble relaxing here," she admitted.

"I've noticed, and I've been meaning to suggest something to you. Why don't you go away for the weekend?"

"With four kids? I don't think that would relax him much. But it was a nice thought."

With a pitiable expression on her face, Jessie shook her head at

Helen. "I *meant* just the two of you. I'd keep the kids, of course, and y'all could make reservations at some place nice. Oh, wait! There's this great country inn over at Nesbit. It's supposed to be very romantic and secluded. How about it?" she prodded.

"Oh, Jessie, that sounds great. But we can't do that to you. It's too much to ask of anybody," she said regretfully.

"You're not asking. I'm telling you to go. For Ray's sanity, if for no other reason. Now let's go see if we can find a telephone number for the inn."

Helen grinned at her. "Ray told me how you liked to have the last word, but I have to confess that I'm glad you do. This would be wonderful!"

Jessie was able to remember the name of the inn, so they got on the Internet and found a web page that gave a telephone number. Without consulting her husband, Helen made reservations for the following Friday night through Sunday morning. The clerk also gave exact directions to the inn. Now all they had to do was convince Ray.

When Helen told Ray that they were going away for the weekend, at first he was not enthusiastic.

"Honey, I'm just not keen on packing up four kids and going to a hotel," he groaned.

Helen gave him the same look that Jessie had given her earlier. "Just the two of us, Ray. Jessie insisted that we go and that she would keep the children. *And* it's not a hotel, but a romantic country inn," she explained.

He still seemed reluctant. "I don't know. That's a lot to ask anybody to do."

"I didn't ask. She *told* me that we were going. It was all her idea."

Ray laughed and gave up. "Then I *don't* have a choice, do I? The last word has been spoken."

Though Maggie and Mara were upset that their parents were going away for two days, they cheered up when Jessie told them what fun the ones staying behind would have.

If the late April weather permitted, she had planned a picnic after they had baked the cookies they would need for it. On Sunday, with their parents' permission, she would take them to church after they had made pancakes for breakfast, and then they would go somewhere special for lunch.

As Ray and Helen were getting ready to leave on Friday afternoon, they hugged each child and said their goodbyes. Then they turned to Jessie, and Helen said, "I don't think you realize what you're letting yourself in for, but thanks."

"We'll be fine. Don't worry. Now goodbye. You kids, have fun, and be good," she admonished as they headed toward the garage.

Ray smiled wickedly and replied, "We don't have to be good. We're married."

"Ray!" Helen gasped in mock horror.

Then they were gone. Jessie wondered again why she kept making ways for Ray and Helen to be together when the very thought hurt so much. Actually, she knew the reason—what was good for *them* was good for Ray. She just prayed for more strength to get her thoughts and heart under control.

The weekend went very smoothly. All of the kids, including Becca, made a huge effort to enjoy themselves. Baking cookies turned out to be somewhat of a circus, with flour all over everything and a few specimens turned to charcoal, but since there were no parents around, no one seemed to mind. The weather turned out to be sunny and mild, so the six of them, dog included, took a picnic lunch down to the pond, where they played games, laughed, and talked for hours.

Sunday morning, after eating delicious heart-shaped pancakes and loading the dishwasher, they got ready for church. They left Sanson lounging on the couch and headed for The First Baptist Church, where Jessie was a member. This was a novel experience for the Hanson children since they never attended church in California. However, they seemed to enjoy the service, especially the singing. Their inquisitive minds had a lot of questions. They wanted to know the meaning behind every little aspect of the service, and Jessie answered as best she could, while trying to maintain a reverent attitude.

When they got back home after lunch, Jessie suggested that they might like to take a nap before their parents got home so that they could be well rested. She knew that she could use one, although none of the children went for the idea.

After everyone had changed clothes and Bret had taken the dog for a run, they settled down in the great room to watch a video that their mother had pre-approved. Before long, they were all sound asleep.

Using Sanson as a pillow, Bret was sprawled on the floor. Becca had curled up in the large overstuffed easy chair, and Jessie sat on the couch, a little girl snuggled in each arm.

Sometime later, they were rudely awakened by the barking dog. The buzzer, which Sanson apparently did not like, was causing the usual reaction. Upon recognizing two short buzzes, a signal that the remote had been used, Jessie realized that Ray and Helen were at the gate.

"Hey, y'all, I think your mom and dad are home!" she announced amidst whoops of delight.

In a few minutes, Helen and Ray appeared in the great room and were rushed by four excited children and a dog.

"Mommy! Daddy! We're so glad you're home!" they chorused. They were all entwined in one big group hug, with the dog right in the middle.

Jessie took a quick peek at Ray's face to see if his weekend had done him any good. To her relief, his expression was one of relaxed enjoyment at the welcome Helen and he were receiving from their family.

With a wide grin on her face, Jessie just stood apart from their reunion and watched silently.

When things had calmed down, Helen extricated herself and turned her attention to Jessie.

"Jessie, how are you holding up? I hope these little terrors haven't been too awful."

She replied, "Not at all. We've had a great time, haven't we, Kids?"

"Yea!!!" they all cheered, including Becca.

Ray said, "I'm glad to see that you're in one piece and that the house is still standing."

"Oh, Daddy! We're not *that* bad!" Becca whined.

"Oh, yeah. Right." he teased his daughter.

"What did you bring us?" Maggie wanted to know.

"Presents for everyone in the car," Ray announced laughingly.

While the children went to the garage to fetch their presents, Ray looked at Jessie and told her, "I have to give you credit, Jessie. This weekend was a great idea. We can't thank you enough."

"You're welcome. Honestly though, I enjoyed myself, and apparently the getaway did you both some good. So it was worth it," she replied.

Helen went over to her and gave her a hug. "Thanks, Jessie."

Jessie smiled and nodded.

The children returned carrying packages bearing their names, and Becca had an extra one. "This one's for you," she said holding a small colorful gift bag out to Jessie.

"For me? But why?" she asked in confusion.

"Just to say thanks for this weekend," Helen told her.

"You already did that."

"We want you to have it," Ray chimed in. "So just accept it and let us have the last word. Just this once."

"All right. Just this once," Jessie agreed, grudgingly. Then she pulled a small jewel box from the bag and opened it. Inside was an exquisite silver rope chain. Dangling from the chain was a filigree heart with a diamond embedded in the center.

"Oh, it's beautiful!" Jessie was deeply touched by the gift. She removed the necklace from the box, unclasped it, and fastened it around her neck.

"Thank you both. I love it," she said sincerely.

"You're very welcome," they replied, seemingly gratified by her sincere appreciation.

Then the children claimed her attention as they displayed their gifts, and everyone got caught up in their excitement.

Chapter 6

It had been Jessie's suggestion to Helen that they move the children just slightly ahead of where they would be in their studies when they returned to school in California. That way, if filming was behind schedule, they would not have to resume home schooling in the fall before returning home and could really enjoy their summer. By the end of May, the children had completed all their work and had taken their final exams.

Then Helen and Jessie began the unending task of trying to keep the kids entertained for several weeks during the hot, humid Mississippi summer. There were several tourist attractions that Jessie wanted them to see, including the Mississippi River, the Pink Palace Museum, LibertyLand, and Graceland. She wasn't sure if children that young would have ever heard of Elvis, but as it turned out, they had.

"Everybody knows about him," they insisted.

In addition, they planned several shopping trips to the various malls located in the city, and children who had grown up on the beach naturally wanted to go swimming. That meant several visits to the water parks. Appearing in public in a bathing suit was not something that Jessie was willing to do. Even though she was willing to chauffeur them and watch the children's antics, it was left to Helen to actually participate. However, even *she* drew the line at the giant water slide.

One afternoon when they had returned from one of their excursions, they were putting Mara and Maggie down for a nap. A smiling Helen watched as Jessie, at the child's insistence, settled Maggie into bed for her nap. She hugged Jessie's neck and said, "I had lots of fun today, Jessie. Thanks for taking us."

"Me, too," Mara chimed in. Then both children kissed her on the cheek.

Jessie was deeply moved by this open display of childish affection. "It was my pleasure, Kidlets," she responded, smiling tenderly at the little girls.

When Helen joined her in the great room, she remarked to Jessie how good she was with children.

"I know you were a teacher. That would explain a lot, but have you never thought of having your own children some day. You'd make a wonderful mother," she asserted, unwittingly hitting a nerve with Jessie.

Jessie was silent for a moment and then admitted sadly, "When I was a teenager, I used to dream about being a mother one day. But then at seventeen, I had to have a hysterectomy, and that kind of put the end to my dream."

"Oh, Jessie, I'm so sorry. I didn't know." Helen thought for a minute and then asked, "What about adoption?"

Jessie shook her head. "I can't feature someone like me landing a husband, and I think kids should have a daddy. So, no, I've never even considered it. But don't get me wrong. I'm not complaining. God has blessed me in so many other ways that I don't have the time or the room to feel sorry for myself."

Helen eyed her in amazement. "Where does that serenity, that contentment that I see in you come from? A lot of people, and if I'm honest I'd include myself, would curse God in your situation."

Jessie saw an opening and decided to step through on faith. "Do you really want to know?"

"Yes, I think I do," she confirmed.

"It comes through faith in Jesus Christ. You see I don't have to worry about my life and the things that happen to me because I know beyond the shadow of a doubt how I will end up. Even if I were to die tonight."

"You really believe that?" Helen sounded skeptical.

"Yes. The Apostle Paul says in the book of Phillipians, 'I have learned in whatsoever state I am, therewith to be content,' and again in 2 Corinthians, 'We are…willing to be absent from the body, and to be present with the Lord.' Do you understand?"

"You mean that when you die you'll go to Heaven."

"Exactly."

"Doesn't everybody who's good go to Heaven?" she wanted to know.

"Those who put their faith in Jesus Christ do. That's what Christians call being saved," Jessie replied.

"Saved from what?" Helen had heard the term before, but no one had ever explained it to her until now.

"Saved from our due penalty for sin. You see the Bible says that we've all sinned and come short of God's glory, and for that we will be punished, which means death and hell. But God made a way for us to escape that by letting His Son take our punishment instead. Jesus died for us. The book of Acts says to believe on the Lord Jesus Christ, and we will be saved."

"That's all you did—believe?" Jessie simply nodded in response.

"That seems so simple, almost too simple," Helen said, her eyes beginning to tear up.

"I believe God kept it simple so that people wouldn't boast about what they did to earn salvation. It's not a matter of credit; it's simply a matter of faith."

"What do I have to do to be saved?" she asked breathlessly.

Jessie was a little breathless herself. This was the most important decision of Helen's life. "In the first place, you have to be convinced that you're a sinner. Then you must confess your sin and believe that Jesus is able to save you from your sin. Finally, you simply accept his free gift and confess Jesus as Savior and Lord."

"How do I do that?"

"If you'd like, I could lead you in the sinner's prayer," Jessie offered hopefully.

"Please."

Jessie got up from her chair and knelt beside Helen. Taking her hands, she said, "Just repeat what I say." Then she prayed, "Lord, I know that I'm a sinner. I confess my sin to you and believe that Your Son Jesus Christ is able to save me. I confess Him as Lord and Savior of my life. Amen."

When they had finished, she looked up at Helen and said, "Now, if you prayed that from your heart, you are now saved. You are born again."

"I did pray from my heart, so I *must* be saved! Oh, Jessie! It's a little bit scary, isn't it? But I feel sort of brand new, as if I'm getting to start over!" she beamed.

"You are." Jessie assured her. "Wait! I want to give you something." She hurried out to the guest suite and came back, carrying a Bible in her hand.

"I'd like for you to have this. I have lots of Bibles, and you're probably going to find yourself wanting to read it." She handed it to Helen.

"Thank you so much, Jessie! Oh, I've got to see that Ray gets saved, too! I can't wait to tell him about this!" she cried.

"Helen, you *should* tell him. But may I give you some advice? You were ready to receive the message I gave you. Some people aren't ready. So don't try to force Ray to make a decision. If he's not ready, he might come to resent you *and* God and fear that your attitude toward him and your marriage will change. That could put up a wall between you and him. And, please, don't develop a holier-than-thou-attitude, as some people do. Sometimes all a wife can do is pray for her husband and love him more than ever before. Let him see the change in you for himself, and if you're gentle and loving with him, you may win him that way."

"You're absolutely right about Ray. He *could* react that way. I'll keep it in mind. Our marriage is getting healthy again—thanks to you—so I certainly don't want to mess it up."

They both stood up, and Helen gave Jessie a hug and declared tearfully, "I don't know what my life would have been like today if God hadn't put you in it, and now I'm certain that He did. Thanks for being there, Jessie."

"You're welcome," she choked, her heart filled with emotion. She patted Helen's shoulder and went to begin preparations for supper.

Ray was unmoved by what Helen had to tell him that night, as they sat in their room. At first, he even appeared angry and complained about Jessie's meddling again.

"Ray, be fair. I *asked* Jessie about it. She didn't force it on me. I can't recall her ever having forced religion on you or anyone else either. Can you?" Helen inquired with equanimity.

He had to admit that, even though she was open about her Christian faith, Jessie had never tried to push it on him. "No, she hasn't done that. But what is this religious thing going to do to you and me? I don't want to lose you," he confessed, concern evident in his voice.

"You won't lose me," she vowed. "If anything, it's going to make me a better wife. And don't worry. I'm not going to force something on you that you're not ready for. *But* you can't object to my praying for you, can you?"

Thinking that there were two people praying for him now, Ray told her, "I suppose not."

Helen got up and sat in his lap. She cupped his face in her hands, pulled his head to hers, and gave him a long, passionate kiss. Holding his wife in his arms, Ray got up from the chair and carried her to the bed.

After having completed filming at several outlying locations, including the nearest, sleepy little town, Ray and his crew were back at Jessie's parents' house. Hopefully, they were in the process of shooting some of the last and most vital scenes and would soon begin to wrap things up.

Jessie hadn't been to the set for quite some time, so that day while Helen and the kids were just lounging around the house, she decided to go see for herself how things were going.

Having been warned in advance that the red light over the door meant 'Do not enter,' Jessie waited on the porch. She knew that filming was in progress. When the light went out, she gingerly opened the door and slipped inside without being noticed.

Strolling around and trying to stay inconspicuous, she heard Ray directing the young woman who was playing the heroine. Curious because she had never actually seen him in action, Jessie sneaked into the back of the room. Watching intently as the scene unfolded, Jessie soon became horrified by what she was seeing and hearing. The woman was practically nude, and Ray was directing her to do things with her male co-star that would be totally alien to one of Jessie's characters.

Jessie was loath to interrupt, but this was one of the reasons that she had fought to maintain rights to her book. Wishing to speak to him privately, she stepped forward to get Ray's attention.

"Excuse me, Ray. Could I talk to you for a minute?" she asked politely.

Startled, he whirled around, and when he recognized her, he said, 'Oh, hi, Jessie. Sure." Then he yelled, "Everybody, take five!"

He walked over to her and said in a businesslike tone, "What can I do for you?"

"It's kind of private. Could we go out on the front porch?"

"Sure." He led the way and ushered her out the door.

"Okay. What's up?" he opened.

"Ray, I cannot—no, I *will* not—go along with the scene you were directing just then!" she informed him, beginning to fume.

"What are you talking about?" he asked, perplexed.

"You are portraying *my* heroine as a slut. I won't allow it!" Her voice was becoming shrill.

"Come now, Jessie. Calm down. This is the big love scene. Moviegoers these days expect a little more sex. It sells, you know," he coaxed.

"I don't believe that. My novels have sold extremely well, and there have never been any scenes like the one I just witnessed. Who would know my characters better than I? And I'm telling you that I won't have something associated with my name portrayed as smut!"

She took a deep breath and tried to calm down. Aware that Ray was getting angry, she said evenly, "I don't believe that I'm out of line here, Ray. You'll just have to rewrite the scene."

"I can't believe you're reacting this way! Obviously, you're more of a prude than I thought you were, Jessie!" he shot back, really angry now. "It's no wonder that you can't get a husband! Even if you *weren't* a dork, no man would ever want a cold fish like you!" he sneered cruelly.

Seething with fury, he watched her, while the light in her eyes just seemed to flicker and die.

As she let her gaze slip to the floor, Jessie began to tremble. She didn't think she had ever been hurt more by a friend's words.

She looked up and gave a weak little smile. "Well, it seems that two out of six Hansons agree that I'm a dork. Maybe by the time filming wraps up, it'll be unanimous, except for maybe the dog." With that, she turned and ran down the steps to the car.

"Damn it, Jessie!" Ray yelled after her.

She reached the car and yanked open the door. With tears in her eyes, she looked up at him still on the porch and in a wounded little voice, told him, "You do what you think best. I'm out of it." Then she climbed into the car and sped away.

Aghast at himself, Ray just stood there. What had he just said to a woman who had been so good to him and his family, who *had* been his friend?

After she'd reached the garage, Jessie sat with her hands covering her face. She took huge gulps of air in an attempt to get control of her emotions before she got out of the car. Now was not the time to think about the hurtful things that Ray had said. She had to get herself shut away in her room first.

When she had calmed down, she got out of the car and entered the house. She had almost reached the French door leading to the screened porch, when Helen called her name.

"Jessie, you weren't gone very long. Filming must have been slow," she guessed. Without turning around, Jessie just nodded her head. She hoped that would be the end of the conversation, but Helen came to stand beside her.

Upon seeing her face, Helen exclaimed, "Jessie! What's wrong? You've been crying!"

All Jessie could manage was to whisper desperately, "I can't talk about it." She fled to her room, locked the door behind her, and closed the blinds. Then she threw herself on the bed and let the tears flow.

Helen thought about going after her but decided against it. She appeared to be extremely upset and needed some time to herself. It was just that she'd never seen Jessie so upset before.

In a few minutes, Ray came striding into the house. Helen went over to give him a kiss, "Hi, Sweetheart. You're home early." He seemed tired and distracted.

"Have you seen Jessie?" he asked wearily.

Uh oh! Helen thought. "She went to her room just a few minutes ago."

He gave her a quick peck on the cheek, and then he went out to the screened porch.

He knocked on Jessie's door. No answer. Then he turned the doorknob. It was locked.

He knocked again and called, "Jessie! I know you're in there! I need to talk to you! Please!" Silence.

"Jessie, please! Let me apologize!" He waited, but still he got no response. Frustrated, he gave up and went back into the house.

In the great room, he lowered himself into a chair and rubbed the back of his neck.

Helen went to stand behind him and began massaging his neck and shoulders.

"Mmm. That feels good. Thanks, Honey."

"Ray, what's wrong? Why is Jessie so upset? I've never seen her like that before," Helen inquired, concerned about her friend, as well as her husband.

He sighed and stood up. "I said something unforgivable to hurt her, but I'll have to tell you about it tonight. I have something that won't wait back on the set." Then he kissed her goodbye and left the house.

Jessie did not come out of her room again that day, so with Becca's help, Helen prepared the evening meal and explained to the kids that Jessie was ill. When Ray got home, he was upset that Jessie had not made an appearance. He looked out toward her room but couldn't see lights or any other signs that she was even in there. He made one more attempt to talk with her. Again, he was met with silence.

That night in their room, he told Helen about the fight they'd had over the love scene.

"Don't you think Jessie might know her characters and her audience better than you?" In an attempt to cheer him up she said, "I think this is when Dr. Laura would ask if this is the hill you want to die on."

But Ray was not smiling. He was completely serious when he said, "It *was* for Jessie. And the awful thing is I took a shot at her, and I think I killed something deep inside."

Then he told Helen what he'd said to Jessie. "While I stood on the porch watching her, it was as if the light in her eyes went out."

He recounted Jessie's words to him. "I just stood there like a jerk and let her go."

His eyes filled with the pain of remorse, he said, "I don't know that she'll ever be able to forgive me. I don't even think *I* can forgive me."

Placing her arms around him, Helen tried to bring him some comfort. "I think you're hurt by this as much as Jessie." She pulled him close and held him as if he were one of her children instead of her husband.

That night, Ray couldn't sleep. Careful not to wake his wife, he got out of bed and pulled on some shorts and a t-shirt. Relying on the moonlight that streamed through the windows, he went into the kitchen. When he glanced toward Jessie's room, he noticed that her door was open.

As he quietly unlocked the French door, he saw movement at the porch swing. Jessie sat there idly swinging herself with one bare foot and staring out into the moonlit night. He moved as stealthily as a cat to join her in the swing.

As he made to sit down beside her, she gave a startled *oh* and then started to rise.

"Please, Jessie! Don't go!" Ray pleaded with her.

She settled back onto the swing but said nothing.

He cleared his throat and began, "I want to apologize for the things I said to you this afternoon. Do you think you could forgive me?"

She was silent for so long that Ray thought she was going to ignore him, but finally she said, "I cried all afternoon, and then I prayed all night. God led me to the conclusion that you said those things in the heat of battle when you saw me messing with your Oscar. You were protecting it like a mother bear protecting her cubs. So, yes, I forgive you, Ray."

Relief washed over him, but he could still feel a distance between them.

"Thank you," he replied as he reached out and took her hand. "You're still hurt though, aren't you?"

"You know the old saying, 'The truth hurts.' I believe it applies in this instance," she responded without rancor.

"I didn't mean it, Jessie. I was angry with you," he lamented, sorrow evident in his voice.

"I know. Don't worry. I'll be fine. I can get past this, but are *you* going to be okay?" she asked.

There she went again! She was concerned about him when *he* had been in the wrong.

"Jessie! What am I going to do with you? Here you are trying to comfort me when you should be making me grovel at your feet!"

"I definitely wouldn't want you to do that, Ray."

They sat there in silence for a few minutes, her hand still clasped in his. He wasn't sure why he had taken her hand, unless he was trying to bridge the distance between them that his cruel words had caused.

Maybe his next words would help. "I rewrote the scene, Jessie.

We're going to do it your way. You'll get the last word, as usual," he told her, a smile detectable in his voice.

"Thank you for that." Then she disengaged her hand from his and stood, saying, "I'm going to try and get some sleep. You'd better do the same. Goodnight."

"Goodnight, Jessie." He sat there for a few moments longer. She'd forgiven him, but he knew that their friendship was irreparably damaged, though Jessie would try not to let it show. That made him sad. Unable to shake the feeling that he'd lost something very special, he went back to bed.

There remained only a few more days of work before filming would wrap. The set was a hive of activity with everyone trying to finish up any last minute details. Jessie had begun to think about how quiet it would be in the neighborhood when all the people and equipment were gone. The thought somehow made her happy and sad at the same time. On the one hand, she would be glad to get started on her next novel. But she knew she would miss her guests, especially the tall, dark, handsome one.

Jessie had truly forgiven him for the cruel things that he'd said to her, and she had tried to return to the friendship that they'd enjoyed before their fight. Though she was unaware of it, there was a part of herself that she held back from Ray and even Helen. The only ones with whom she appeared to be her old self were the children and the dog.

Helen noticed the change right away. It wasn't that she was cool toward them. There was just this indefinable aloofness that seemed to hang between them. One night, Helen mentioned it to Ray.

"You've noticed it, too? I thought I was the only one. I'm sorry, Sweetheart. I didn't mean to hurt you in all this," he denied, a note of sadness in his tone.

"I know. I guess it's a good thing we'll be going home soon. Maybe she can get back to the way her life was before we dropped into it."

They lay in bed, both lost in thought. Then Helen remarked wistfully, "I'm going to miss her so much. Do you realize how much she's done for the Hansons, Ray?"

"The closer we get to wrapping, the more I think about it—the fact that I have my family, the film, everything. I owe it all to Jessie." After a pause, he groaned, "And she asked for nothing in return, except that I treat her novel with respect." He pulled his wife closer for comfort.

The day that filming wrapped, Ray threw a party for the cast and crew. Also he invited everyone in the area who had assisted in anyway. Of course, his family and Jessie were invited as well. Helen was half afraid that Jessie wouldn't attend, but she readily accepted the invitation.

Before the party actually got underway, Ray stood up to make a speech. He thanked the cast and crew for a job well done. Then he thanked their hostess. "I want to thank Jessie Martin, who made this film possible—first by writing a novel called *The Sixth Commandment* and allowing me to film it; secondly by allowing us to use her parents' house for the setting; last by being a good friend. Thanks, Jessie."

Amidst thunderous applause, Jessie just smiled shyly and nodded. Then he continued, "If we can keep things on schedule, we can premiere before the December deadline." Then Ray got the party started.

That very day, the crew would begin packing up and hauling all the equipment off the location site. Most of the cast would be leaving for the airport. It would take another day or so to complete the clearing up of the site. Jessie had told Ray not to worry about it because she'd take care of it, but he insisted that he would leave her parents' house the way he had found it.

Ray would fly back to California on the huge transport plane with the crew, equipment, and especially the film, since he was not about to let *that* out of his sight. Knowing this, Jessie had offered to return his family to the airport. They would be leaving the following day. Once again, she was proving indispensable to him.

As he was preparing to leave, Ray kissed his wife and children goodbye. Maggie piped up and asked, "Daddy, when your movie starts, can Jessie come to see it with us?"

Ray glanced at the discomfited expression on Jessie's face. Obviously she had never expected the question.

He smiled at his youngest daughter and replied, "Sure, Sweetie, if she wants to."

He looked questioningly at Jessie, who shook her head. "I don't think Hollywood and I would mix too well. It's bad enough when I have to go to New York, but Hollywood is way out of my league. I'll just wait and see it when it opens back here."

Then she held out her hand to Ray. "I wish you the best. I'll be praying when the movie opens and when the Oscar nominees are announced. I hope you realize your dream, Ray," she told him, smiling.

He studied her for a moment and then said cryptically, "You're not going to get off that easily."

Then he grabbed her shoulders, pulled her toward him, and kissed her soundly on the mouth.

"Thanks again for everything, Jessie. Bye." Waving goodbye to everyone, he climbed into his car and was gone.

Helen stood there with the kids, waving until Ray was out of sight. Then she turned to look at Jessie, who wore the saddest expression on her face that she had ever seen. Helen had a flash of intuition. Suddenly it all became clear to her. This sweet, loving, funny, kind, giving, selfless, albeit unattractive, woman was in love with Ray! That would explain the hurt over their fight and the wall she had put up between them. Helen felt an instant empathy for her and the things she was going through.

Later that night after the kids had gone to bed, Helen went out to the screened porch where Jessie sat in the swing. She pulled the French door shut behind her. "Can I talk to you for a minute, Jessie?" she began.

"Sure." Jessie motioned for her to sit beside her on the swing.

"First of all, I wanted to thank you for all you've done for us, for me especially. You have totally changed my life, in many ways. You led me to Christ. My husband loves me again, and you made it possible for us to be together. You home schooled my children. I could go on." She leaned over and gave her a hug. "I'll never forget you, Jessie," she went on with a definite catch in her voice.

Jessie was having trouble controlling her emotions, but she managed to reply in a husky whisper, "I won't forget y'all either."

"Your secret is safe with me, you know," she informed her gently.

"What secret?" Jessie breathed in confusion.

"I saw the look on your face this afternoon when Ray kissed you. You're in love with him."

Jessie covered her face with her hands and gasped in startled disbelief, "How did you know?"

"I told you. I saw your face. And, besides, I know the devastating effect that Ray can have on women. It's just that the usual reaction is that the women throw themselves at him. To the best of my knowledge, he has never caught one though," Helen joked.

"Helen, I'm so sorry! I didn't mean for it to happen!" she cried in remorse.

"Don't worry about me. I understand completely. It's not your fault." She paused and then continued, "When *did* it happen?"

Jessie knew exactly when it had happened. "I think I started falling for him the first time I talked to him on the phone. His voice is almost like a velvet caress, isn't it? Then when I met him, it was all over," she confessed, blushing at the admission she'd just made to the man's wife.

"Then why in the world did you work so hard to save my marriage?" Helen was astonished.

Jessie hung her head and quietly responded, "Ray wasn't ever going to be interested in someone like me—married or not. Besides, there were you and the children to consider. If I could do something to help save y'all pain, I had to try. And then there was Ray. I knew the best thing for him was to be in love with and married to the mother of his children."

"You're one in a million, Jessie Martin!" Helen marveled. She patted Jessie's hand and got up from the swing.

"I'd better get to bed. We've got to get an early start tomorrow. Goodnight, Jessie."

"Goodnight, Helen," she called after her. Then she rose and went to her own room.

Jessie pulled up to the airport's loading zone so that the Hansons could unload their bags and their dog. Embracing the children, she gave them a tearful goodbye. Then she turned to Helen.

"I want you to know how much I've enjoyed your stay and how much your friendship means to me," she said, a wobble evident in her voice.

"Thanks, Jessie. I wish you would reconsider about coming to the premiere, but I understand why you can't. I'm going to miss you. We all are," she replied.

"I'll miss y'all, too."

Just then a car horn got her attention. "Oh, I've got to get out of the way now. Bye, everybody!"

As she got into the car and pulled away from the curb, she was thinking that she would probably never see them again. The thought made her want to cry.

Chapter 7

Getting back into a daily routine proved difficult at first. Jessie's home had never seemed so quiet before, and she hadn't experienced such loneliness since her mother had died. However, she knew she had to suck it up and get on with her life. Finally, she was able to start the novel she'd had on hold for so long.

A few weeks later while preparing her supper, Jessie had the TV on the Channel 3 news and heard a report on the upcoming premiere of a movie filmed in nearby Marshall County, Mississippi, and based on the novel by local author, Jessica Martin. The film would premiere in Hollywood the second week in November and nationwide Thanksgiving weekend.

It was only a few weeks away, but it seemed like a lifetime to Jessie. She didn't think it would ever happen, but finally the film opened in Memphis. Friends had asked her to go to the movie with them on opening night, but Jessie declined. She explained to them that she needed to see it alone with no one around asking her what she thought and opted to go to another theater and be inconspicuous instead. Perhaps because the movie was based on the work of a local author, the theater was practically sold out by the time Jessie got there. She found a seat on the back row, where she would be able to watch other people watching the film. She sat there, nervously awaiting the dimming of the lights, which would signal the start of the movie. Then her breath caught in her throat as she watched the words *Hanson Pictures, A Raymond Hanson Film* appear on the screen before her. That affected her more deeply than seeing the title of her own work.

After the opening credits, the camera zoomed in on a beautiful Victorian house in the country—her parents' house. Just as in her novel, the action began immediately and held the audience spellbound. She watched in awe as the plot unfolded before her and Ray's directing talent became evident. He had masterfully portrayed every scene just as Jessie had envisioned when she had written the words. It was as if he had read her mind. The actors that he had cast in the leading roles *were* her characters.

Then came that fateful love scene. Almost afraid to see what was coming next, Jessie closed her eyes for a moment. Then she opened them to observe the most beautiful portrayal of true love that she had ever seen on film. It was totally different from the scene she had witnessed that awful day. Tears began to well up in her eyes as she realized the effort to which Ray had gone to undo the mistake that he had made with her. She felt the hurt begin to heal, and the wall she had unwittingly put up between them crumbled.

When the film was over and the closing credits were scrolling up the screen, Jessie just sat there, exhausted by the emotions she had experienced that evening. She listened to the comments of the people filing past her on their way out of the theater. "Fabulous!" "Best movie I've ever seen!" "I'm coming back tomorrow night!" "I'm glad you forced me to come to this movie!" They were all positive. She prayed that the movie would be this well received all over the world.

She was so proud of Ray! He had made a wonderful movie, and somehow she just knew that he was going to get his Oscar!

The drive home that evening did nothing to dull her excitement over Ray's film. Later, unable to sleep, she lay in bed thinking about it. Suddenly, she wished that she could talk to him. Glancing at the clock on her night table, she saw that it was 11:30 PM, 9:30 in California. Before she could change her mind, she pulled the telephone book from the drawer and looked up the Hansons' number where she had written it down. She picked up the phone and dialed the number.

"Hello." She recognized Helen's voice.

"Helen, hi! It's Jessie Martin."

"Jessie! It's great to hear your voice! How've you been?" she asked, her tone warm and welcoming.

"Pretty good. How about the Hanson clan? Everybody okay?"

"We're all fine here." A short pause then, "I bet you saw the movie tonight, didn't you? What did you think?"

"Oh, Helen! It was just beautiful! I'm so proud of Ray!" she rhapsodized. "Will you tell him for me?"

"You can tell him yourself. He's right here," she replied.

After a pause while she handed Ray the phone, his voice came over the line. "Hello, Jessie," he said softly.

She was more affected by the sound of his voice than she'd thought she would be, but she answered calmly enough, "Hi, Ray. I saw the movie tonight, and I just wanted to tell you how beautiful it is."

"Thanks, Jessie. That means a lot coming from you," was his response.

"You're welcome. And, Ray?"

"Yes?"

"Thank you for…you know." She couldn't bring herself to say the words, but Ray knew what she meant, nonetheless. "Yes, I know, and you're welcome."

"Oh, Ray! I'm so happy for you! I know you're going to win an Oscar—two, in fact—one for Best Picture and one for Best Director, at the very least, possibly more," she informed him with confidence.

"I'll settle for Best Picture. Does this show of confidence mean that you'll come out here and be our guest for the Oscars?" he asked her.

"I don't think so. I just can't see myself hobnobbing with the glitterati of Hollywood, so I'll just take my front row seat in front of the TV. Also I'm going to start praying now that the members of the Academy will see the merits of your work and will nominate the film. I'll be thinking about y'all the whole time."

"But, Jessie…" he began.

"No, Ray. I just wouldn't be comfortable. It's for the best. Well, I've got to go now. My prayers are with y'all. Bye." She hung up.

The ensuing weeks until the Oscar nominees were announced dragged by. Jessie was so tense that she could hardly work.

In the meantime, 'The Sixth Commandment' broke all the records at the box office for five weeks straight. It had exceeded all their expectations. And per their agreement, Jessie received the sizeable payment for the rights to her novel.

Realizing that this did not mean an automatic nomination, Jessie kept on praying until the deadline for mailing in ballots had passed. Even then, she kept praying over Ray's movie.

At last, the February announcement date arrived. As Jessie sat in front of the TV, which she had kept tuned in to the Entertainment channel all day, she began to think that the suspense was going to kill her. What must it be doing to Ray and Helen?

The cameras were trained on an empty stage setting. After what seemed like an eternity, a nondescript, executive type gentleman stepped up to the microphone and read off the list of the nominees.

He began with the least recognizable categories and worked his way up to the most significant.

She heard 'The Sixth Commandment' nominated for Best Cinematography, then Best Screenplay, Ray's female lead for Best Actress, and his male lead for Best Actor. Finally, Best Director and Ray Hanson was the first name called. Jessie thought her heart would burst.

"For Best Picture, the nominees are…" All she heard was 'The Sixth Commandment,' and she almost collapsed onto the floor, moaning over and over, "Thank you, Lord! Thank you, Lord!"

Six nominations! Jessie was so overcome with emotion and gratitude and happiness for Ray!

The ringing of the phone brought her back down to earth. As she reached for the receiver, she wondered who could be calling her at a time like this.

"Hello," she said faintly.

"Jessie! Did you see? Six! Count 'em—six nominations!" It was Ray practically shouting into the phone. She could hear Helen sobbing in the background.

"Yes! I saw it! But I have to remind you that I told you so, Ray." She pretended that she was calm, though she was anything *but* calm.

"So you did! I can't even think straight right now, but I wanted to call and share some of the excitement with you."

"Now you're supposed to be gracious and say it's enough just to be nominated," she told him with a chuckle.

"I've always thought that was a load of crap. *I want to win!* Now I have to start my campaign to do just that. In about six weeks it could be a reality! Oh, Jessie! I'm so excited!"

"I know, Ray. Apparently, so is Helen if that sobbing I hear is anything to go by."

"She lost it when the final category was read. I may have to give her a sedative tonight. Heck! We'll both probably need one!" He wasn't kidding either. As a matter of fact, Jessie thought she might need one herself.

"I'll talk to you later, Jessie. I think I'd better go try to calm my wife. Goodbye."

"Bye, Ray. And congratulations!" Then he was gone.

If the last ten weeks had been tense, Jessie hated to think what the next six weeks would be.

Jessie made a superhuman effort to concentrate on her writing during the next weeks, and it took all her strength of purpose to get anything accomplished. However, she was able to make some headway, since she had an agent and a publisher, both breathing down her neck from New York.

She had to take a couple of days and go to Memphis for a physical exam. Knowing her family history for heart problems, her doctor had strongly recommended that she go to a cardiologist to determine whether or not she was susceptible to the same condition. Jessie wasn't sure if she wanted to know or not, but she decided to take her doctor's advice.

After completing a battery of tests, the cardiologist held a consultation with her in his office. On the surface, the doctor seemed like the kindly, fatherly physician that anyone would appreciate. And he *was* that way, at least at first.

When she was ushered into his office, he smiled benignly at her and began with, "Well, Miss Martin, I am happy to tell you that you do not appear to have inherited your mother's heart condition. Fortunately, your heart is strong and healthy."

Recalling the long illness through which her mother had suffered, Jessie heaved a sigh of relief and returned his smile, "That's really good news, Doctor..."

But he wasn't finished, "However, young woman, do you have any idea what you are doing to your body? Your current diet and lack of exercise may kill you faster than any inherited heart disease. You are at risk for stroke, diabetes, cancer, or any number of other ailments. I'm going to recommend a strict, healthful diet for you—not one of these starvation diets—and an exercise regimen that will take the weight off and keep you healthy. You have a choice to make here. I hope you make the right one. I can't do this for you; only you can." He paused to let that sink in and then asked, "Do you have any questions?"

"No, Sir," she replied meekly. "You've made yourself pretty clear."

"Good. Then I want to give you this packet of information so that you can get started right away."

On the way home, Jessie thought about what the doctor had said. It *had* been her choice to start overeating when she was in her late teens, and it was her choice whether or not to continue. She knew that the problem was tied to her great disappointment at not being able to have children, and somehow she had turned to food for comfort in compensating for that loss. If she expected to obey doctor's orders and lose the weight, she was going to have to come to grips with that fact.

That night, she spent a lot of time talking to God about the weight issue and pleading for strength. Finally, she came to the conclusion that she could do it—she *would* do it—with God's help and started that very day.

It took a lot of discipline not to consume her usual foods in the usual portions, and she had to force herself to exercise. To help stay on track, Jessie simply had to get everything except her diet foods out of the house. Also each day before she began her work, she would exercise, moderately at first, but working her way up to a more rigorous pace. If she felt a craving for a snack, she'd have a carrot or an apple instead of the usual candy bar. In a couple of weeks, she could begin to tell the difference in how she felt and how her clothes fit. She was actually able to put in more hours on her writing because she felt better physically.

Dieting had given Jessie something else to think about besides the Oscars, but the closer the day loomed, the more nervous and anxious she got.

Finally, the big day arrived. Jessie didn't even pretend to write that day since she knew it was a lost cause. She could concentrate on exercise and housecleaning. Even with the frenzy of activity with which she tried to occupy herself, it seemed as if the day dragged by.

Hoping to catch a glimpse of Ray and Helen arriving at the Pavilion, at 7:00 PM she turned the TV to the Entertainment channel and sat on the floor directly in front of the set. Before too much time had elapsed, she was rewarded. There were Helen, gorgeous in some fabulous designer gown, and Ray, equally gorgeous in his tuxedo. The reporter asked Ray which parties he and his wife would be attending after the ceremony.

"None. My youngest daughter is sick, and we'll be going straight home to be with her when it's over," he replied like the concerned father that he was.

Maggie's sick? Poor baby. I hope it's nothing serious, Jessie crooned to herself.

Eight o'clock at last! Jessie switched the channel to ABC and remained glued to the set in her position on the floor. After a while, Jessie had to get up and move around. Besides, the presentations had not yet gotten to the awards in which she had an interest.

Realizing the host had just announced the presenters for Best Cinematography, Jessie ran back to her vigil in front of the TV. The presenters, two people with whom she was unfamiliar, read the list of nominees, and then said, "And the winner is…" It wasn't 'The Sixth Commandment' that was called. Jessie was so disappointed. She felt as if she'd just had the air let out of her lungs.

Next came the award for Best Screenplay. Jessie fretted, *I don't know how much of this I can take!* She felt a little better when she actually recognized one of the presenters this time. "The nominees are…" Of course, Jessie only recognized one title. "And the winner is 'The Sixth Commandment!' Jessie jumped up in excitement. Naturally, Ray wouldn't go up to receive the award because he had not written the screenplay, but he had been involved in part of it—the part of which Jessie was the proudest. Still she listened attentively as the screenwriter made his speech.

Several awards later, they came to Best Actor and Best Actress. The young star who had played Jessie's heroine so beautifully won her Oscar! Though disappointed for the young man, Jessie was ecstatic over the other win.

Jessie was certainly glad to know that her heart was in good shape. Otherwise, she didn't think she would have been able to watch the next two awards.

Praying the entire time, she sat there on the floor within inches of the TV screen. "The nominees for Best Director are…and Ray Hanson for 'The Sixth Commandment.' " A dramatic pause for effect and then, "Ray Hanson…" That was all that could be heard due to the roar that went up at the announcement.

Jessie watched as Ray pulled Helen close and kissed her before he went up on stage. She placed her hand on the television screen as if she were really able to touch him. He looked so handsome and seemed so sincere as he humbly thanked his wife Helen for her patience and support and everyone who'd had a part in making him look good. Jessie was so happy for him! But she knew that this was not the prize about which he'd dreamed so long.

Best Picture. The suspense was debilitating. And Jessie was having trouble breathing as if she'd just run a marathon. "The nominees are…" They showed a poignant excerpt from each picture, which naturally heightened the suspense even further. Now Jessie couldn't breathe at all. "And the winner is…'The Sixth Commandment!' " Tears of relief and joy began pouring down her cheeks as she thanked God and watched the sheer exultation on Ray's face as he kissed Helen again and went up on stage, accompanied by his assistant and several cast and crew members.

When the applause had died down, Ray began thanking everyone for the second time that night. He ended by saying, "And finally, I'd like to thank Jessica Martin, the author of *The Sixth Commandment,* for letting me use her novel for my picture and for all that she did to make the whole filming process more pleasant for the entire cast and crew, my family, and me." Then he looked directly into the camera as if he were talking to her alone and said with a secretive smile, "Thanks, Jessie, for always having the last word." Then he backed away from the podium and was escorted from the stage.

Jessie fell over and sobbed into the rug. She was so happy for Ray! He had realized his dream!

Too exhausted from her emotions to move, she just lay there on the floor as the presentations came to an end. Idly she wondered what Ray had planned next and knew that whatever he attempted he would be successful. He was so talented, and tonight that talent had received the ultimate reward!

Jessie had just gone to bed when the phone rang. She reached to turn on the bedside lamp and answered after the second ring.

"Hello."

"Hello, Jessie," the husky voice on the other end of the line responded.

"Oh, Ray!" And she just started crying again.

"I didn't mean to make you cry," he said, but she could sense the unseen smile.

"It's just that I'm so proud of you and so happy that you won," she defended her tears.

"Thanks. I really can't believe it's over and it turned out so well. I played by the rules, and I actually won – *we* won, Jessie! Thanks to you! It doesn't always work that way."

JESSIE'S WAY: THE LAST WORD

"All I did was write a novel. I didn't do anything else for your film," she denied quietly.

"You just stuck to your principles. Jessie, if I had left that scene the way it was, it would have hurt the picture. Your fans would have hated it. The Academy would have hated it. There would have been no Oscar," he admitted, brutally honest with himself.

"Is that what you were referring to in your speech?"

"Yes."

"Then I'm glad I'm so obstinate," she laughed. "How's Helen taking it?"

"She's doing pretty well. She's sitting right here holding a sick child in her arms."

"Oh, I heard that in your interview before the Oscars began. Can I talk to them?"

"Here. You'd better talk to the little one first. She's about to fall asleep." He put Maggie on the phone.

"Hi, Jessie," the sleepy voice mumbled.

"Hi, Sweetheart. I heard you were sick. I hope you get to feeling better," Jessie sympathized with the child.

"I have a fever and a tummy ache, but Mommy says I'll be okay," she said, though she sounded pitiful.

"I'm glad, Maggie. Would you let me say hi to your mommy?"

There was a pause while the phone was handed to Helen. "Hi, Jessie! Isn't it wonderful? I'm still walking on clouds! I'm so excited about the whole thing! I haven't stopped praying since the nominees were announced!" she gushed, finally pausing for air.

Jessie jumped in, "I know what you mean. I've been praying, too."

"Well, it worked. I'm going to give the phone back to Ray and go put this little bundle back in her bed. Talk to you later, Jessie." Another pause.

"Jessie?"

"Still here. You missed all the parties tonight, didn't you, Ray?" she queried.

"I'm right where I want to be. I'm not missing them at all," he informed her.

"Spoken like a good daddy. Maybe your next award will be Father of the Year," she teased him.

"Cute," he replied. "I'm going to let you go now. I probably woke you out of a deep sleep, but maybe you'll overlook such rudeness for a special occasion. Bye, Jessie."

"I was awake. Goodbye, Ray."

He had hung up, but she kept the receiver to her ear. For some reason, she felt that if she hung up the phone, she would never hear from the Hansons again. And she knew that she probably wouldn't.

Chapter 8

One important decision that Jessie had made was to sell her parents' house. It had been difficult to let go, but she'd become convinced that the house needed a family living in it. So she had listed it with a realtor. The fact that the property had been well maintained meant that it had sold quickly. In a few weeks, a nice family of five would be living there, and she prayed that the children growing up there would be as happy as she had been.

The decision to diet hadn't been easy for Jessie either, but she stuck with it, nonetheless. By the end of April, she was feeling so energetic that she decided to volunteer in some of the summer youth programs sponsored by her church. She was honest enough to admit that one of the reasons she wanted to be involved with young people was that she still missed the Hanson kids, as well as their mother and especially their father. This was a constructive way to take her mind off her loneliness.

Since she had been a fairly good softball player as a young teenager, she felt that helping to coach the girls' softball team would be something that she could handle. When school was out for the summer, the practice would get under way, and a couple of weeks later, the season would begin.

Jessie had to study the softball rules to help her recall the fine points of the game. After all, it *had* been almost eighteen years since she'd last played at fourteen. But by the time the season started, she was expert enough to assist the head coach. Besides, winning wasn't the coaches' main purpose. Teaching good sportsmanship and giving kids a feeling of self-worth, win or lose, in an atmosphere of Christian love were their goals.

Arranging her daily schedule so that she could get a reasonable amount of writing done, she was able to assist in the mornings and write in the afternoons and evenings. So far, it had worked out well for her.

With the first game approaching, the team buckled down to practice and was ready when the day finally arrived. Trying to get the team up for the game, Jessie acted more like a cheerleader than a coach. Some of the kids weren't very good athletes, but they played just the same. All that was required of them was that they do their best and be good sports. Even though the team lost that first game, Jessie let them know how proud she was of them all. Though they were disappointed, they were ready to try again next time.

Jessie had noticed at practice that one of the girls—Jodi—was quite aggressive, and if she struck out or made a mistake, it was always someone else's fault. However, during the first couple of games, she became just plain vicious. She cursed at the umpire and the pitcher and threw the bat at the catcher. Not wanting to kick her off the team just yet, Jessie and the coach decided to talk with her parents and her about the bad behavior.

When they met with them, it was plain where the child's aggression came from. The mother was rude and insulting to both coaches and insinuated that her daughter's problem was the coaches' fault and not hers or her husband's. If Jessie and Marian, the head coach, would do their jobs better, their child would be fine.

Despite the parents' unwillingness to improve the situation, the coaches decided to give Jodi one more chance. That would prove to be a mistake.

For a while the team was on a semi-winning streak. They would win a few and lose a few, the way most of the teams in the church leagues did. Noting a slight mellowing in Jodi's behavior, Marian and Jessie felt that she'd improved enough so that she could remain on the team.

By the end of the season, however, the team was in a slump, and Jodi's behavior began to backslide. On a particularly hot August day, they were playing the toughest team in the league. Jessie's team was behind 7-5. Jodi was at bat, and the opposing pitcher seemed to be having a bad day. On the first pitch, she came close to hitting Jodi with the ball. On the second, she *did* hit her. Totally losing control of herself, Jodi went after the girl, swinging her bat.

Marian and Jessie ran out onto the field to stop her. Since she was younger, Jessie reached the pair first just as Jodi took a full swing at the pitcher. Fortunately, she was able to duck, but unfortunately for Jessie, the full brunt of the swing was delivered to her face right on her nose. She felt excruciating pain and fainted dead away.

When she came to, she was in a hospital emergency room, and she was still in a great deal of pain. As she tried to speak, someone came over to the gurney where she was lying. The woman appeared to be a doctor rather than a nurse, although Jessie couldn't see her too well. Her nose had already started to swell and was blurring her vision. Though she could see fairly clearly for everything except reading and close work, she felt lost right now without her glasses, which had been destroyed by the bat.

"Just lie still, and don't try to talk. You're in the ER at Baptist Central Hospital. You've suffered severe trauma to the nose, probably resulting in a serious fracture. There's a great deal of swelling and bleeding. For now, all we can do is try to keep you comfortable. We won't be able to determine the full extent of your injury or proper treatment until the swelling goes down, probably in about a week, and to be on the safe side, we're going to keep you here at least overnight, perhaps longer."

The doctor spoke to another woman, presumably a nurse, and then turned back to Jessie.

"Are you allergic to any drugs?" she needed to know.

Jessie made the mistake of shaking her head *no* and groaned from the resulting pain.

"Excellent. Then I've ordered Demerol for you. That should help you to rest. In the meantime, we'll admit you to a room.

That was all Jessie knew until the following morning.

This time, the pain in her head woke her up, but Jessie thought that she felt a little better than she had the day before, even though she had to breathe through her mouth and had trouble seeing what was going on around her.

About mid-morning a doctor came to talk to her. He informed her that if she had someone at home to take care of her she could be released by the following afternoon. Otherwise, she would have to stay where she was. Since there *was* no one, she'd have to stay put.

It looked as if Jessie's coaching days were over. Fortunately, softball season was almost over, too. She truly regretted the incident that had caused her injury—more for Jodi's sake than anything else. What was going to become of the child if she couldn't learn to control her temper? Hitting Jessie had been an accident, but she had intentionally tried to hit the other girl. Right now all Jessie could do was pray for her.

Bearing flowers and balloons, Marian came to the hospital to see her that very day. Jessie asked her what had been done about Jodi.

"Of course, she's off the team for good. But unless you want to press charges against her for assault, I guess nothing else can be done," Marian opined.

"Did she seem remorseful at all?" Jessie wondered out loud

"Not at first. In fact, she said it was your fault that you got hit. But then she started crying and asked me if you were going to be okay. I think she truly regrets the entire incident. There may be hope for that girl yet," she informed Jessie with a smile.

"Oh, I believe there is. That's why I won't be pressing any charges. This makes me feel better," Jessie admitted.

Then there was a timid little knock at the door. After Jessie called a weak *come in*, the door opened and in walked a shame-faced Jodi, carrying a gift box. When she saw Jessie's face, she put her hand to her mouth and cried, "Oh, Jessie! I'm so sorry that I hit you!"

"I know you didn't mean to hit me, so it's okay; I forgive you. Come over here and give me a hug," she ordered her.

Jodi did as she was bidden and went over to the hospital bed to give Jessie a gentle hug.

Straightening back up, she meekly told Jessie, "I brought you a gift. I hope you like it." She handed her the box.

Opening it, Jessie found the sweetest music box fashioned out of hammered copper in the shape of a church. When the steeple was wound, the tune that floated out from it was "Amazing Grace."

"Jodi, I love music boxes, and this is the nicest, sweetest one I've ever seen. Thank you so much," Jessie offered admiringly as she wound the steeple again.

Jodi looked as if she would cry, so Jessie asked, "Sweetheart, what's wrong?"

"I was afraid you wouldn't like it. My mother never likes any of the gifts I get her. But I think you really mean it, don't you?" she inquired as if she couldn't quite trust Jessie's answer.

"It's a beautiful and thoughtful gift, Jodi. And I *really* mean it." She wondered how some women ever got to be mothers. What would a little positive feedback have cost Jodi's mother?

"I'm glad. Well, I'd better be going. My mother's waiting in the car for me. Bye, Jessie, I hope you feel better soon. Bye, Marian." Jodi left with a tearful smile on her face.

Marian had been silent during the entire visit, but when Jodi had gone, she asked in astonishment, "Well, what do you make of that? Will wonders never cease?"

All Jessie did was smile and thank God for an answered prayer.

Several days later, the swelling on Jessie's nose had gone down enough for x-rays to be taken. That afternoon, the doctor, accompanied by a plastic surgeon, came by her room to talk about her options.

Pointing out the fracture in the bone, the surgeon showed her the x-rays and explained, "Both Dr. Kyle and I believe that without surgery you will always have problems breathing correctly. However, if I go in and correct the break, you should be your old beautiful self in a few months."

Jessie smiled wryly. "That may not be as good as you think because my nose was pretty unattractive to begin with, and the rest wasn't that great either." She was under no illusions about her looks.

"If you're not happy with your appearance and as long as we're in there anyway, why don't we fix it for you?" the surgeon suggested.

"Oh, I don't think so. I'm not much one for messing with what God gave me," she declined, shaking her head.

"You're not exactly the one who's been messing with it, now are you? Maybe this is God's way of giving you something that he wants you to have at this particular time," Dr. Kyle pointed out.

Jessie had always thought that plastic surgery was out of the question for her, but now she wasn't so sure. Maybe Dr. Kyle was right. She *did* have to have surgery anyway if she wanted to avoid breathing problems.

"Can I pray about this and give my decision tomorrow?" she compromised.

"Certainly. In the meantime, shall we go ahead and schedule the reparative surgery?"

"Yes. Do that. I can see from the last few days that I don't want to go through any more breathing discomfort than I have to," she replied.

The time that she was awake during the night Jessie spent praying about the surgery. What it came down to was the feeling that she was being given another chance at a life. Lately the old one had just seemed stalled on one particular person with whom she'd never had a chance in the first place. She had already lost thirty pounds, and if she changed her appearance for the better when she had the opportunity more or less thrust upon her, then maybe she would have the confidence to go out and meet someone special.

Deciding that was what she would do, Jessie felt at peace when she told Dr. Kyle about her decision the next morning.

"Excellent. I'll inform Dr. Simon of your decision, and he'll come by to discuss the cosmetic changes with you. He has scheduled your surgery for tomorrow morning at eight o'clock."

Dr. Simon came in later that day to discuss the changes. Basically what he was going to do, other than setting the fracture, was smooth out some here and take a little off there.

In jest, he told her, "In a few weeks, I can have you looking like Gwyneth Paltrow." Jessie didn't know who that was, but she hoped she had a nice nose.

"I don't know her, but her nose has to be better than Jimmy Durante's," she remarked, only half kidding.

The doctor smiled at her and said, "You won't be making jokes like that much longer. I promise."

Jessie was slightly apprehensive about the surgery, but she'd had lots of visitors to come and help take her mind off of it. Marian had come back. Her pastor and several others from her church had been by to check on her and pray with her.

By the time she was prepped for surgery, she was calm and ready to get it over. The operation, which took a couple of hours, proceeded without any problems. She went to recovery and then to a room, where she would remain for a couple of days. Then she would be able to return to her home. However, it would be weeks before the bruising and swelling would clear up. Also there was the incision, which would have to heal with resulting scarring for which Dr. Simon would give her a salve. So she wouldn't really be able to tell the final outcome of her surgery until then.

Since she felt and looked like a zombie, Jessie stayed close to home for her recuperation. After a while, she felt well enough to put in some time writing. Though she hadn't been in contact with her agent or her publisher for weeks, she felt that her mind was turning to mush and that work was the cure. Fortunately since her glasses had been destroyed by the impact of the bat, Jessie had older pairs to read by.

Discovering that she was actually seeing fairly well without wearing glasses all the time, Jessie was forced to admit that perhaps she'd been using them as a crutch, something behind which she could hide her insecurities about her looks. Now that there was the hope of some improvement in that area, she felt she should look into alternatives to glasses. Having her glasses smashed into her face was not something that she wanted to experience ever again. Contacts were a possibility, but she'd never really liked the idea of placing foreign objects in her eyes.

Then there was laser surgery, which wasn't always successful and, in some cases, had to be repeated after a while. Besides, she didn't want any more surgeries of any kind any time soon.

That left her with one other alternative—a program that she'd heard about on the radio, which strengthened the eye muscles, thereby reducing the need for glasses. Since Jessie had some time on her hands, she decided to try that. As it turned out after only a few weeks, she had a good deal of success with it and was able to wear her old glasses for reading and work only.

After her first check up following surgery, Dr. Simon had reduced the dressing on the wound to a sterile strip and told her that healing was coming along nicely, despite what the mirror might tell her. He told her that she could resume mild exercise but to keep it simple.

Within a few more weeks, her nose was healed, and Jessie was able to study the difference between then and now. Then, she'd had the large, crooked nose with a bump right on the bridge that had always made her feel so unattractive. Now, her nose was straight, minus the bump, and a lot smaller. She decided that it was a nice enough nose.

So here was a new Jessie, emerging like a butterfly from a cocoon— a Jessie with a slim body, down to what her cardiologist called her ideal body mass; a Jessie without horn-rimmed glasses; and a Jessie with a new nose.

She studied herself in the mirror and had trouble reconciling the reflection that she saw with the physical likeness she used to see. She was still the same Jessie on the inside, but almost totally different on the outside, except for her hairdo, lack of make up, and frumpy clothes. Unpinning the tight little knot at the back of her head, she let her hair fall past her shoulders. It really had no style or life, so she decided that to keep up with the new Jessie she needed a more modern, carefree hairstyle. Memphis was a good place to take care of that, and while she was there, she would get some new make up and maybe some new tailored, non-baggy clothes, too.

Two days later, during a quick trip into the city, she got her new hairstyle – still past her shoulders, but layered so that it looked softer and fuller. Then she stopped by the make up counter of her favorite department store, where a helpful saleslady assisted her in choosing make up to suit her complexion. She bought everything from make up base to eye shadow. After a few helpful hints on how to apply everything, Jessie, satisfied with her purchases, was on her way to the clothes department.

She really felt strange looking for clothes in petites. She hadn't been in such a department since she'd been a teenager. She was used to shopping in the women's plus sizes. *But never again!* she vowed to herself.

Jessie had a field day buying several dresses, tops, jeans, and slacks. Also she decided to get new underwear, and, of course, she needed new shoes. By the time she left the store, she was loaded down with purchases. Then she was ready to go home.

Once there, she hurried to her bathroom mirror to experiment with the new make up. Some of the things she'd bought would take practice for her to be able to apply, but overall she thought she'd done a pretty good job of the application. Then she went to the bedroom and put on one of the new dresses and a pair of heels that she'd purchased as well.

Back in the bathroom, she brushed her hair and then stood back to take a look at the complete picture.

"Who *are* you, and what are you doing in my bathroom?" she asked her reflection. The dramatic change was mind-boggling!

Now what she wanted—what she needed—to keep moving on with her life was to meet someone who could help her move past her feelings for Ray.

Chapter 9

After sixteen months of being a *new* woman, Jessie still hadn't met that special someone. Even though she'd been out a few times with some nice men from her church and friends of friends, there'd never been anyone to whom she was physically attracted. It was her fault. She knew that much. In the meantime, she'd begun to pray that she would stop comparing every man she met to Ray. Having been in love once, she now wanted a man who could love her in return. She would just have to quit being so picky.

During those months, Jessie had really gotten into exercising. She'd joined a health spa in town where she could get out and meet people and enjoy all types of exercises, especially in the winter months. She made it a point to go to the spa at least three times a week.

One morning in April, she rushed into the spa to escape the cold spring rain that was falling. Hurrying over to the reception counter to sign in, she greeted Chuck, the spa manager, with a warm smile and then went to the treadmills.

Greg Robertson, who had been leaning on the far end of the counter and talking to Chuck said, "Wow! Who is *that*?"

"Oh, that's Jessie," he replied.

"What do you know about her?" he asked, obviously intrigued.

"Not much. She's a patron." Making it a practice not to talk about his patrons or give out information, Chuck was very noncommittal.

"Oh, c'mon, Chuck. You can trust me," he coaxed.

"Sorry, Greg. You're on your own," he refused. For some reason, there was something about Greg that he just didn't trust, something that he couldn't put his finger on. He was new to the area, too.

Greg looked in the direction in which Jessie had gone and sauntered that way.

He found her walking at a fast pace on a treadmill and decided to get on the one beside her.

After a few minutes, he slanted his gaze over at her and giving her his most charming smile, began, "I don't believe I've ever seen you around here before. I think I'd remember if I had."

Jessie glanced at the handsome man walking in time beside her and returned his smile. Then she replied, "Oh, I've been coming here for several months. It's just that I'm here at a different time today. Maybe that would explain it."

"That's probably it then."

They talked amiably for a while, and Greg noted that she wasn't wearing a wedding ring. Then Jessie moved on to the stationary bikes. Following her with his eyes, he could tell that she was the kind of woman who would take things slowly. That was why he hadn't asked her out right away, but, even after such a short time, he knew that he was completely fascinated by her and determined that he would do whatever it took to get to know her. Unaware that his reaction might be in the least strange, he began to make plans about how he could see her again.

Watching for a time when Chuck would leave the reception area unattended, Greg went over and sneaked a look at previous entries in the logbook to check for Jessie's usual exercise time. *Ah! This must be it. Jessie Martin – 9:00 AM*, he said to himself. Satisfied, he resolved to be there, too.

It was another week before Jessie was able to get back to her regular exercise schedule at the spa. Upon arriving, she signed in and warmed up. With the intention of doing some leg curls, she went over to a weight bench.

She'd completed several sets when the handsome man that she'd talked with several days ago came and sat on the bench next to her.

He smiled at her, and Jessie thought what a nice smile it was.

"Hi. We've got to stop meeting like this." Then he grinned broadly and admitted, "Yes, I know it's a corny line, but is it working?"

Jessie returned the smile and came back, "It depends on what you were going for."

"I just wanted to strike up a conversation with a beautiful woman," he tried.

"Well, when you find one, let me know how it works," she responded, unaffected by his obvious attempt at flattery.

"What do we have here – a shrinking violet? You have to be aware of the effect you have on the opposite sex," he countered.

Jessie did not much appreciate the trend that this conversation was taking. Aside from the few minutes when they had exchanged polite chitchat before, they were total strangers. Jessie was old-fashioned in her views on relationships between men and women and didn't want to give him the impression that she was an easy pick-up. Apparently, the look she gave him conveyed that message because he backed off.

"I'm sorry. I meant no offense," he said, trying to undo his mistake. Greg could see that he was going to have to take this even more slowly than he'd imagined, though on this second meeting, he was more certain than before that she was worth the effort.

"I accept your apology," she answered after a slight hesitation.

"Let's start over, shall we? Hi. My name is Greg Robertson." He held out his hand to her.

Jessie hesitated again then taking his outstretched hand opted for, "I'm Jessie."

Greg noted the omission. Boy! Was she going to be a hard case or what? She really didn't trust strangers easily at all. If she knew that he'd already garnered a lot of information about her, she'd never trust him, so he'd better tread carefully.

"Maybe sometime I can get a last name to go along with that, but for right now, it's nice to meet you, Jessie."

Greg engaged her in conversation for a few more minutes and then thought it wise to move on. But he had every intention of continuing. By now, he knew that some day she was going to be his. He vowed that nothing would get in his way.

After a few more *chance* meetings at the spa, Greg maneuvered into the position of asking Jessie out on a date, and Jessie promptly declined. Though disappointed, he wasn't about to give up and persevered.

After one more refusal, she finally said yes to meeting him in Memphis at a well-known Italian restaurant, where they would go Dutch treat.

Jessie wasn't sure why she was being so careful about starting a relationship with this man. He seemed nice enough, and, setting comparisons to Ray aside, he appeared to be quite a catch. But there was just something about him that bothered her. She had even prayed about what she considered to be an abnormal reaction on her part. Still, she got no sense of peace about going out with him.

Their date – if one could call it that – went pretty well. The food was excellent, and they got along well. As the evening was winding down, Greg began tentatively, "Jessie, when can I take you out on a real date? I would love to come pick you up at your house as a true gentleman should, and I would love to know your last name."

Jessie gave him a brilliant smile, which caused his heart to turn over, and relented, "Martin. And I suppose the next time you ask me out I'll say yes."

"How about next Friday then? I'll pick you up at your house, and we'll go some place special to mark the event."

"All right," she agreed, though she wasn't exactly excited about the idea.

"Great! How do I get to your house?" he wanted to know.

Jessie gave him as precise directions as she could, realizing that he would probably get lost. Somewhat perversely, she didn't care if he did. If he didn't, that was okay, and if he did, that was fine, too.

The truth was that Greg had already been to Jessie's house. As she'd left the spa a couple of days ago, he had secretly followed her to her driveway. Of course, she would never know that. It was just insurance in case she kept brushing him off. He was not a man who accepted rejection.

Several times during the next week, Jessie thought about canceling the date, but she didn't have Greg's number. In the end, she decided just to get it over with. After all, it was only one date, not a lifetime commitment. At least for now, she wanted to keep things platonic.

As Jessie began getting ready for the date, she decided to tone it down a little. Instead of wearing her hair loose as she'd been doing for months, she wore it in her former knot. Also she chose to wear pants instead of a dress. When she'd finished dressing, she felt that she had achieved the effect for which she'd been striving – conservative, not in the least provocative.

Promptly at six o'clock, the gate buzzer announced Greg's arrival. Jessie was a little surprised that he had been able to find her house so easily. When she opened the front door for him, she remarked on that.

"I've always been good at following directions," he avoided. Then he asked her if she was ready to go.

"Sure. Just let me get my purse." Since she never liked to leave the gate open, she'd put a remote in her purse.

He held the door open for her, waited as she locked the deadbolt, and then escorted her to the passenger side of his black Mercedes.

He handed her carefully into the seat and then went around to the driver's seat.

When they reached the entrance, Jessie pulled out the remote and opened the gate, closing it after they'd pulled through.

Once they were on their way, Jessie asked, "Where are we going anyway?"

"It's a surprise for a special occasion – our first date," he informed her with a secretive smile.

She would have preferred knowing their destination, but she decided not to press him on the issue.

Before long, they entered the suburbs of Memphis, and Greg pulled the Mercedes up to a quaint looking building surrounded by cars and parked some distance from the door.

Inside, the atmosphere was romantic, a sense that was heightened by the candles flickering on each table and the love songs playing over the intercom. This made Jessie really uncomfortable because it seemed as if Greg might have placed more significance on this evening than she had. Strengthening her resolve to remain platonic, she kept the conversation on an impersonal level.

"What kind of work do you do Greg?" she opened.

He gave her what should have been a disarming smile, but it left her totally unaffected. Supposing that a lot of women would be bowled over by the attention Greg was showering on her, Jessie wondered at her indifference. Could her distrust of him be the only problem, or was she still comparing the men she dated to Ray?

"I'm managing my dad's factory – Robertson Manufacturing, at least I am when I don't get better offers, like pursuing a beautiful woman." he replied.

She ignored the obvious compliment and remarked, "Oh, you're *that* Robertson."

"Yes. And what do you do for a living, Jessie?" He already knew the answer, but he pretended ignorance for her benefit, since he had no intention of her ever knowing how he'd had her checked out.

"I'm a writer," she answered, leaving out the fact that she was quite accomplished and well known.

"Wait a minute! You're not *the* Jessica Martin, the novelist?" he kept up the subterfuge.

"I guess that would be me," she responded modestly.

"I'm impressed! Beautiful *and* talented!"

More flattery. The more he talked, the more uncomfortable Jessie became. He must have sensed her discomfort because he abruptly changed the subject. Grateful that their food arrived soon, Jessie was able to relax a bit and concentrate on eating.

While they ate, the conversation was pleasant enough. However, it began to degenerate when Greg commented on her clothes and her hair.

"I wish you'd worn your hair loose tonight. I think I prefer it that way. And I think women look much better in dresses than they do in pants – more feminine. Maybe you'll remember that on our next date," he advised her. It seemed more like an order than a suggestion.

Open mouthed, Jessie stared at him. He was trying to manipulate her, to control her! This was their first date, and here he was trying this stuff on her. *This* was not good! Unable to bring herself to respond to his remarks in any way, Jessie kept her eyes on her water goblet. Determining that this relationship was over before it even began, she started wishing that the evening were over already.

When Greg asked for the check, she heaved a sigh of relief. After paying the check, he asked if she was ready to leave and escorted her to the car. Once there, he suggested that they could go to a club and dance for a while.

"Oh, I don't go in for the club scene. Besides, I'm sort of tired. I think I'd like to go home now," she hedged, trying to avoid a direct refusal of his suggestion.

"It's not a school night, you know. C'mon. Live a little. If you'd give me the chance, I bet I could make you in to a party girl," he cajoled.

She sensed that he was trying to control her again and came back with, "No thanks. I'm content with the way I am. I really prefer going home."

He looked as if he might try to argue further, but thought better of it. "If you insist," he said politely enough.

Jessie could tell that he was put out with her, but she didn't care. All she cared about was getting this evening over soon.

When Greg stopped in front of her house, evidently he expected her to invite him in. Jessie thanked him for dinner and got out of the car. Greg stared at her in disbelief. Then he got out and hurried around the car to the front door, where she stood with the key in hand.

"That's it? Don't I get invited in for a cup of coffee?" he inquired with a tight smile.

"I don't drink coffee, and I told you I'm tired. So goodnight," she stood there, looking pointedly at him.

"Goodnight then."

He tried to take her by the shoulders and draw her close for a kiss, but to ward him off, Jessie put her hand against his chest and sternly protested, "No! This is our first date! I don't even know you!"

For a moment, it seemed as if he was going to kiss her in spite of her protest. Then he came to his senses.

"Okay. I can take things slowly, if that's the way you want it. *And* I can take *no* for an answer." *For now,* he said under his breath.

"Goodnight, Jessie," he called as he went to his car and drove away.

Shivering despite the warmth of the May night, Jessie just shook her head and went inside, double-checking that she'd closed the gate.

Why had she ever agreed to go out with him? He gave her the creeps.

Chapter 10

Since the weather was so nice, Jessie decided to exercise at home by either walking or jogging along the driveway. The things Greg had said to her the night of their date really causing her concern, she'd decided that it was a good idea to avoid the spa, where she would most likely encounter him. There would be no more dates with Greg Robertson.

This particular sunny late May morning, Jessie had just finished her walk and had gone inside to settle down to writing when the telephone rang. Afraid that it might be Greg, she let it ring a few times before she answered it. Then realizing that it was foolish to be fearful of a telephone, she picked up the receiver.

Wishing that she'd remembered to turn on the answering machine, she said, "Hello." She was going to have to get Caller ID to avoid situations like this one.

"Hi, Jessie. It's Ray Hanson," the voice on the other end replied softly.

Jessie felt as if her heart had stopped. *Ray! I haven't heard from him in over two years! Why is he calling now?* The chaotic thoughts just kept rushing through her mind. Then she got control of her mind, as well as her tongue.

"Ray! It's so good to hear your voice! How are you? How are Helen and the kids?" she asked excitedly.

There was such a long pause on the other end that but for the fact there was no dial tone she would have thought that the line had been disconnected.

"Ray?" she queried tentatively.

He cleared his throat and stated bluntly, "Helen was killed by a drunk driver almost twenty-one months ago."

Jessie couldn't stop the sob that rose in her throat as she cried out in disbelief, "Ray, no!" And she began to weep as she clutched the receiver to her ear.

He just let her cry.

When she'd gotten herself under control again, she whispered, "Why didn't you tell me?"

"I thought you knew," he replied, his tone solemn.

"You thought I knew, and what? That I didn't care?" she choked, the hurt evident in her voice.

Silence. Then, "Yes. It was all over the news. I thought you were too busy or maybe you were still mad at me," he admitted.

"I didn't know, Ray!" she wailed and trying to control her emotions, said, "I'm so sorry. I knew her for such a short time, but I loved her all the same." She covered the mouthpiece and cried again.

"I know that," Ray allowed.

She took a deep breath and asked, "How are you holding up?"

"Naturally, it's been very difficult, but I thought we were over the worst. That is until Mother's Day. This one was particularly hard for the kids," Ray explained.

She could relate to that and commiserated, "From my own experience, I can tell you that the second year is often worse than the first. I don't know why."

"Which brings me to the reason for my call. After I witnessed my children having such a hard time with Mother's Day, I decided to send them on a fun trip as soon as school is out. When I asked them where they wanted to go, they all four voted for Mississippi to see Jessie."

Send, not bring, Jessie thought.

"Where will *you* be, Ray?" she wanted to know.

After a slight hesitation, he stated, "I have a business trip up the coast, and then I'm going to take some time for myself."

Time for himself? That probably means with a woman – one in particular, she guessed.

"So how *is* Alissa anyway?" she asked, trying her best not to sound sarcastic, obviously failing miserably.

Her question was met with a stunned silence. Then, "She's fine."

"Does she like kids, Ray?"

"I don't believe that she's overly fond of them. What's your point?" He sounded slightly irritated with Jessie.

"Don't dump your kids for Alissa, Ray," she advised him.

She heard him suck in his breath. Finally, he replied in anger, "I'd almost forgotten how much you like to interfere in other people's lives. Look! I didn't call you to get a lecture! Just forget it!" The longer he spoke the angrier he became.

"Ray! Don't you hang up on me!" she demanded. "Don't take your anger at me out on the kids!" She took another deep, calming breath and said reasonably, "I would love to see your children. When do you want them to come?"

She heard a heavy sigh. "School gets out tomorrow, so the day after that. Will that work for you? They won't be interfering with your writing, will they?"

"No. I'll call my agent and my publisher and tell them I'll be on hiatus for as long as you'll allow them to stay – the entire summer if that's what they want."

"You're being your usual generous self, Jessie. But let's just wait and see how it goes. I'll make their flight arrangements and get back to you later today."

"That'll be fine. I'm looking forward to seeing the kids again," she said, trying to sound positive in spite of their earlier disagreement.

"Thanks, Jessie. Talk to you later. Bye." The line went dead.

Jessie hung up the phone. Then she put her head on her arms, resting on top of the desk, and let the tears flow again. She grieved for the children because they'd lost their mommy. Then she grieved for Ray because he'd lost his beloved wife. Then she grieved for herself because she'd lost a special friend. And finally she grieved for them all because Ray was seeking comfort with a woman who might never love the Hansons the way they needed to be loved.

After she'd spent her tears, she dialed Mark Sanders' number in New York and told Him that she needed to take time off.

"Is it *that* important, Jessie." He didn't sound too pleased.

"I'm going to have company, maybe all summer. Ray Hanson's children," she informed him.

"Oh, right. That was terrible about their mother, wasn't it?" he sympathized.

"You knew, and you never thought to tell me?" she complained to him.

"I thought you had heard about it. It was all over the news."

"So I understand. But I just now found out about Helen's death. Anyway, they want to see me, and I'm going to make it happen, so just get over it. Okay, Mark?"

"I guess I'll have to," he responded, acceding to her wishes.

"Good. I'll get back to work as soon as I can. Bye."

Ray called back later that afternoon to give her the kids' flight number and ETA. "Thanks again, Jessie. They were really excited when I told them that they could go for a visit. Oh, and Jessie, they want to bring the dog, too," he warned.

"Well, of course. What would vacation be without Sanson? I'm glad for their sakes that it worked out, Ray."

"Me, too. Well, I'd better let you go. You probably have a lot to do. Bye now."

In a flurry, she began cleaning the house – changing the beds, scouring the bathrooms, dusting everything in sight, and vacuuming. Then she made a quick trip to the grocery store to stock up on what she hoped were still the kids' favorite foods. With little time to spare, she was ready for her visitors.

Jessie arrived at the airport just a few minutes before their flight arrived and waited by the gate for the Hanson children to walk through.

When she saw the four of them, she recognized them right away, even though they had grown. Noting the sadness that still etched their faces, Jessie's heart went out to them.

She smiled a welcome and waved at them, but they didn't seem to notice her. They stood there, searching timidly for a familiar face.

Suddenly she realized, *Oh! I forgot! They won't recognize me!*

She called their names and went over to them. "It's me – Jessie. I'm so sorry, y'all. I forgot to tell your dad about how I'd changed."

"Jessie! You sound the same! But you look so different!" Becca cried.

Maggie gazed at her in wonder. "You're so beautiful, Jessie!"

"Wow!" Bret and Mara chimed in together.

Then they all rushed her and tried to hug her at the same time. As best she could, Jessie put her arms around them and held them.

"Oh! I am so glad to see y'all!" she murmured hoarsely.

The reunion was proving to be quite emotional for everyone, so Jessie suggested with a grin, "Let's go pick up your luggage and that silly dog you brought with you."

The suggestion was met with a chorus of *okays*.

Once they had retrieved everything and trekked to the car, it was just about lunchtime. Feeling that it was too hot to leave Sanson in the car while they ate, Jessie decided that they should go to a fast food drive-thru. There was a nice park with picnic tables and a restroom on the way home.

After they'd gotten their food and some water for the dog, Jessie drove to the park and found an area in the shade. The children helped her set out the food, and then Jessie asked the blessing.

They had begun their impromptu picnic and were chatting about their flight from California when Maggie piped up out of the blue with, "Jessie?"

"What, Sweetheart?" Jessie returned.

"Why didn't you come when my mommy died?" she inquired sadly.

Jessie almost choked on the bite of salad that she'd been chewing. She glanced around the table and saw five pairs of accusing eyes staring at her. Even the dog seemed to blame her.

"Oh, Kids, I'm so sorry! But I didn't know about your mommy until your dad called the other day. If I'd known, only something very serious could have kept me away. I've been told that it was all over the news, but since I started writing, I rarely ever watch anything except local news. I figure that your mommy's accident happened while I was in the hospital," she tried to explain.

Mara asked fearfully, "Did you have an accident, too?"

"Not like the one your mom had," she hurried to clarify. "I had an argument with a softball bat and lost. That's why I have a new nose. I was in the hospital for a while, and then I had to have surgery."

Sitting beside her, Maggie reached up and touched Jessie's nose. "It's a pretty nose. Did it hurt?"

"A little," Jessie admitted. "But I got over it." She paused then asked huskily, "So will y'all forgive me for not being there for you?"

Maggie threw her arms around Jessie and wailed, "Oh, Jessie! It wasn't your fault! We forgive you!" Then the other kids gathered around her, and Becca answered for them, "Now that we know the reason, we forgive you."

Sanson nosed between them and, placing his front paws on the bench, licked Jessie right in the face on her new nose.

"Yuk!" she complained, wiping away the wetness with the back of her hand. This caused the kids to burst into a paroxysm of laughter.

Enjoying the sound of their laughter, Jessie said with a wry smile, "I'm glad y'all think that's funny. I wonder if you'd think it was so funny if I were to *tickle you!*" And she made a grab for the nearest child – Mara. Mara squealed with delight and collapsed onto the grass. Jessie left her holding her sides and giggling.

Then she went after Becca. "No, Jessie! I'm too old for this!"

"Let's see if you are!" Jessie threatened and grabbed her and tickled her until she begged for mercy.

Bret had backed away with the intention of outrunning Jessie, but by now, Sanson was in on the game and caused the boy to fall in a heap on the grass, where Jessie was able to get him good.

Maggie had been shrieking with laughter during the entire escapade, but then Jessie turned to her and said with an impish grin,

"Your turn, Missy!" She tried to run, but Jessie caught her around the middle and tickled her, too.

Mara shouted, "Let's get Jessie!" Then all four children ganged up on her and tickled her until she fell to the ground with the dog barking at their antics and trying to lick her face again. "Stop! No fair – five against one!" she protested, trying to sound stern, which was hard to pull off amidst all the laughter.

"All right, y'all, we need to finish our lunch and go to my house," she commanded, still chuckling over the tickling she'd just received.

They all agreed, and soon they finished eating and were on their way home.

———————

Upon arriving at Jessie's house, they unloaded the car and took their bags to their rooms, the same ones they'd had last time. With Jessie's assistance, the kids unpacked, and then they all gathered in the great room to discuss what they wanted to do for fun during their visit.

When she discovered that Becca had graduated from high school the week before, Jessie insisted that they go back to Memphis the next day and shop for a gift. After they'd eaten a special lunch, they would stop at the grocery store and buy the ingredients for the cookies they wanted to bake for their picnic on Thursday.

After supper, the younger children got ready for bed. Jessie went into the bedroom to tuck in the little girls and give them a kiss goodnight. Maggie threw her arms around Jessie and said, "I had a good time today. I love you, Jessie!"

"Me, too!" Mara chimed in and joined in the hugging.

"I love you, too, Sweeties." Jessie suspected that the little girls didn't want her to leave, so she lingered while they snuggled down under the covers. Then turning out the light, she left the door ajar and went to check on Bret, who was bedding down in the study again.

When she knocked on the door, he called, "Come in!"

Opening the door, she smiled at him and the dog and asked, "Need anything, Sweetheart?" She knew that might seem sort of mushy to an eleven-year-old boy, but she had sensed a need for comforting in all four children.

"No, we're fine, Jessie," he replied.

"Do you mind if I kiss you goodnight, Bret?" she asked.

"I guess it'd be okay." He didn't want to seem too eager.

She went over and gave him a quick hug and a peck on the cheek.

"I think Sanson wants one, too," he said, looking at the dog, whose tail was wagging furiously.

"We wouldn't want him to feel left out, would we?" She bent and gave the dog a hug and kissed the top of his head.

"Goodnight, you two. See you in the morning."

She returned to the great room, where Becca sat, watching TV.

"Well, I think they're all settled for the night," she told her.

"Good. I was afraid they might not sleep without Daddy here. Especially Mara and Maggie. He tucked them in every night after Mom…" she trailed off.

"I know it's been difficult for y'all, Sweetheart. I still miss my mom, and it's been over eight years. But it gets easier," she promised.

"I hope so," she replied wistfully.

They chatted a while longer, and then, because Jessie wanted to get an early start in the morning, they both went to bed.

After she'd gotten ready for bed, Jessie decided to check on the little girls one more time before turning in. Relying on the hall light, she pushed the bedroom door open and peaked in. She heard Maggie crying with Mara trying to comfort her.

Jessie turned on the light and hurrying over to the bed, sat down beside Maggie. Still crying, the distraught child threw herself into Jessie's arms.

"Maggie, what's wrong, Sweetheart?" she asked her.

"I miss my daddy!" she wailed pitifully.

"Oh, I'm sorry, Sweetie," Jessie crooned as she held her close.

Becca appeared at the bathroom door and with a worried frown inquired, "What's wrong?"

"Maggie misses her daddy," Jessie explained.

"Oh," was her only response.

"Would it make you feel better if you girls came and slept in my bed with me?" Jessie offered.

Maggie hiccupped and gave an almost inaudible, "Yes."

Jessie pulled back the covers, and the little girls hopped out of bed to follow her. Maggie turned back to look at Becca, "You come, too," she begged her older sister.

"Maggie, I'm too old for that kind of thing," she replied, though she sounded as if she would really like to accept.

"It's a big bed," Jessie reminded Becca.

"Okay then," she capitulated.

As they were on their way to Jessie's room, Bret came out of the study and asked, "What's up?"

Maggie answered, "We're going to sleep in Jessie's room with her. You come, too. It's a big bed," she quoted.

He looked questioningly at Jessie, and she said, "You might as well. Bring the dog, too."

When they entered the bedroom, Jessie announced, "If anyone needs to go the bathroom or to get a drink of water, now is the time." Of course, everyone needed something.

Once they were finished, all six of them piled into the bed with Jessie in the middle. Mara and Maggie were on either side snuggled up to her. Becca and Bret were on the outsides, and Sanson was relegated to the foot of the bed. Becca turned out the bedside lamp.

"Jessie?" Maggie said.

"What, Sweetheart?"

"Do you think my mommy's in Heaven? I asked my daddy, but he didn't know," she added as an afterthought.

The question almost broke Jessie's heart, but she answered evenly enough, "I believe with all my heart that your mommy is in Heaven right this minute."

"Really? So she's happy and safe?" Mara chimed in.

"She's with Jesus. There couldn't be a happier, safer place," she explained, hoping that they would understand.

"That makes us feel better. Thanks, Jessie," Becca added.

"Yeah, thanks," they all said, beginning to get drowsy.

"You're welcome. Now everybody go to sleep. Goodnight, y'all," she ordered, smiling to herself.

There was a chorus of sleepy goodnights and then, except for the sound of breathing and the dog's gentle snoring, silence.

In the morning, Jessie had to disentangle herself from Maggie and Mara and crawl over the foot of the bed to get out. She was able to accomplish that feat without disturbing a child. Sanson wagged his tail, but, otherwise, did not move. Then she went into the bathroom to shower and dress.

When she'd finished dressing, Jessie went to wake up the kids.

"Okay! Everybody up! Let's go!" The only human response she got was a couple of sleepy groans. However, the dog jumped down off the bed and went to Jessie for some attention.

"Good morning, Boy." She said as she rubbed his ears. "At least *you're* awake. C'mon. Help me get these sleepyheads up." She called him over and got him to jump into the middle of the bed and teased him until he started barking and frolicking all over the bed, making it practically impossible to sleep. When he started licking their faces, the kids gave up and got out of bed, though not without complaint.

"I thought you'd see it my way," Jessie told them, tongue-in-cheek. "Now, y'all get dressed while I fix breakfast—bacon, scrambled eggs, and toast. Okay?"

"Okay." And they all scattered to their rooms.

After breakfast, the kids helped Jessie clean up the dishes. Then when they'd all made their beds and brushed their teeth, they were ready to go. On the way out, Mara asked if they could drive by Jessie's parents' house.

"We can drive by, but it doesn't belong to me anymore. I decided that it needed a family living in it, so I sold it to a man with a nice wife and three children," she explained to them.

"That's good. I bet the house is happy now," she replied.

"I like to think so," Jessie acknowledged.

By the time they got to Memphis, it was ten o'clock, the time when most stores opened. Jessie asked Becca what kind of graduation gift she wanted.

"Oh, anything will be fine," she hedged.

"Daddy gave her a car," Bret offered.

Jessie gave a low whistle of appreciation and said, "Wow! Now that's a nice gift! You're first car?"

"Yes. Daddy didn't think I was old enough until I graduated, but he knew I would need one for college. So that's what he gave me," Becca allowed.

"Well, congratulations, Sweetheart! What kind is it?"

"Thanks. It's a Jeep Grand Cherokee. He wanted me to have something big and rugged."

"Wise man." Jessie continued, "Well, how about jewelry? Do you need a watch or anything like that?"

"Well, I have a watch, but it *is* kind of fancy to wear to class. It's got diamonds on it. Maybe a practical watch would be good," she responded.

"That sounds great. I know of a nice jewelry store in the mall. We'll go there first. Okay?"

"Okay," Becca agreed readily.

The jewelry store in question had a good selection of watches and a helpful salesclerk. Knowing that Becca would try to be frugal and choose the least expensive watch, Jessie tried to judge her reaction as she was shown a wide variety.

Before long, the clerk showed them a plain, but beautiful watch with a brushed gold band. Becca touched it and said, "Oh, this one's so pretty! How much is it?"

"If that's the one you want, it doesn't matter how much it costs," Jessie told her. "Is it?"

"I love it," she responded simply.

"Then we'll take it." And she handed the clerk her credit card.

While the clerk rang up the sale, Jessie helped Becca take the watch out of its case and fasten it around her wrist.

Then Becca threw her arms around Jessie and cried, "Oh, thanks, Jessie! You're so sweet! It's just beautiful!"

"You're very welcome, Becca! Happy graduation!"

The other three kids had been very well-behaved during the purchase of the watch, so when they'd finished in the jewelry store, Jessie told them, "Let's see. There's another store right around here that I need to go to." She led them into a toy store.

"Ooh! What do you need in here?" Maggie had to ask.

"I don't need anything, but you three younger kids need to pick out a toy for yourselves. Let's call it a welcome-to-Jessie's-house present, shall we?"

"Oh boy!" the trio shouted.

Bret found a computer game that he could play on Jessie's computer. Mara fell in love with a delicate little doll in a frilly dress. Since Maggie missed her stuffed animals back home, she decided on an extra soft, squeezable teddy bear.

"Gee, thanks, Jessie!" they effused over their gifts.

Content with their purchases, the five shoppers headed for the restaurant where they had decided to eat lunch. After studying the menu, the kids all decided to have hamburgers and French fries (What else?), but Jessie opted for a salad.

During the meal, Jessie told them that they should be planning their menu for their picnic the following day. She informed them that she'd had a picnic table placed down by the pond, so it should be a great place to go. Theirs would be the christening picnic.

They decided to bake chocolate chip cookies the next morning before the picnic. Peanut butter and jelly sandwiches, potato chips and soft drinks would finish out the menu.

Since no one had any more shopping to do, they decided to head back home and stop at the grocery store in town.

Jessie, trailed by the four kids, was pushing the cart around the store when she heard someone call her name.

"Jessie!"

She turned to see Greg Robertson striding toward her. *Oh no!* She was just barely able to stop herself from saying the words out loud.

"Oh, hi, Greg."

"I haven't seen you at the spa lately, and you haven't returned any of my calls," he said in an accusing tone.

"Oh, yes," she replied in an offhand manner. "The weather's been so nice that I've just been exercising at home," she went on to explain. "And I've been busy with company." She waved her hand toward the kids. "These are the Hansons. Kids, this is Greg."

"Hi, nice to meet you," the four of them replied simultaneously.

"Hi," was Greg's unenthusiastic response. Evidently, he didn't care for anyone who took Jessie's attention off him.

Eyeing Jessie's hair pulled back in a ponytail and the blue jeans she wore, he frowned and asked,

"When can I see you again?"

Perversely, Jessie was glad that she was dressed in a way that he did not like, and she had no intention of ever going out with him again. Rather than get into that in the middle of a grocery store, she simply excused herself by saying that she was too busy with her guests.

"I'd really like to take you out, Jessie," he persisted.

"I can't leave the children alone, and they might be here all summer. So I'll have to decline. It was nice to see you though, Greg." *Now why did I say that? It's just not true,* she thought. He appeared to be extremely possessive of her, though she had no idea what she'd done to make him that way. His attitude completely unnerved her.

As she started to wheel the cart away, he put a detaining hand on her arm.

"You can't seriously mean that you'd prefer tending to someone else's brats to going out with me!" he said through gritted teeth.

Now he was beginning to scare her. His words sounding almost like a threat against the children, she felt that a little diplomacy might work better.

"No. That's not it, Greg. It's just that I haven't seen the kids in such a long time, and we're having a nice, long visit. I'm sorry," she threw in for good measure.

He seemed to be somewhat mollified by her reassurances.

"Well, I can understand that, I guess. Can I call you later?"

Not wishing to risk further outbursts in front of the children, she just gave in, "Sure."

Greg gave her a charming smile and said, "Later then." Totally

JESSIE'S WAY: THE LAST WORD

ignoring the kids, he quickly left the store.

The four gathered around Jessie. Maggie verbalized their sentiments, "I don't like him. He's mean."

Becca added, "We're sorry if we're in the way. Your boyfriend didn't seem to like our being here at all."

"You're wrong on two counts, Sweetheart. First, you're not in the way in the least little bit. Secondly, he's not my boyfriend. I've gone out with him once, and I didn't enjoy it at all," she clarified for them.

Jessie noticed the concern on their faces and declared, "Come on! We're not going to let someone like him spoil the lovely day that we've had, are we?"

Her question was met with a chorus of *nos*.

"Good. Let's get these groceries home," she suggested. Jessie was trying to be positive for the kids' sakes, but she felt the need to send up a silent prayer for God's protection and vowed to be on her guard against Greg.

Chapter 11

Since he had finished his business in San Francisco ahead of schedule, Ray decided to take an earlier flight home and call Alissa to let her know that he was back.

On the flight home, he began to reflect on the past. It had been over three years since he'd seen Alissa. This was the woman for whom he'd almost left his wife. He thought about the way she was then: the beautiful, seductive blue eyes, the long, jet-black hair, and the warm, curvaceous body. She had been more than willing to start an affair with him back then, but, thankfully, he'd been unwilling to be with another woman while he was still a married man. He was grateful that he'd done nothing that could have led to the end of his marriage.

That recollection caused him to think about Jessie. Ray smiled wryly as he remembered the argument that Jessie and he'd had over his marital problems. If she hadn't interfered in his private affairs, he would not have had over a year and a half of happiness with his family intact before his wife had died.

Then he thought about Jessie's uncanny ability to read his intentions, even from two thousand miles away. Just like last time, she'd made him angry, but this time, she'd really crossed the line. He was a single man with nothing to keep him from pursuing a relationship with an attractive woman. Not having been with a woman since his wife had died almost twenty-one months ago, he felt that he was ready to begin such a relationship. Even though Jessie was doing him a huge favor by allowing his children to visit, she had no business meddling again.

When he got home, Ray noticed how quiet the house was, and he realized that it was not a good thing. He turned on the TV so that there would be some noise. Then he called Alissa. Apparently, she wasn't home yet, so he left a message on her answering machine. With that accomplished, he sat down in front of the TV to watch cable news.

As he sat there, he became lonelier and lonelier. Then it hit him. He missed his kids! Really missed them! He missed the laughter, the tears, the noise, the arguing, the constant need for attention! So what was he doing here without them? Why wasn't he with them in Mississippi? All of a sudden, he had a strong desire to be with his children and to see Jessie again, even if she was trying to interfere in his life. That was part of her charm.

It dawned on him that she might have been right yet again. If he had a relationship with a woman who didn't like kids, how would that make *them* feel? They'd already lost their mother, and they didn't need to be made to feel that they were losing him as well.

Lost in thought, he was shaken from his reverie by the chirrup of the telephone. It was Alissa.

"Hello, Ray," she said softly. "I've been looking forward to this evening for over three years. I can't wait to see you again."

"Alissa, I'm sorry. I was just about to call you back. There's been a sudden change of plans."

"What are you saying, Ray? Do you want me to come to your house?" she hinted.

Having come to a sudden decision, he explained to her, "No. I have to cancel altogether. I've discovered that I miss my children, and I'm going to Mississippi to be with them."

"What?" she yelled into the phone. "You're dumping me for your children? Are you sure there's not another woman? Didn't they go to visit that writer you were involved with?"

Ray laughed outright at the thought of Alissa's being jealous of Jessie. "Believe me Jessie's not the type of woman you need to be jealous of. Besides, I'm not dumping you. I'm simply putting *us* on hold for a while."

"Ray, you overestimate your charms. I'm warning you. I will not wait around for you. There are plenty of men who want me. And by the time you get back from *Mississippi,* of all places, I'll be involved with one or more of them," she advised him, quietly threatening.

He didn't like her tone. Perhaps he'd had a lucky escape, after all.

"Well, you do what you have to do, and so will I," he told her without hesitation.

"Goodbye, Ray!" And she was gone.

Not waiting around to wonder if he was doing the right thing, Ray dialed the number of the airport. The earliest nonstop flight that he could get was six o'clock the following morning, so he booked a seat, even though it meant getting a very early start. With the phone in hand, he started to call Jessie to advise her of his plans, but then he decided that he liked the idea of surprising the kids. Once he arrived in Memphis, he would rent a car and drive to Jessie's house.

The decisions made, Ray had one more call to make to his assistant. There was nothing that would require his attention for several weeks, if necessary. Because he hadn't taken a break since Helen's death, he decided that he needed a long vacation *with* his children and not without them. Then he went to pack his bags for an extended visit.

———

At eleven thirty the following morning, the preparations for their picnic were well underway. Recalling the last time that this crew had made cookies, Jessie couldn't help smiling. The scene was exactly the same – the ingredients and paraphernalia for making chocolate chip cookies concealed the island top; flour and sugar covered the floor; the smell of burned casualties filled the air. Fortunately, they'd had enough successful batches of cookies to feed a small army.

Jessie recruited volunteers to help with the clean up, and the rest were instructed to start making the peanut butter and jelly sandwiches.

They were all working and chatting happily together when the gate buzzer went off.

Of course, Sanson started barking. He never had liked that buzzer.

Leaving the kids with their work, Jessie went to check the monitor. She didn't recognize the vehicle at all and couldn't make out the identity of the driver. She pushed the intercom button and asked, "May I help you?"

The person behind the wheel replied, "Hi, Jessie. It's Ray. I wanted to surprise the kids."

Ray! Jessie felt lightheaded for a second, before she responded calmly, "They're occupied, so you ought to be able to come on up without their knowing it." Then she opened the gate for him.

After making sure that no one would notice her absence, she tiptoed to the front door, unlocked it, and sneaked out onto the front porch to greet Ray when he drove up in front of the house.

As he emerged from the vehicle, Jessie just stood there drinking in the sight of him. Aside from the few lines that sorrow had evidently etched into his face, he hadn't aged a bit; he was as devastatingly handsome as ever.

She pulled herself together and with a wide grin, accused him, "You missed your children, didn't you?"

Ray looked up at the young woman who had just spoken to him as if they knew each other. He didn't think that he would have forgotten such a gorgeous creature.

He looked at her in confusion. "I beg your pardon. Do I know you?"

Jessie chuckled and apologized, "I'm sorry. It's me – Jessie. I keep forgetting that the Hansons haven't seen the new me before."

By this time, Ray had joined her on the porch. His jaw dropped as he stood there and allowed his gaze to travel over her. He noted the perfect fit of the blue jeans and red t-shirt on her slim body. Her long blonde hair had been allowed to fall in a modern, carefree style to just below her shoulders. Her previously large and unattractive nose was now cute and even pert. Gone were the horn-rimmed glasses, which had obscured the lovely hazel eyes. This was *not* the Jessie that he remembered!

"Jessie? No way! I don't believe it! Say something that is truly *Jessie* so that I'll know it's really you!" he said, still doubting her.

"As long as I get the last word," she told him with a laugh.

"It *is* you!" Grabbing her, he gave her a bear hug.

"Oh, it's so good to see you, Ray!" Jessie whispered in his ear. Then she just shut her eyes and enjoyed the moment for as long as it lasted.

"You'll have to give me some time to get used to the new you," he responded, shaking his head as if to clear away cobwebs.

"Take all the time you need, but for now we'd better get in there to see what your children are up to," she warned as she pulled away from his embrace.

"Right."

Jessie led the way inside to the kitchen, where the children were still busily at work, oblivious to the fact that their father was standing there.

Ray surveyed the scene for a few moments before remarking with a broad smile, "Now this is what I like to see – my children, hard at work."

Four startled faces looked in his direction. "Daddy!" they squealed in unison. Then they rushed him and threw themselves on him, with Sanson joining in the fun.

"Daddy! What are you doing here?" Maggie cried. "We missed you so much!"

"I missed you guys, too! That's why I'm here. I was hoping to surprise you, and apparently I succeeded."

Jessie observed their reunion with tears beginning to well up in her eyes. *Oh, Ray! I'm so proud of you! Your kids really needed you here, and you didn't let them down after all,* she thought.

"Oh, Daddy! We're so glad you're here! You can come on our picnic with us. We're almost ready to go," Mara informed him.

"A picnic? It sounds like fun," he replied.

Bret piped in, "We're having peanut butter and jelly sandwiches."

"And *we* made the chocolate chip cookies," Becca told him proudly.

"My favorites," was his serious response, as he looked over their heads at Jessie and winked.

Hiding a smile, Jessie suggested, "What say we help your dad bring in his bags, and then we'll pack up the food and head down to the pond. Okay?"

"Okay!" they responded willingly.

"Are you sure you have enough room for me, Jessie? I can go to a motel."

"Don't be silly. Of course, there's always room for you in my house. You'll have the guest suite. In fact, it's ready for a visitor," she asserted, making it clear that his unexpected visit was welcomed.

"Thanks." Ray thought that Jessie might look different on the outside, but inside she was the same sweet, generous person that she'd always been.

Judging by the number of bags that Ray had brought with him, his visit was not going to be a short one. That thought gave Jessie much pleasure.

Once they had Ray's gear stowed in the guest suite, they packed their picnic lunch and trouped down to the pond. It was a lovely early June day, not yet too hot and humid to enjoy being outdoors for a long period of time.

Despite the fact that there were globs of peanut butter mixed with grape jelly oozing out the sides, Maggie and Bret were extremely proud of the sandwiches they had made. After Jessie had said the blessing, everyone else seemed to enjoy them, too, along with the conversation buzzing around the picnic table.

When they had reached the dessert stage, Maggie told her daddy, "We met Jessie's boyfriend yesterday."

Ray looked at Jessie in surprise and queried, "Boyfriend?" For some reason, the thought that this new, beautiful Jessie might have a boyfriend hadn't entered his mind. Oddly, he found the thought unpleasant.

"He's *not* my boyfriend. We've only had one real date, and we're not likely to have any more. If I can help it," she added as an aside.

"Why? You two didn't hit it off or something?" He had felt relieved at her words.

"It's kind of hard to explain. It's like he thinks he owns me, even after only one date. He tried to tell me how to dress and how to wear my hair," she offered.

"He's mean, too," Mara piped up. "He called us brats. We didn't like *him* either."

With raised eyebrows, Ray looked at Jessie. She could read the question on his face and replied, "He became irate when I told him that I couldn't go out with him and leave my guests alone. That's when he called them brats. I tried diplomacy with him to calm him down, but I'm more certain than ever that I don't want to see him again," she replied, leaving out the part about how he'd scared her.

But Ray could detect the concern in her eyes and voice. *This guy must really be a piece of work to frighten somebody like Jessie,* he thought. Then he felt a little ashamed because he hadn't always treated her that well himself.

When they'd finished their picnic, Jessie asked, "Now what do y'all want to do?"

Ray couldn't help smiling at her *y'all* and thought back to the last time he'd heard her use that Southern expression. It had been a happier time for him and his children. Glancing around the picnic table at them, suddenly he realized that there had been a softening of the tension and sorrow in their faces in the few days that they'd been there. They appeared more relaxed than he'd seen them in twenty-one months, and he wondered if it was the different setting or if it was Jessie's influence. As he watched her with the kids, he thought it was probably the latter.

Mara wanted everybody to lie on his back in the grass to watch the clouds and guess their shapes. Out in the open area, where she suggested this game take place, there was plenty of shade cast by the trees.

Since Jessie'd had the area treated with an all-natural bug spray that was non-toxic to humans and pets, she didn't think they would pick up any tick bites. It seemed to be an idyllic way to pass an afternoon, so she voted for Mara's suggestion.

"I don't know," Ray came back, tongue-in-cheek. "I think I liked it better when you guys were hard at work."

"Oh, Daddy! We've worked hard today. We deserve a rest," Becca whined.

"So you do," he readily agreed.

All seven of them, including the dog, stretched out in the grass and gazed up at the clouds.

Jessie lay between Mara and Maggie. Becca was beside Maggie, and the guys manned the outsides, with Sanson lounging at their feet.

"I haven't done this since I was a little girl," Jessie admitted with a reminiscent smile.

"Oh really? And just how long would that be?" Ray wanted to know.

Jessie raised herself up on her elbows and gave him a look. "I'll tell my age if you tell yours first," she challenged him.

"Forty-one," he accepted the challenge.

Jessie grinned wickedly at him and responded, "Twenty-three."

Sitting up straight, Ray scolded her, "Jessie Martin! Don't fib in front of my children!"

His children were giggling at the exchange between the two adults. Maggie said, "You guys are funny!"

"The truth, Jessie!" Ray commanded her.

"Thirty-four," she finally admitted her true age.

He studied her animated face for a few moments and decided, judging by her serious tone, that this time she was telling the truth, though the smooth, clear skin and laughing eyes made her seem younger.

"That's more like it," he replied and lay back on the grass.

They spent quite some time gazing at the clouds and guessing their shapes, which ranged from the usual cotton candy and snowmen to sheep and cows. Some of the clouds even looked like *clouds* – of all things. After a while, there was silence. Raising herself on an elbow again, Jessie saw that they were all sound asleep, including Ray. Having never seen him in this vulnerable position before, she studied his face, now innocent in sleep, and realized that her feelings for him were as strong as ever. It was no wonder that none of the men that she had dated, most especially Greg Robertson, had measured up to him.

Jessie lay down again and prayed that she would have the strength to keep from making a fool of herself over him and thus ruin her life, not to mention the kids' vacation. Also, she would hate to embarrass

Ray.

Unable to sleep like the others, Jessie got up and began repacking the picnic leftovers. Pretty soon the others began to rouse.

"It's about time you sleepyheads woke up," she told them, as she finished the clean up.

Now that everyone but Ray was up, Maggie said, "Come on, Daddy! Time to get up!"

"I'm too comfortable to move," he replied sleepily.

Maggie took that as an invitation to sit on his stomach and screamed in mock terror as he grabbed her and began tickling her. "Is that any way to treat your old dad?" Then he picked her up as he rose from the grass and swung her around, as she giggled with delight.

"That was fun, Daddy!" She reached her arms out for him to pick her up so that she could give him a hug. "I love you, Daddy," she said against his neck.

"I love you, too, Pumpkin," he murmured. I love all you kids more than anything in the whole world!"

The other kids came and got in on the hugging. "This has been the best day ever, hasn't it?" Bret asked no one in particular. Everyone agreed that it had.

Not wishing to intrude, Jessie just stood there, smiling at their family moment.

Then they headed back to the house.

That night, Jessie stayed in the great room while Ray tucked in his children from the oldest to the youngest. Becca showed her dad the watch that Jessie had given her for graduation.

"It looks expensive, but she wouldn't tell me how much it cost. It was okay to accept the gift, wasn't it, Daddy?" she asked, uncertain about his reaction.

"If Jessie was determined to give you the watch, I'm sure the decision was out of your hands. I learned a long time ago about her penchant for always getting the last word," he remarked with a wry smile.

"Oh, good," she said, relieved at his response.

Ray kissed the top of her head and told her not to stay up too late. Then he headed through the bathroom to Mara and Maggie's room.

Already in bed awaiting their father, Maggie was squeezing her teddy bear, and Mara was straightening her new doll's dress. As Ray entered the room, the girls said, "Daddy, look at what Jessie bought us. She said they were welcome-to-Jessie's-house presents." They held the gifts up for his inspection.

"They're just adorable," Ray declared, after he'd looked over each toy.

"I think she really bought them to cheer us up though," Mara offered with a nine-year-old's wisdom.

"Cheer you up? Were you sad?" he asked, suddenly feeling a twinge of guilt.

"The first night we were here, I started crying 'cause I missed you so much, Daddy. Then Jessie came in here and took us to her room and let all us kids and Sanson sleep with her. It's a big bed, you know," she clarified for him.

Ray remembered the bed. At first, the thought of that bed made him feel sad, but then he got a mental picture of the five of them plus the dog, and he couldn't help smiling.

"That must have been very cozy," he replied, grinning at his two young daughters.

"Oh, it was! I felt so much better. Last night I slept in here with my new teddy, and I was fine," Maggie assured her father.

"I'm glad, Sweetheart."

He hugged both little girls and kissed them goodnight.

As he headed for the door, Mara told him with a serene expression on her face, "Daddy, Jessie says that Mommy's in Heaven with Jesus, and that she's happy and safe."

Ray shut his eyes as he felt a flash of pain. All he said was, "I hope so, Pumpkin." He hadn't known what to say to his children when they'd asked the question. He might have guessed that they would ask Jessie about it and that she'd have an answer.

He wished them goodnight and turned out the light. Leaving the door open a crack, he passed the great room on his way to Bret's room. "One to go," he told Jessie in passing. He knocked on the door and entered.

Bret was playing on the computer when his dad came in. Sanson lay on the floor beside him.

"Hi, Dad," he greeted before turning back to the game he'd been playing.

"I'm playing this game Jessie bought me yesterday. It's great!" he told him eagerly.

"A welcome-to-Jessie's-house gift?" Ray asked him.

"Yes, Sir. You want to play?" he invited.

"Sure." He looked over his son's shoulder and followed his instructions. Of course, by now, Bret had mastered the game and handily beat his dad.

"Well, that's all for me." He patted Bret on the back. "Goodnight, Son. Another half hour, then it's lights out. Okay?"

"Okay," he agreed without complaint.

Ray went out to the great room and sat down opposite Jessie.

She smiled across at him. "It takes a while, doesn't it?"

"It does. Helen used to take care of all the tucking in, but since she...well, I, of course, took over, and I've found that I really enjoy it," he admitted ruefully.

"I can understand that. It's a sweet time of the day, " she echoed his sentiments.

"Exactly." After a pause, he continued, "Jessie, about the gifts."

"Oh, you're not going to make them give back their presents, are you? I wanted to give them something—a memento of their visit..."

He cut her off, "Jessie, calm down. I just wanted to thank you for them. It was sweet of you to do something to cheer up my kids."

Relieved, Jessie responded, "You're welcome."

"Whatever you've been doing with them has made a definite difference. They seem happier and less tense," he confided to her.

"I think your presence here today is more responsible for that than anything I've done," she demurred.

He eyed her for a moment before he spoke. "I have to apologize to you for the way I snapped at you on the phone the other day. I know you were only looking out for the children when you told me not to dump them for Alissa."

"And you, too, Ray. I want what's best for you all. Maybe if you take things slowly and let the kids get to know her, she'll come to love them, and it'll work out for y'all," she offered, twisting a knife in her own heart.

"That's not going to happen. I don't think she wants anything to do with me now. When I told her that I was canceling our date to come here, she actually said that I was dumping *her* for my kids! I think that I've had a lucky escape," he informed her, amazed that anyone could have an attitude like Alissa's.

"I'm sorry, Ray," she replied, feeling like a hypocrite because she wasn't sorry in the least.

Ray knew it, too. "No, you're not. You were right again, and you know it. It took me a while to admit it because I just can't bear to let you have the last word every time," he confessed.

She smiled at him and said, "Apology accepted. And, Ray, I'm sorry about not being there for y'all when Helen died. I figure it happened while I was in the hospital with this," she remarked, touching her nose.

"Cosmetic surgery *is* important," he said with a note of sarcasm.

Jessie realized that he didn't know the true story about her new nose, but he might have given her the benefit of the doubt.

"For your information, my nose was badly fractured in an argument with a softball bat. I was in the hospital for a couple of weeks waiting for the swelling to go down and then for reparative surgery. Because I was in a lot of pain and had severe headaches to boot, I couldn't bear to have the TV on. That's probably why I didn't hear about it," she explained, trying to subdue the quiver in her voice.

Ray got up from his chair and went over to kneel in front of her. Taking both her hands in his, he pleaded, "Jessie, forgive me for assuming the worst—just now *and* when Helen died. I should have known there was a good reason for your not being there. I'm so sorry." He felt really bad about the misunderstanding.

Jessie was completely disarmed by his actions, which caused her to feel quite breathless. But she was able to murmur, "I forgive you, Ray. It was an awful time for you and the kids."

"Yes, it was, but, thanks to you, we all have a lot of good memories of the months prior to the accident." After a slight pause, he added with a charming smile, "It's a beautiful nose, by the way."

"My surgeon said that it would look like Gwyneth Paltrow's nose," she told him.

"I wouldn't have thought that you knew who she was," he laughed.

"I don't, but she has to have a better nose than Jimmy Durante," she replied with a giggle.

All of a sudden, Ray had to fight the urge to take her into his arms, so he got off his knees and sat back down in his chair.

"She does, but I don't know that there's any comparison except that you're both gorgeous blondes," he emphasized.

"Oh, right!" she automatically doubted the sincerity of the compliment.

"I mean it, Jessie. It's an astounding metamorphosis," he assured her.

"I'll take your word for it, since you're somewhat of an expert," she conceded reluctantly.

In mock surprise, he said, "You mean that I get the last word this time?"

"Enjoy it while it lasts," she came back with an impish grin.

After a while, they said their goodnights and went to bed.

Chapter 12

After breakfast on Sunday, Jessie asked if anyone wanted to go to church with her. Ray declined. No surprise there. And she fully expected that the children would want to stay with their dad, though Maggie appeared to be torn. Sensing her indecision, Jessie suggested that she stay with her dad this time and that she could go with her to church some other time.

With the problem solved, Jessie went to her room to get ready. After carefully applying make up and brushing her hair, she donned a light green linen dress with a scooped bodice and a short, flared skirt. Without thinking, she fastened her silver heart necklace around her throat. Finally, she added a pair of white heels, and she was ready to go.

Then she went in search of her guests and found them out on the deck. When she opened the French door, everybody glanced her way.

"Oh, Jessie, you look so pretty!" Maggie cried.

"Thanks, Sweetie," she responded.

Ray thought that was an understatement. As he eyed her slim form in the green dress, her shapely legs, and her lovely face, the word *gorgeous* kept coming to mind.

Becca remarked, "Isn't that the necklace that Mom and Daddy gave you the last time we were here?"

Covering the heart with her hand, Jessie looked over at Ray and apologized, "I'm so sorry. I wear it to church almost every Sunday, and I didn't even think about it." She reached up to remove the necklace.

"No. Leave it. It's perfect with that dress," Ray declared, somewhat misty-eyed.

"Thanks," she replied to the compliment and changed the subject. "I'll be back sometime after twelve. Then I'll fix us some lunch."

Ray answered, "I don't think so. When you get back, I'm taking us out for lunch."

She started to argue, but seeing that it would do no good, opted for, "Seems as if someone is getting used to having the last word around here."

He smiled, "It's heady stuff, too. I can see why *you're* so fond of it."

Jessie laughed out loud and shook her finger at him. "On that note, I'll be leaving now." She grabbed her purse and Bible and went out to the garage.

Involvement in a heated, but friendly, discussion in Sunday school caused Jessie to be late getting into the worship service. Thus she ended up having to sit in the very back under the balcony. As she craned her neck to see the pastor when he stood up to preach, she noticed a man sitting a few rows in front of her. He appeared to be scanning the crowd of worshippers, searching for someone.

Jessie gave an inaudible gasp. It was Greg Robertson! What was he doing here? She tried to get her racing thoughts under control. After all, this was a public place. He had a right to be there if he wanted. But she just could not shake the feeling that he was there looking for her.

After seeing Greg, she couldn't concentrate on the sermon. She kept wondering about his motives in being there. So during the prayer before the invitation, Jessie decided to slip out before Greg had a chance to see her.

When she got outside, she practically ran to the parking lot and locked her car door as soon as she was safely inside. Jessie didn't know if she was being paranoid or not, but she sped away from the church with a feeling of relief, though still she felt the need to keep glancing in her rearview mirror on the way home.

As she drove up in front of the house, she saw the entire Hanson family sitting on the front porch. Maggie climbed out of her daddy's lap and affirmed, "Oh, Jessie! We're so glad you're home!"

"Really, Sweetheart?" she replied as she strolled up onto the porch. "Hungry, are you?"

"Yes," she answered truthfully.

"Well, let's get ready and go fill you up then," she suggested.

In a few minutes, everyone had gathered out at her vehicle. Mara and Maggie wanted her to sit with them, so she gave Ray the keys and asked him to drive. Becca sat in front with her dad, and Bret sat on the back seat.

"Where to?" Ray asked as he started the car.

"Memphis. We can decide what kind of food on the way there," she said.

Once they had cleared the gate, Ray headed toward Memphis.

To save time, Jessie had not changed her Sunday clothes. As a result of sitting in the middle on the second seat, she kept having to tug her skirt over her knees.

"Okay. What kind of food does everybody want?" Jessie began.

For the entire drive, the discussion was centered on food. In the end, everybody voted for Italian, with Jessie abstaining, so she directed Ray to a well-known restaurant on Winchester Avenue.

The place was crowded, but they didn't have to wait long to be seated at a large circular booth with Ray and Jessie posted on the outsides. Once the waitress had taken their orders, they munched on bread and salad while they awaited their main course. An indulgent smile on her face, Jessie listened as the children all tried to engage their dad in conversation.

After the food arrived, Jessie inquired if they minded if she asked a blessing. Ray looked at her in surprise. He'd never thought about people wanting to pray in a public restaurant before, but he had no objection.

She bowed her head and prayed, "Lord, we thank you for our safety and for the food we are about to receive together as good friends. In Jesus' name, amen."

In the few days that the children had been with Jessie, Maggie had gotten into the habit of echoing her *amen*, which she did now.

Ray appeared to be moved by the prayer but made no reference to it. Instead, he asked Jessie about her latest novel as they began their meal.

After she'd finished outlining it for him, he told her, "It sounds like a winner. Maybe we can work together again sometime."

She smiled her agreement, "I'd like that." Then, "What have you done recently?"

He admitted that he hadn't been directing much lately. "I've kept it simple since Helen's death. I wanted to be close to home for the kids."

Jessie's eyes teared up at the idea of Ray's being so considerate of his children's needs during this time. Actually, he really had deserved some time for himself, but he'd chosen to be with them instead.

The kids joined in the conversation, which caused the meal to pass noisily, but quickly. When the check came, Ray pulled out his credit card to pay. Glancing at the card, the waitress stopped in her tracks and asked excitedly, "Are you the man who directed that movie based on Jessica Martin's novel?"

Jessie watched in amusement as Ray trained his considerable charm on the pretty, young waitress, who couldn't have been much older than Becca. In fact, Jessie had noticed her flirting with Ray every time she'd been by their table.

"Yes, I am," he acknowledged with his most charming smile.

"Oh, Mr. Hanson, can I have your autograph?" she practically drooled.

"Certainly. If you'll call me Ray," he invited in a seductive tone.

"Daddy! How embarrassing!" Becca complained.

Jessie had to cover her mouth with her napkin to keep from bursting out laughing. While the waitress went to find a piece of paper, Jessie asked, not even trying to hide her amusement by now, "Would you like for us to wait in the car so that you two can be alone?"

Ray just grinned at her and asked innocently, "Oh, do you think I'm overdoing the big Hollywood director routine?"

"Well, *yeah!*" she replied as if to someone who was totally clueless.

"I never get this kind of attention back home. I think I like it," he confessed.

At that moment, their waitress returned, bringing several other young women in her wake, all of whom wanted Ray's autograph. He took the time to oblige them all.

One of them asked him, "The next time you see Jessica Martin, will you please tell her how much I admire her work?"

"Why don't you tell her yourself? There she is," he pointed toward Jessie.

The girl looked at Jessie in confusion and then gushed, "Oh, Miss Martin, you don't look anything like your photo! You're so beautiful! Can I get your autograph, too?"

Biting her tongue to give herself something else to think about, Jessie mimicked Ray's earlier reply, "Certainly. If you'll call me Jessie." Then she autographed the piece of paper with a flourish.

After the young women had gone back to their work, the children didn't even try to control their laughter. Becca was laughing so hard that tears rolled down her face. Ray tried to look offended but failed miserably when *he* burst out laughing as well.

"Let's get out of here," he suggested, still laughing at himself. They took a leisurely drive back to Jessie's house.

That night when everyone was supposedly in bed, the children came to Jessie's bedroom door. Upon seeing her light still on, someone knocked timidly.

"Come in," she called, curious as to what they wanted at this time of night.

The four of them and the dog, of course, came and got on her bed.

"Can we talk to you, Jessie?" Bret asked.

"Sure. What can I do for you?" she offered.

Mara spoke up, "Well, you know that next Sunday is Father's Day, and we want to do something special for our daddy."

Becca took up the explanation, "Yeah. But we don't have much money of our own, and we don't want to ask Daddy for money to spend on a present for him."

Maggie took a turn, "We wondered if you could help us think of something that we could do for Daddy."

"Oh, y'all, that's so sweet! Let me think here a minute." Jessie thought back to Father's Days of the past. It had always been a very special day for her dad and her, and she'd never had much money to spend either. They'd always taken one day before Father's Day when just the two of them would do something together – something that cost little or no money. No one else, including her mother, was invited. It wasn't until after his death that Mrs. Martin told Jessie how much those special days had meant to her dad. They had helped form a bond between father and child that even death could not break.

"Y'all could do what I used to do with my dad." She went on to explain, "Instead of one day, you could each take a day, maybe starting on Tuesday, and go fishing or roller blading or whatever you like with your dad, just so that you have alone time with him and can talk to him. Then on Saturday, you could do something together as a family with Sunday as a day set aside for whatever your dad wants to do. What do y'all think?"

"What would we talk about?" practical Mara needed to know.

"It'll come to you, but just let him know how much you love him and tell him what you're thinking about. That sort of thing." She had another idea. "We could even make up some invitations on the computer," Jessie suggested.

"I like it!" Becca piped in.

"Sounds good to me!" Bret replied.

The little girls added their approval with Sanson contributing a sleepy *woof.*

"Good. Then tomorrow morning we'll make up five invitations – one for each of you plus the group thing on Saturday. In the meantime, y'all decide what to put on your invitation. Okay?"

"Okay," they all agreed.

"Now, y'all get back to bed before your dad comes looking for you and gets suspicious," she warned them.

"Thanks, Jessie. We knew you'd be able to help us." They all gave her a hug and then trouped back to their rooms.

When they'd left her room, Jessie couldn't help smiling and saying out loud, "Now how precious is that?" Then she turned out her light and went to sleep.

After breakfast the next morning, Bret, who was the computer expert, and Jessie worked on their invitations, while the rest of the kids kept Ray busy. They had decided that the special 'Dad's Days', as they called them, would begin with the youngest child and end with the oldest.

By that afternoon, Bret and Jessie had designed and printed the invitations, which covered a variety of activities. Being first, Maggie had decided to invite her dad to a tea party, which would be held in Jessie's sunroom. This would require that the others make themselves scarce that day. Mara wanted to take her dad fishing at the lake that they had visited the first time they came to Jessie's house. Bret's idea was that he and his dad would shoot some hoops at the church's outdoor basketball court, and Becca was going to take her dad horseback riding at a farm belonging to a friend of Jessie's.

With all of the details worked out in advance by Monday evening, the children were ready to present their invitations to their father. He was sitting in the great room, watching TV, when Jessie came into the room and, without a word, walked to the set and turned it off.

"Excuse me, Mr. Hanson, but there are some people who want a word with you," she explained to him as he looked up at her.

Maggie came in first and handed Ray her invitation.

"What's this?" he inquired, suspicion evident in the question.

"Read it," Maggie commanded him.

He read aloud, "In honor of Father's Day, you are cordially invited to a tea party hosted and attended by Miss Maggie Hanson in the sunroom at Jessie's house on Tuesday at 11:00 AM. Semi-formal attire requested. RSVP."

Ray glanced at Jessie, who gave him an imperceptible nod to indicate that Maggie was serious. Then he looked at his daughter, standing before him. He put his arms around her and said, "I would be honored to attend your party, Miss Hanson."

"Oh, good! Eleven sharp, Daddy." She ran back to her room.

Next came Mara. After she'd handed her daddy the invitation, he read it out loud, too. "In honor of Father's Day, you are cordially invited to Mitchell's Pond on Wednesday at 10:00 AM for a day of fishing and enjoying a sack lunch in the company of Miss Mara Hanson. Casual attire requested. RSVP."

Ray declared, "Fishing? Are you kidding? I would love it! Thanks, Pumpkin! Uh, Miss Hanson!" He gave her a hug.

This one was followed by two more invitations, which Ray also readily accepted. After the kids had finished with their invitations and Ray had tucked them in, he came back to the great room and flopped into a chair.

Sensing his gaze on her, Jessie looked up from the book she'd been reading.

"What?" she asked when he didn't say anything.

With a lazy smile he questioned her, "Whose idea was this? Dr. Laura's?"

"No, but I'm certain she'd approve. My dad and I used to do this for Father's Day—just the two of us. So when the kids wanted something special so that they wouldn't have to ask you for money, I suggested this. I hope you don't mind," she qualified, a little uncertain of his reaction.

He studied her face before answering. Then he cleared his throat and responded, a definite huskiness in his voice, "I don't mind. In fact, I'm really touched by the kids' wanting to do something like this for me. Thanks, Jessie."

"They're *your* children. I just made a suggestion," she refused credit. Then smiling, she told him, "You've got a busy week ahead of you. Better rest up."

"I think you're right. I'd better keep up with these," he said, holding up the invitations. "I'd hate to miss an appointment." With that, he said goodnight and retired to the guest suite.

Maggie spent the next morning getting everything ready for her tea party with Jessie assisting in the food preparation. Then she went to put on her prettiest dress and brush her hair, while the others, including Sanson, left for parts unknown. A few minutes before eleven with all the preparations made, she sat in the sunroom, waiting for her daddy.

Promptly at eleven, Ray, dressed in a coat and tie, knocked on the sunroom door. Opening the door to her daddy, Maggie ushered him into the room and asked him to sit at the table.

"I'm so glad you could come, Daddy."

"Me, too, Sweetheart," he replied as he held her chair for her.

After she asked the blessing, Maggie served him some tea and some of the chicken salad sandwiches that she had made with Jessie's help. Dessert, consisting of chocolate cake, followed. During their meal, they chatted comfortably, mainly about things at a seven-year-old's level.

Once they'd finished eating, Maggie had Ray sit beside her on the sofa. She took her daddy's big hand in both of her little ones and said, "Daddy, I miss my mommy so much. Sometimes I think my heart is always going to hurt."

He pulled her up onto his lap and held her close. "I know, Sweetheart. Sometimes I feel the same way," he assured her.

"But, Daddy, I love you more than ever 'cause you've been there for us kids. And you let us come here to see Jessie. I think I do feel a little better. You're the best daddy in the whole world!" she declared.

"I love you, too, Maggie," Ray choked. At that moment, he was unable to say anything more because he was so filled with emotion.

They spent another little while talking about important things. When they heard the buzzer announcing the fact that the others were home, Maggie remarked, "They're back. Daddy, this *has* been fun, hasn't it?"

"Yes, Sweetheart. If I may say so, you really know how to throw a tea party," he replied solemnly.

"Thank you, Daddy. I'm glad you liked it."

They went out to the kitchen where the others had gathered.

Maggie went to Jessie, threw her arms around her waist and cried, "Oh, Jessie, we had such a nice party! Thanks!"

"You're welcome, Sweetie," she said, risking a quick glance at Ray, who just wore an enigmatic smile and made no response.

That night after saying goodnight to his children, Ray came into the great room and stretched out on the couch with a satisfied, though tired, groan.

Curiosity was eating at Jessie, but she refused to ask him about his time with Maggie.

"Tired?" was all she would say, as she looked up from her book.

"What you really want to know is how Maggie and I got along today, isn't it? I've noticed the questioning glances you've been throwing out all evening," he responded with a sardonic inflection in his voice.

"No. It's really none of my business," she denied quietly.

"If you say so," he said and shut his eyes as if he would go to sleep.

"Ray Hanson, are you going to tell me or not?" she asked impatiently.

He opened his eyes and chuckled. Sitting up, he recounted the events of the tea party. "I think this has been the most memorable time that I've ever spent alone with my youngest child. I don't know which one of us got more out of it, but it was very precious."

"After my dad was gone, my mother told me how much our special days had meant to him. It's a gift y'all will always cherish," she said, a nostalgic look in her eyes.

"I know," he replied huskily. Then with a grin, "It's much better than a tie."

Jessie smiled and queried, "Ready for round two?"

"I'd better be." Then he went to bed.

At 9:45 the next morning, Ray drove Mara to Mitchell's Pond with careful directions supplied by Jessie. It was really a small lake, but for some obscure reason, it had always been called Mitchell's Pond, perhaps after the original owner. Jessie had gotten permission for Ray and Mara to fish there as long as they wanted.

Equipped with Mr. Martin's fishing poles, a sack lunch of cheese sandwiches, apples, cookies, and soft drinks, and a blanket for sitting on the bank, they were all set for the anglers' paradise that was

Mitchell's Pond, which was stocked with trout. Mara had even dug up some worms for bait.

After parking his rental car in a shaded area, Ray and Mara chose a bank with lots of trees and sat down on their blanket to start fishing.

Ray pretended that he didn't like to touch the worms.

Mara offered helpfully, "Let me put it on the hook for you, Daddy." And she proceeded to do just that with ease.

"Thanks, Pumpkin. I appreciate that."

Talking quietly, they fished for a while without so much as a nibble. Then Mara felt a pull at her line and pulled up a small fish. Even though it was too small to keep, she was excited to have caught the first fish.

"Congratulations, Sweetheart! You're a better fisherman than your old dad," Ray told her.

"Keep trying, Daddy. You'll catch some, too," she encouraged him.

Ray hid a smile at her consideration for his feelings. She was right though. In a few minutes, he caught a huge trout, one that wouldn't have to be thrown back. Ray took it off the hook and put it in the cooler that they'd brought along.

"See, Daddy, I told you so!" Mara reminded her daddy.

They fished for a while longer with both of them catching some fair-sized trout. Then they decided that they were hungry. Mara unpacked the lunch that she had prepared. She asked Ray if he wanted to say the blessing.

"I'd rather hear you say it, Mara," he replied.

"Okay. Let's hold hands." Then she prayed, "Dear God, I thank you that my daddy and I can have this time together and thank you for our food. Amen."

"That was very sweet of you, Pumpkin," Ray said in a hushed voice.

"I love you, Daddy!" she replied, as she reached over to give him a hug.

"I love you, too." He knew grown men shouldn't cry over stuff like this, but he felt as if he could at the least provocation. Fortunately, he was spared that.

After they'd finished their lunch, the pair fished a while longer. When the cooler was full of trout, Ray leaned back against a tree, and

Mara leaned on him. They talked for a while and then decided that it was time to go home.

As they were packing up, Ray told his daughter, "Thanks for my day, Sweetheart. I've never had such a nice fishing trip before."

"You're welcome, Daddy." She gave him another hug, and then they went back to the car.

———————————

Early the next morning before the heat of the day had settled in, Bret and his dad went to the basketball court. Jessie had cleared it with her pastor in advance so that there would be no problems.

The two hadn't shot hoops together in a couple of years, though Bret had played with his buddies. As a result, Bret was able to out shoot his dad. But then Ray, who had been quite an accomplished athlete in high school and college intramurals, got warmed up and began sinking baskets.

While they took a break and drank the bottled water that they'd brought along, they sat on a bench in the shade.

"Dad, could I ask you a question?" Bret began tentatively.

"Sure, Son."

"If I decide that I don't want to be in the movie business like you, will you be proud of me anyway?" he needed to know.

Ray wondered where that question had come from and asked, "Why do you ask, Bret?"

He explained, "Billy's dad already wants him to go into business with him when he grows up, and he doesn't even like messing with cars. They fight about it a lot."

"I see. Well, Son, I can honestly tell you that anything you decide is fine with me. I just want you to be happy, not a carbon copy of me."

"That's good to know," he replied, the relief evident.

"You have a few years before you have to decide, but have you given any thought to the career you *would* like?"

"I love animals so much that I think I might want to be a vet," he answered.

Ray was proud of that. "That's an excellent choice, Son. I know you'd make a great one. I've seen how you take care of Sanson when he's sick or hurt."

"Gee, thanks. Dad?"

"What, Son?"

"I love you," he said, his eyes beginning to water a little.

In spite of the fact that boys his age might not appreciate being hugged by their dads, Ray reached over and gave him a big one.

"I love you, too, Son." This time Ray could not prevent a tear from escaping from the corner of his eye.

Before it got too hot, they decided to shoot a few more hoops. Then Bret treated his dad to a hamburger at a local drive-in.

As he was driving back to Jessie's house, Ray told him, "I had a great day doing guy stuff with you, Son. Maybe we can do it again sometime soon."

"I'd like that. I like hanging out with you, Dad," he confessed.

Ray smiled and squeezed Bret's shoulder.

In consideration for the horses that they would be riding, Becca and Ray started out on their outing before eight on Friday morning.

"Since I know the way, can I drive, Daddy?"

Jessie had to laugh at Ray's fearful expression and said, "If you're going to let her drive a horse, surely you can let her drive a car."

"Thanks for the input, Jessie," he responded, sounding anything but grateful.

"Please, Daddy!" Becca wheedled.

"Oh, all right, but be careful," he admonished his daughter.

Becca was actually a very good driver, so Ray's fears proved unfounded.

When they got to the farm, Jessie's friend Ed took them to the horse barn. On an earlier visit, Becca had picked out two fairly spirited quarter horses for her dad and herself. Since they were both experienced riders, the mounts proved to be excellent choices.

Ed told them to give the horses their heads and they would take them to the path that his riders usually preferred to use.

With Ed's admonition to have fun ringing in their ears, they set off side by side at a slow trot. They rode in silence for a while, and then Becca told her dad that she'd finally decided what she wanted to major in at USC.

"What? I'm afraid to ask," Ray replied, teasing his eldest child.

"Seriously, Daddy. I want to be an actor like you, and maybe some day I'll be a director, too. Maybe we could even work together, or I could be the first woman director to win an Oscar. Just think of it!" she told him proudly.

"There's not a doubt in my mind that you could do it. And I would be honored to work with you some day, Honey," he told her, amazed at how much alike they were.

"Thanks, Daddy. I think you mean it."

"I do," he said simply.

They picked up the pace and brought the horses up to a fast trot for a while and then settled down to a walk.

"Daddy, do you remember when you filmed 'The Sixth Commandment'?"

"Sure, Sweetheart. Why do you ask?"

"You and Mom had been having marital problems before then, hadn't you?"

Ray wondered where this was leading, but answered truthfully, "Yes, we had."

"I remember how difficult I was being about coming here and how mean I was to Jessie back then. I even called her a dork to her face," she confessed, ashamed of herself now.

Join the club, Ray said to himself.

"Mom hit the roof and would have punished me, but she let Jessie handle it instead. When Jessie told me about how important it was to your marriage and to us kids for all of us to be together, I understood. When you were gone for so long before that, I missed you so much and was afraid that we couldn't be a family anymore. I settled down then and even started to have fun. It scares me to think that we could have missed that time together."

"Me, too, Becca," he admitted, his throat tight.

"Jessie says that she still misses her mom but that it gets easier. I hope that's true."

"I believe it will. It's just going to take time, Becca."

She reined in her horse with Ray doing the same. Reaching over, she threw one arm around her dad's neck. "I love you so much, Daddy! Thanks for caring so much about us!"

"I love you more than you could ever imagine, Sweetie!" he said, placing an arm around her waist.

They continued at a slow pace, allowing the horses to cool down. Then they headed them back to the barn. When they got back, Becca thanked Ed for letting them ride his horses.

"Oh, you're welcome. Any friends of Jessie's are friends of mine. Any time y'all want to ride, just give me a call."

"Thanks, Ed," they both responded to his generous offer.

After they'd cooled the horses and brushed them down, they took their leave.

Ray took his daughter's hand and led her back to the driver's side of the car. "I feel like being chauffeured again," he stated with a smile.

"It would be my pleasure, Sir."

"Thanks for today, Honey. It's hard for me to fathom how grown up you are. You're not my little girl anymore."

"I'll always be your little girl, Daddy."

Chapter 13

There still remained two 'Dad's Days.' The kids had planned a picnic in the park for Saturday. As Jessie assisted them in getting the food ready, they chattered effusively about the fun that they'd had so far.

"I'm glad it worked for y'all. But it's not over yet. You still have today and tomorrow," she reminded them.

"You're coming with us, aren't you?" Becca asked.

"Oh. No, Becca. This is a family thing just for your dad and his kids. He's not my father. No, I'll stay here and get some work done," she excused herself.

At that moment, Ray came in from the screened porch. Maggie bemoaned the fact that Jessie refused to come with them.

"She says it's a family thing and that you're not her father," Becca informed him.

"You could pretend that she's your daughter, couldn't you, Daddy?" Maggie suggested, hopefully gazing up at him.

Ray cast an amused glance at Jessie, who was making a super-human effort not to burst out laughing. "Well, she *is* like family. I vote that she comes if that's what you guys want," he added his support.

"Yea! She's coming then!" they all agreed.

"I suppose I'm outnumbered," she surrendered.

"Hurts, doesn't it?" Ray asked her.

"What are you talking about?"

"Not getting the last word," he replied, grinning at her expression.

They loaded everything into Jessie's car and headed for the park. Even Sanson was allowed to come as long as he remained on his leash.

It was a small park located in the middle of town, but they were able to find a picnic table under a nice big oak tree. After Jessie had spread out the tablecloth, the kids helped put out the food. Mara wanted them all to hold hands while she said the blessing.

Sitting by Maggie on one side and Ray on the other, Jessie was dismayed at the thought of holding his hand. Of course, she said nothing as he reached for her hand, but she hoped he hadn't noticed the slight tremor that went through her body as he'd taken her hand in his.

With the blessing said, they began eating the food that they'd all helped to prepare. They chatted happily and just enjoyed each other's company. It turned out to be another great "Dad's Day.'

That night before bedtime, the kids asked Ray what he wanted for Father's Day breakfast. He considered their question for a moment before deciding that pancakes and bacon were his favorite breakfast foods. Jessie heaved a sigh of relief. This was something that they could handle.

When he had finally gotten the tucking in done and the goodnights said, Ray came back to the kitchen where Jessie was busy checking on the ingredients for breakfast. Fortunately, she had everything on hand.

"You've gone to so much trouble for my Father's Day, Jessie," he remarked as he sat at the island and watched her work.

"It's been fun seeing the kids try so hard to make this a memorable gift for you, Ray. I haven't minded in the least," she told him honestly.

"I have to admit that this week has tired me out, but I wouldn't have missed it for the world. I've gotten a lot of insight into the way my kids think and feel. It's priceless."

"I'm glad. 'Dad's Days' has been a success then," she said with a smile.

"Is that what they call it?" he asked.

"Yes. Cute, huh?"

"Cute," he echoed her sentiments. Then, "Thanks again, Jessie. Goodnight."

"Goodnight, Ray."

The next morning, the kitchen was a hive of activity. Becca fried the bacon, while Jessie allowed the younger kids to help her mix the pancake batter. Even though Maggie and Mara begged her to let them flip the pancakes on the griddle on top of the commercial style range, she had to take a firm tone with them.

"I just don't like the idea of you girls standing in a chair over this hot stove. What fun would it be if you were burned in the process?"

"Okay. We understand. Can we set the table instead?" they asked.

"Now that would be a big help," she replied, and they happily began their task.

Soon the bacon and more than enough pancakes for six were ready. Ray came into the dining area and looking at the huge stack of pancakes, remarked, "Well, this is enough for me, but what are the rest of you guys gonna eat?"

"Daddy! You can't possibly eat all of those!" Becca replied, shocked by his question.

"I wouldn't be so sure about that if I were you," he said with a twinkle in his eye.

"Oh, pooh! You're just teasing," she realized as she went to give him a hug.

The other kids went to hug him, too, as a chorus of 'Happy Father's Day' reverberated around the room.

As they all gathered at the table, Maggie decided that she wanted to say the blessing. When she had gotten everyone to hold hands again, she prayed, "Dear Lord, I thank you for this food, and I thank you that we have our daddy and Jessie to love us. Amen."

Jessie was deeply touched by the child's simple prayer. Smiling, she echoed Maggie's amen. Then they began their meal. The mountain of pancakes began to disappear along with the bacon and orange juice that accompanied it.

As they were finishing up breakfast, Bret asked his dad what he wanted to do that day since the rest of 'Dad's Days' was his choice.

After giving the question due consideration, Ray responded, "What I want us to do is help Jessie get the dishes cleaned up. Then I want us to get ready to go to church with her. After that, I'll take us all out to lunch. How does that sound?"

Jessie looked at him in total surprise. This was something that she had never expected. "You really want to go to church?" she sounded skeptical.

"I really want to go with you," he came back sincerely.

"All right. Let's get moving then," she ordered.

Everyone pitched in as they began clearing the table and loading the dishwasher. With all the help, they made short work of the clean up.

Jessie dressed in a light blue skirt and yellow, short-sleeved blouse. After applying make up and brushing her hair, she donned white high-heeled sandals. Then she went to see if anyone needed her assistance in getting ready. Both little girls wanted help in buttoning their Sunday dresses and then insisted that she brush their hair.

By nine thirty, everyone had gathered in the great room. They were all looking good in their Sunday best, especially Ray in his tan sports jacket and colorful tie.

Then they all went to the garage and got in Jessie's car. Since Mara and Maggie wanted their daddy to sit with them, Jessie drove them to church, where they arrived in time to get situated in a Sunday school class on time. Jessie wasn't sure how the kids would react to being separated and put in classes with strangers, but they seemed to take it in stride. Becca was thrilled to see some cute young men her age in the Young People's Class, and there were plenty of friendly boys and girls in the other kids' classes.

Ray decided to go to the Singles' Class with Jessie. She knew exactly what was going to happen. The single women in the class would swoon over him.

Smiling, she warned him, "I hope you're prepared for the sensation you're going to cause. If you enjoyed the attention at the restaurant the other day, you really ought to have fun today."

"We Hollywood types learn to go with the flow," he assured her, tongue-in-cheek.

"Oh, right," she grinned

As they entered the class, Jessie could tell right away that she had assumed correctly. Ray was an immediate hit with the women. When they had found two empty seats together, every woman in the class turned to stare at him. One of them came over to introduce herself.

"Who's your friend, Jessie?" Lexy Carter wanted to know. She was the prettiest woman in the entire church.

Jessie hid a smile. The other class members didn't call her Sexy Lexy for nothing. Right at this moment, she was really pouring on the charm for Ray's benefit.

"Ray Hanson, S...Lexy Carter." She just did catch herself before making the slip.

As Ray stood up to acknowledge the introduction, Lexy held out her hand and responded in a soft, seductive voice, "Nice to meet you, Ray."

"It's my pleasure," he returned.

"Are you the Hanson who turned Jessie's novel into a movie?" she asked, flashing him a brilliant smile.

"Yes, I am," he answered.

"Oh, this is so exciting! It was a wonderful movie! We were so proud of our little Jessie!" she gushed.

If the class hadn't started just then, *little* Jessie thought she might have been sick.

The women all reluctantly turned their attention to the Sunday school teacher, John Walters, who was trying to make an announcement about some meeting or other and finally captured their attention.

Class proceeded without any further incidents, but after the closing prayer, the women in the class swarmed Ray.

Jessie stood back and watched for a few minutes and then said, "Excuse me, Ray. You stay here and chat while I go collect your children from their classes."

As she turned to leave, he reached out and grabbed her arm. "No, wait! You ladies will have to excuse me. I need to go with Jessie. Nice meeting you all," he said, encompassing them all with one charming smile.

When they got out in the hall, he whispered, "I can't believe you were ready to abandon me in there."

"Oh, I thought you were going with the flow," she teased him.

"Not *that* much flow," he quipped.

Jessie laughed out loud at his response.

After collecting the children and hearing about the fun they'd had in their classes, they went to the sanctuary for the worship service. Fortunately, they were able to find a vacant pew at the back with enough space for six, with Ray sitting on one end and Jessie sitting on the other end.

Someone came up to Jessie on her side close to the wall. As she looked up at the person who stood there, a feeling of dread came over her. Greg! She'd been fortunate enough to avoid him ever since the grocery store incident, but apparently her good fortune had run out.

"Hi, Jessie! Can I talk to you for a minute?" he opened.

"The service is about to begin," she made the obvious excuse.

"It'll only take a minute," he pressed her.

She sensed that he would make a scene if she refused, so she resigned herself to speaking with him.

"All right." She cast a look of helplessness in Ray's direction and rose from her seat.

Ray eyed the two as they left the sanctuary for the vestibule. He leaned over to speak to Becca. "Do you know who that is?" he asked her.

"Greg, the boyfriend," she whispered.

"We don't like him," Maggie reminded her daddy.

Out in the vestibule, Greg accused Jessie, "Who's *that* guy?"

A heavy unease settled in her as she thought, *Now he's going to be angry at Ray!* To counteract that possibility, she carefully chose her words. "Who, Ray? Oh, that's the children's father. He came to be with them."

"Where's their mother?" he asked, as if it were his business.

Rather than adopt an adversarial attitude with him, she just said, "She died."

"Oh. When can I see you, Jessie?" he took up where he had left off the last time.

Though at a loss as to how to deal with him, she needed to break off their relationship – whatever *that* was. Most definitely, she was not going anywhere alone with him, but neither did she want him to come to her house without talking to Ray about it first. She didn't want him or his children exposed to Greg without advanced warning.

"Look. The service is starting, and I need to get back in there. Call me this evening, and we'll get together tomorrow," she compromised.

That seemed to satisfy him because he replied, "Okay. I'll call this evening." Then, not even pretending to be there for the service, he turned and left the church.

Somewhat shaken by the encounter, Jessie went back to her seat. Ignoring Ray's questioning look, she took a hymnal from the holder on the pew in front of her and sang along with the rest of the congregation.

After a young woman with a beautiful voice had sung 'My Father's Eyes,' the pastor got up to preach. In honor of Father's Day, he spoke about how a child's first impression of his Heavenly Father was based on his image of his earthly father and that dads ought to behave accordingly. Ray sat there with his arm around Maggie and took in every word.

Jessie glanced at him and saw how intently he was listening to the pastor. Sometimes she sensed a spiritual hunger in Ray, but she still hesitated to talk about such things with him. Not knowing how far Helen had gotten with him before her death, Jessie didn't want to scare him off. She would just have to pray for him and wait for God to present the right moment.

When the service was over, Lexy Carter cornered Ray and, giving him a coquettish smile, asked him to lunch at her house. Jessie's jaw dropped at her effrontery in excluding everyone else from her invitation.

Choosing to misinterpret Lexy, Ray reached out and put his arm around Jessie's waist. "Thanks. It's very kind of you to invite us, but we have other plans," he excused himself, flashing her a smile that took the sting out of his refusal. Then, shaking hands with the pastor on their way out, he led Jessie and his children to the car.

"What was that all about?" Becca asked. Her curiosity was definitely aroused.

"It seems that your dad has made another conquest. I believe this one was just a little bolder than he might have expected though," Jessie explained, suppressing a grin.

"That's an understatement. I don't know what all she had in mind, but I certainly got the impression that I was on the lunch menu. I thought that Southern women were supposed to be old-fashioned and let the men do the chasing." He shook his head in bewilderment.

"Daddy, it's the twenty-first century, and you're fresh meat to these women. Grow up," Becca chided him.

He stopped in his tracks and looked at his oldest daughter. Seeing the twinkle in her eyes, he realized that she was teasing him. "You're not too old to spank, you know," he warned, unable to hide his amusement.

As they approached the car, Jessie couldn't stop the giggle that escaped her mouth. Ray shot her a look and said, "That goes for you, too, young lady!"

"Yes, Daddy," she replied meekly.

The kids were all laughing by this time as they headed to Memphis for the last of the 'Dad's Days' activities.

They enjoyed a delicious lunch at a popular family restaurant, which served all kinds of food. Afterwards, Ray suggested that since it was Father's Day and *his* choice he would like to take a drive to see the Mississippi River. He'd only seen it from the air and would like to see it up close. Because he was unfamiliar with the area, Jessie drove.

They drove down Riverfront and then enjoyed a leisurely stroll around Tom Lee Park. It was a very pleasant way to spend an afternoon. But it was getting late—time to leave.

As they started for home Ray declared, "This has been a very special Father's Day, and everything leading up to it just proved to me what a lucky man I am. I'll never forget it, you guys. Thanks, Kids...and

Jessie."

Sitting beside their father, Mara and Maggie each gave him a hug as everyone, including Jessie, replied, "You're welcome, Daddy!"

Later that afternoon when she had a chance to talk to Ray alone, Jessie told him about her dilemma with Greg.

"I don't know what to do. I need to talk to him and break it off, though, for the life of me, I can't see what there is to break off. I'm leery of being alone with him, but I also don't want to expose you and the kids to any more of his odd behavior. Any suggestions?" She eyed him, hoping that he could come up with something.

"Want me to beat him up? I'm bigger than he is, so I think I can take him," he said, trying to lighten her mood.

"My hero!" she smiled.

He returned her smile and proposed, "Seriously though. Why don't you invite him to supper here tomorrow night? Surely he can behave himself that long. And then afterwards, maybe you could go into the sunroom to have your talk while the kids and I do the dishes and hover discreetly in the background."

She sighed heavily. "It's probably the best solution, but I still don't like the idea of his being here with y'all."

"Let me worry about us. Okay?" He thought for a minute, and then asked, "What's this guy's full name? I'm going to call a friend of mine at LAPD and see if he checks out on the computer. I have a feeling that this isn't the first time he's done something like this."

"You think so?" she asked with a worried frown then added, "It's Greg Robertson. He manages his father's plant – Robertson Manufacturing. Actually, I believe he's relatively new to the area."

"Hmm. Interesting. I think I'll make that call now," he responded.

That evening, Jessie received the call that she'd been dreading. Even though Greg appeared none too pleased about having supper at her house with others present, he sensed that this was as far as she was prepared to go and took what he could get.

Chapter 14

As she prepared for the meal that evening, Jessie could not escape the feeling of unease that had come over her when Greg had accepted her invitation. However, she knew that this situation needed immediate attention before it escalated. While she was dressing, she felt compelled to send up a prayer for Ray, the kids *and* herself, that they would all be kept safe.

Keeping in mind that Greg preferred her in long hair and a dress, she left her hair loose and put on a white flared skirt and a navy blouse. Since she didn't want to start the evening off by making him angry, she decided that discretion was the better part of valor in this instance.

After carefully applying makeup and a flattering shade of lipstick, Jessie put on low-heeled sandals and went out to the kitchen to set the table and check on the food. Mara and Maggie offered to help her with any last minute details. Though she didn't really need any help, she was grateful for their presence and readily accepted their offer.

At seven o'clock, the gate buzzer sounded. Jessie checked the monitor and then she pushed the button that would open the gate for her guest. Taking a deep, steadying breath, she walked around the great room to wait for the doorbell.

Ray came in from the guest suite, took one look at her expression, and said, "My offer still stands. Just say the word."

"Ray! Don't make jokes! This situation has me really worried, so be on your best behavior," she scolded.

He promised her, "I will. I'm just trying to get you to lighten up some."

At that moment, the doorbell rang, and she went to let Greg in. She greeted him with a bright smile and a warm handshake, an action, which he did not seem to appreciate. If he had thought that she would have a more intimate greeting, he was sorely disappointed.

"Come in, Greg," she invited and led him to the great room, where Ray was sitting on the couch with Mara and Maggie. Ray stood up, which caused him to tower over Greg, who was at least a head shorter and had a less muscular build.

She introduced, "Greg, I believe you've met Mara and Maggie. This is their dad, Ray Hanson. Ray, Greg Robertson."

Ray shook hands with Greg and replied politely to the introduction, "Nice to meet you, Greg."

"Same here," was the only response Greg made.

After she had Greg sit in a comfortable chair, Becca entered the room, followed soon by Bret.

Even though Ray tried to be his most charming toward Greg and attempted to engage him in conversation, the situation remained awkward. His only interest being in Jessie, Greg was not trying at all to be sociable.

When a very short time had passed, Jessie decided that it was time to serve the meal. She excused herself and went to put the food on the table. Then she had everyone come and take a seat. Since the children seemed to be ill at ease around Greg, Jessie said the blessing and did not request that they hold hands.

Having decided that Greg was going to be no help, Ray engaged his children and Jessie in their usual mealtime banter, a fact that Greg did not seem to appreciate.

Bret had a question for his father. "Dad, Jessie says that we can go to LibertyLand sometime. Can we?"

"What's a LibertyLand?" Ray asked somewhat bewildered.

"Oh, Daddy, it's a fun place!" Maggie chimed in. "They have lots of rides and food!"

"Yeah! And a kid at church yesterday said they have a new ride called The Rebellion. It takes you way up high and then just sort of drops you to the ground!" Bret enthused.

"Ooh!" the other kids responded.

"You have to be a certain age to be able to ride it though," he qualified.

"I'm not riding it!" Mara and Becca declared together.

"And you want to ride this contraption by yourself, Son?" Ray inquired, indicating that he wouldn't be riding it either.

"I will if I have to," he replied, undeterred.

"What a bunch of wusses!" Jessie chided the others. "*I'll* ride it with you, Bret."

"Gee thanks, Jessie," he said, giving his family a smug look.

Ray just looked at them both and shook his head. Then he stated practically, "Jessie, I hope that you ride it *before* lunch and that your insurance is paid up."

Laughing, she made a face at him and came back at him, "Thanks for your sincere concern."

Everyone, except for Greg, laughed with Jessie. As the meal progressed, his expression became more and more dour.

When the meal was finished, Ray took that as a cue to suggest that Jessie and Greg retire to the sunroom, where they could talk privately while the rest of them cleared up the dishes and got ready for bed.

At last! Something that seemed to meet with Greg's approval had been proposed. He stood up and took her arm to lead her away from the table. As Jessie led him to the sunroom, the sense of unease, which had abated during the meal, now returned full-force.

Ray, who had been watching the pair as they retreated, turned around to see his oldest child eyeing him.

"What's going on, Dad? Jessie looked very nervous, and I didn't think she wanted to date *him* anymore." Becca got right to the point.

Ray decided to be honest with her and so explained in a hushed tone, "That's what she's going to try to tell him, but she's worried because she doesn't know how he's going to take it."

"In that case, we'd better stay close," she cautioned.

"I don't want the younger kids to witness any unpleasantness, so I'm going to get them ready for bed right away. You stay here. Okay?"

"Okay. I'll work on these dishes while you're gone," she offered.

"Thanks, Honey." He was impressed by his daughter's mature attitude. Then he told the three youngest Hansons to get ready for bed.

While Becca worked, she kept her ears alert to any disturbance coming from the sunroom.

Jessie turned on the table lamp and nervously sat down on the couch. Greg sat right beside her and took her hand in his, an action that she did not like at all. The times that Ray had held her hand, though taken by surprise, she had found herself enjoying the experience. This was not a pleasant experience, so she disengaged her hand from Greg's clammy grasp. That angered him even more.

"Why don't you want me to touch you, Jessie? This is our third date, and I don't think it's unreasonable to want to touch a desirable woman like you," he complained.

Jessie stood up to face him and just said it straight out. "I don't want to go out with you any more, Greg."

He was silent for a moment and then asked quietly – too quietly for Jessie's liking, "May I ask why not?"

Wringing her hands, Jessie eyed him warily and replied, "I'm just not attracted to you."

At that, Greg jumped up from the couch to loom over her. "You're sleeping with *him*, aren't you?"

"I don't know whom you're talking about, but I can assure you that I have never *slept* with anyone!" she denied, raising her voice for emphasis.

"Oh, come on! You expect me to believe that you have this guy in your house and you're not sleeping with him! What do you take me for?"

"You're talking about *Ray*? His children are here, for Heaven's sakes! Besides, he doesn't think of me that way," she told him.

"I get it. He doesn't think of you that way, but that's how *you* think of *him*. Is that what you're saying?" he prompted.

"I'm saying nothing of the sort!" Realizing that things were getting out of control, she took a deep breath and said calmly, "This conversation is pointless. All you need to know is that I don't want anything more to do with you."

"Well, that's too bad!" he ground out and made to grab her.

Jessie was able to elude his grasp, but that made him even angrier. He backhanded her across her cheek hard enough to knock her onto the couch.

"Oh!" was her shocked response as she put her hand to her stinging cheek.

With a glint of fiendish intent in his eyes, he lunged at her, and, grabbing her blouse, ripped it open to reveal the lacy slip underneath.

"No! Stop it!" she cried as she struggled with him. Uppermost in her mind, was the fact that if she let out a scream she would frighten the children. She didn't want to do that, but neither did she want his assault on her to continue.

He sat down beside her, and pulling her close, crushed her mouth with his, grinding her lips against her teeth, as she continued to struggle. When he raised his head, she slapped him hard and shrieked, "Let go of me!"

Infuriated, he threw her back against the arm of the couch and began to rain kisses on her neck and lower. She tried to push him away as she cried out again, "Stop it!" But his weight was too much against her puny efforts. She could hardly breathe for fear.

Suddenly his body jerked away from her.

Concerned as she was, Becca hurried over as close to the sunroom door as she could without being detected and listened intently. Behind the closed door, she heard voices, raised in anger, though she couldn't make out what they were saying.

Then she heard it. *Whack!* It sounded as if someone had been struck.

153

Panicking, she ran to get her dad. At that precise moment, he came out of the girls' room

He took one look at Becca's face and pulled the door shut all the way.

"I think he just hit her!" she whispered desperately.

Galvanized into action, Ray sprinted to the sunroom door and burst in. He saw Greg on top of the struggling Jessie. He grabbed his arm and the collar of his jacket and wrenched him away from her, sending him into a heap on the floor. When he made as if to get up, Ray punched his jaw. Then he pulled the moaning Greg to his feet and hauled him to the front door.

Ray considered throwing him through the door but thought better of it. After jerking it open, he grabbed Greg up and tossed him so hard that if he hadn't clutched at the porch rail, he would have ended up in the flowerbed.

Righting himself, Greg threatened, "This isn't over! She's mine! Do you hear me?"

Ray said softly through clenched teeth, "It had *better* be over. She doesn't want you. Now get out of here, and leave Jessie alone, before I finish the job I started and then call the sheriff and have you arrested!"

Greg had enough sense to see that he couldn't win a fight against Ray. Muttering threats, he stumbled to his car and left, burning rubber as he sped away. After he shut and locked the door, Ray remembered to hit the button that would open the gate. Greg was just insane enough to ram it. Checking the monitor, he saw the man drive through the open gate. He shut the gate and went to check on Jessie.

As Ray entered the sunroom, he saw Becca kneeling beside the couch and trying to comfort the shaking Jessie, who was curled up into a tight, quivering ball. With one hand, she clutched the edges of her ripped blouse, and the other was pressed against the welt on her cheek, where Greg had struck her.

Kneeling in front of her, his voice husky with concern, he asked, "Are you okay, Jessie?"

She couldn't quit shaking, but answered as best she could, "I-I'm n-not s-sure."

Ray pulled her hand away from her cheek. When he saw the angry welt, which proved that Becca's assumption that Greg had hit her was correct, he seethed with rage. He wished that he had really put a hurting on the man when he'd had the chance.

"Becca Honey, go open the door to Jessie's bedroom and turn back the bed covers, please," he instructed his daughter.

"Sure, Daddy."

Then he gathered Jessie up into his arms and carried her to her room, where he gently placed her in the middle of the bed. After unfastening her sandals and removing them from her feet, he pulled the covers up to her chin. Seeing that she was still shaking, he sat down beside her on the bed.

Becca suggested, "I think I should get some ice to put on her face."

"That's a good idea. Thanks, Sweetheart," Ray responded. Then he reached over and caressed her red cheek with his forefinger and lamented, "I'm so sorry, Jessie! I should have done a better job of protecting you!"

Jessie sat up, clutching the covers to her chest. She threw one arm around Ray's neck and cried, "Oh, Ray! It's not your fault! If you hadn't been here, he would h-have... He t-tore my blouse and then k-kissed me! I didn't want him to t-touch me!"

Ray's arms had come up around her to hold her, as he crooned soothingly, "It's okay, Jessie. He can't hurt you now." Then holding her away from him, he asked, "Why didn't you scream?"

As she gazed into his eyes, Jessie confessed, "It ran through my mind, but I didn't want to frighten the kids. They've been through so much, and I didn't want them to get involved in this."

Ray held her close again. Concern for his children had almost cost her dearly. If Becca hadn't been so cautious, this entire situation could have ended tragically.

At that moment, Becca returned with the ice in a plastic zip bag, which she handed to her dad.

"Thanks, Honey," he said as he held it against Jessie's cheek.

As the cold touched her face, she winced in pain. Noticing her reaction, Ray swore under his breath and then admitted, "I wish I *had* beaten him up when I had the chance!"

Jessie smiled at him and reminded him, "You're *still* my hero."

"You can thank Becca for that. While I was putting Mara and Maggie to bed, she was listening at the sunroom door, just in case, and warned me when she thought you were in trouble," he informed her.

Jessie glanced at Becca and responded with a wide grin, "Thanks, Becca. I'm grateful that you're nosey. Just like your dad."

"You're welcome. I am, too," she replied.

"Hey! How did I get in on this?" he wondered, feigning offense.

Becca and Jessie just laughed at him.

Laying her back against the pillows, Ray queried, "Are you going to be all right in here. Do you need something to help you sleep?"

"I think I'm okay. I just want to take a shower and wash where he…where he…" Jessie couldn't make herself finish the thought.

Ray bent and tenderly kissed her forehead. "Goodnight then. Let Becca or me know if you need anything."

Coming over to give her a hug and a kiss on the cheek, Becca echoed her dad's offer. Then they left the room.

Jessie lay in bed for a few minutes and thought about the awful things that could have happened to her earlier. She thanked God that she had been spared the trauma of rape. Realizing that there was only one man who she ever wanted to touch her, she was truly grateful that Ray had been there to prevent Greg's doing anymore than he had. As it was, she still felt dirty. Getting out of bed, she went into the bathroom and took off her clothes. Instead of putting them in the hamper, she threw them in the garbage. She didn't want those clothes around to remind her of this night. Then she stepped into the shower.

After a restless night, Jessie rose early to survey the damage to her face. With careful application of make up, she thought she might be able to conceal most of the effects of the events of the previous night.

Once she was satisfied that she'd done her best to cover the bruises, Jessie went to the kitchen to start breakfast. Ray was already there. Looking up as she entered, he scanned her face to see how she looked that morning.

When he had pulled out a bar stool for her, he commanded, "Sit."

"I'm just going to start some breakfast," she protested.

"No. I'm doing breakfast today," he told her.

"You? Can *you* cook?" she marveled.

"Sure. I'm one of the world's great cooks," was his facetious comeback.

"For real?" Jessie asked, sounding dubious.

"No, but my cooking *is* edible. My kids look healthy enough, don't they?"

"True," she admitted, as she took the stool he offered.

"How are you feeling this morning?" Ray wanted to know.

Avoiding his gaze, she assured him, "Oh, I feel fine."

"Liar," he responded, reaching over and lifting her chin with his fingers. He studied her face for a few moments and then guessed, "I'd say that you didn't sleep very well last night. Even though you did a masterful job of concealing your bruises, your eyes look big and frightened, sort of like Bambi caught in headlights."

"I'm okay," she reiterated, flustered by his touch.

"I'm not buying it, Jessie. Regardless of how you claim to feel, I want you to take it easy for a few days. You've been through a very traumatic experience, and the rest will do you good," he informed her.

"But what will the kids think? I don't want to worry them," she voiced her concern.

"We'll tell them that you're a little under the weather. That's all. Let us take care of you for a while," Ray proposed.

"I don't know..." Jessie began, but he interrupted her.

"I'm having the last word on this, Jessie. So give in gracefully and just accept it. The whole process will be a lot less painful," he advised, evidently enjoying himself.

"It seems that I don't have a choice," she concluded.

"Good girl! Now you're getting it!"

He went to the refrigerator and poured her a glass of orange juice. Handing it to her, he said, "By the way, I talked to my friend at LAPD again last night, and he was able to dig up quite a lot of information on

Greg Robertson. I was right. This wasn't the first time his behavior towards women has crossed the line. His father apparently owns factories all over the country. Whenever son Greg gets into trouble, Dad buys his way out of it and moves him to another location. Some of his victims haven't been as fortunate as you were." He paused and then continued, "He raped them."

Jessie buried her face in her hands and moaned, "Oh, those poor women!" Her hands began to tremble.

Ray came around the island and, swiveling the stool so that she faced him, put his arms around her. "I'm sorry! I didn't mean to upset you. I just thought you should know."

"I'm okay. I just realized again how grateful I am that I had you and the Lord looking out for me. It would have been devastating for my first..." she stopped short.

"Your first what?" he prodded.

"Never mind," she hedged, not really wanting to have this conversation with Ray.

He tried coaxing her, "Finish the thought, Jessie."

"No! You'll just think I'm a cold-fish dork," she replied, her face flaming at the recollection. She couldn't look Ray in the eye.

It wouldn't have made any difference because her words had caused him to shut his eyes in pain as he recalled their significance.

"Jessie! I *didn't* think it back then, and I couldn't possibly think it now! Besides, I believe you said that you'd forgiven me for that remark," he reminded her, tightening his arms.

She apologized, "I did, and I'm sorry. I shouldn't have said that."

He accepted her apology but, not letting her off the hook, continued, "First *what*?"

Realizing that he wasn't going to give up, Jessie hung her head to hide her embarrassment and finished in a muffled voice, "My first time...with a man."

The amazing revelation finally sank in. This dear, sweet, beautiful woman was saying that she was still a virgin! Ray found that fact strangely provocative and appealing. His growing concern to protect her from harm had just been magnified at least ten times.

He curled his forefinger under her chin and forced her to look up. Bending his head to rest his forehead against hers, he said huskily, "Virginity is nothing to be ashamed of, Jessie. In this day and age, it's a rare and precious thing for a young woman."

"You don't think I'm a dork then?" she asked breathlessly.

He raised his head and smiled into her eyes. "Never!" he vowed. Resisting the sudden urge to kiss her, Ray let his arms fall to his sides. "I'd better get breakfast started."

Jessie took a shaky breath. Being that close to him just reinforced her feelings. She would have given anything if he'd wanted to kiss her just then, but she knew that he thought of her only as a friend.

When the aroma of sausage frying on the griddle and biscuits baking in the oven drifted to the children's rooms, they began to straggle into the kitchen.

"Smells good," Bret mumbled sleepily.

The kids noticed that their dad was doing the cooking. Mara asked, "Why are *you* cooking, Daddy?"

"Don't you like your dad's cooking, Pumpkin?" he replied with a grin.

"You're a good cook, Daddy," she confirmed. "But what's wrong with Jessie?"

Glancing at Becca, who had just entered the room, Ray answered, "Jessie's a little under the weather, so while she gets some rest, we're going to help her for the next few days. Okay?"

Maggie climbed onto the bar stool beside Jessie and patted her shoulder.

"I'm sorry you don't feel good, Jessie," she comforted. Then she asked anxiously, "Are you going to be all right?"

Jessie put her arms around the little girl and reassured her, "I'll be fine, Sweetheart. When I get better, we can take that trip to LibertyLand."

"And the water park, too?" Mara piped in.

"Sure. We can do both," she promised.

After breakfast, Becca lingered to talk to Jessie. "Are you really okay?" she asked, concern evident in the question.

She said, "I'm fine. Truly, but your dad is insisting that I rest some. You know how he can be."

"Yes, I know, but *this* time I think he's right," Becca agreed.

With eyebrows raised, her dad complained, "You two are acting as if I'm not standing here, taking in every word."

"It wouldn't make any difference if you weren't, Daddy." She ducked the towel that he threw at her and started clearing away the breakfast dishes.

All that week, the entire Hanson family refused to allow Jessie to do any kind of work. Ray and Becca took care of the cooking. Bret and the little girls helped with the cleaning, while they all pitched in to change the beds and do the laundry.

When it came time for grocery shopping, Ray insisted that everyone go along, including Jessie. Until the situation with Greg was cleared up, he was wary of leaving her alone in the house. The man was just too dangerous. That was a fact that he was about to rediscover.

Chapter 15

By Monday of the next week, Ray deemed that Jessie was fit enough to go to LibertyLand the following day. In fact, they decided to make it a full day and go to the theme park in the morning and the water park in the late afternoon.

Before they began their fun day, Jessie made sure that everyone had a cap with a wide brim and that there was a large bottle of sunscreen. They were going to be out in the hot late June sun for several hours, and she didn't want anyone suffering from sunburn.

After packing the car with bathing suits and beach towels, they said goodbye to Sanson, who was lounging on the couch, and then headed for Memphis.

Anticipating the terrific new ride at LibertyLand, Bret reminded Jessie that she'd said she would ride it with him.

"A promise is a promise," she told him, wondering what had been in her mind at the time.

Ray just shook his head. "You two need professional help," he declared.

When they arrived at the park, Jessie passed out caps and insisted on applying sunscreen to everyone's bare arms and legs. Then they strolled around for a while before coming to the kiddy rides.

Making a beeline for the merry-go-round, Mara and Maggie wanted to start there. Becca and Bret refused to ride anything so juvenile, but the little girls begged their daddy to ride it with them.

"Oh, Daddy, please, ride it with us!" they implored, gazing up at him with hopeful expressions on their little faces.

Jessie clenched her teeth to keep from laughing at the picture of the big Hollywood director on a merry-go-round, but he seemed to know what she was thinking anyway.

"Sure, Pumpkins. And so will Jessie," he volunteered for her.

She retorted, "They didn't ask *me* to ride it."

"Will you, Jessie?" Maggie asked her.

Ray stood there with a smug look on his face, which dared her to refuse.

Knowing that she was trapped, she childishly stuck out her tongue at him and said, "I'd be honored to ride it with you girls."

While the quartet waited for their turn on the merry-go-round, Becca and Bret parked themselves on a bench in preparation for watching the adults on the kiddy ride.

When their turn finally came, they were able to find two vacant horses side by side. Mara didn't need any help mounting her wooden horse, but Ray picked Maggie up and deposited her on the saddle. Then he and Jessie stood beside them, making sure that they were holding on tightly as the ride started up.

"I haven't been on one of these since I was Mara's age," Jessie admitted, thinking back to the time that her own father had ridden with her.

"That *has* been a long time then," Ray agreed, chuckling as she took a playful jab at his stomach.

As the merry-go-round unexpectedly lurched forward, Jessie grabbed hold of the nearest pole. The ride proved to be really quite enjoyable since it didn't involve any thrills, just the steady up and down rhythm of the horses as they went around.

When the ride was over, Ray suggested that they move on to something that the older kids would enjoy. That turned out to be The Pippin, a scary wooden roller coaster, which Becca and Bret were content to ride alone.

Thank goodness! Jessie thought. She needed to save all her energy for The Rebellion, Bret's horrific new ride.

When the roller coaster ride was over, they discussed what to do next. Jessie suggested that since it was getting close to lunchtime, perhaps she and Bret ought to get their ride over. They would probably have to wait in line, so they went searching for it.

Spying it in the distance, Bret announced excitedly, "There it is!"

Jessie gulped. What had she gotten herself in to? The Rebellion, a gargantuan monster, rose several hundred feet straight up into the air and, at this very moment, was dropping approximately twelve screaming daredevils to the ground. At almost the last second, their seats seemed to land on a cushion of air.

Bret grabbed her hand and started pulling her toward it. "Come on, Jessie! Let's go get in line!"

Ray eyed her pale face and said with an understanding smile, "It's not too late to back out. You don't have to do this, you know."

She took a deep breath and replied steadily, "Yes, I do. I promised Bret." Then, leaving her purse with Ray for safekeeping, she allowed herself to be pulled along to stand in the line of people waiting to board the ride. The others found a bench to watch with awe the monster's performance.

While they waited, Jessie tried to concentrate on Bret's excited chatter, but all she could really think about was how very high up they were going to be. At last, there was room enough for the two of them. Jessie and Bret sat in the seats, which left their feet dangling in the air. Then the attendants came by to check that their padded safety bars were securely in place.

As the machine began its ascent, Bret looked around and saw his family waving at them. Jessie couldn't see them, probably because she had her eyes shut.

"Look, Jessie! They're waving!" he exclaimed, pointing them out.

She made the mistake of opening her eyes and muttered, "Ohhh!" Then she valiantly returned their wave, as the monster rose higher and higher.

Finally, they reached the top. After a short pause, they began their swift descent. Feeling as if her stomach were in her throat and other effects of the G-forces on her body, Jessie closed her eyes again and promised the Lord that if she lived through the experience she would never ride The Rebellion again!

Though it was over in a matter of seconds, it seemed like an eternity until they were gently delivered to the base of the monster. When it came to a complete stop, the safety bars were released and they were able to leave their seats. Jessie's legs were so shaky that she had to hold on to Bret to keep from falling.

"Gee! Wasn't that great? You want to go again, Jessie?" he asked, apparently enthusiastic about the prospect.

"No. Not in this lifetime. Thank you very much," she vowed.

The rest of the Hansons hurried over to question them about their experience. "What was it like?" Becca wanted to know.

"Were you scared?" was Maggie's question.

Noting the way that Jessie was holding on to Bret for support, Ray asked, "Are you okay, Jessie?"

"I'll be fine. I'm just trying to get over the urge to kneel and kiss the ground," she replied, not altogether joking. However, the others thought she was extremely funny.

When she let go of Bret, her legs almost gave way, causing Ray to place a steadying arm around her waist.

"You're not ready to go again?" Ray chuckled at the look she shot him. "I'll take that as a *no*."

Mara piped in, "I'm hungry. When are we gonna eat?"

Since it was after twelve, they decided that now was a good time to eat and went looking for food.

———————

Watching from his hiding place as Jessie and her guests left for Memphis, Greg waited for a while to make sure that they would not return unexpectedly. Then he walked over to the gate, tossed the bag he was carrying to the other side, and climbed over with ease.

When he got to the front porch, he pulled a crowbar from the bag and forced open the door. Of course, this roused Sanson, who came to investigate the noise. At first, Sanson growled at him, but then he seemed to recognize Greg from before. Having forgotten about the dog, Greg decided to keep him out of the way by letting him out of the house. He might interfere with his plans, and besides, he liked dogs. There was really no need to hurt him.

Carefully proceeding down the hall that led to the garage, he took the crowbar and broke one of the bulbs in the light fixture. With that accomplished, he went into every room, including the guest suite, and unplugged every phone as well as the fax machines and computers. He didn't want any phone calls upsetting his plans. His last step was to take out a pair of pliers, the ends wrapped in electrical tape to avoid creating sparks. After extinguishing the stove's pilot light and turning the burners to the ON position, he loosened the fittings of the gas log inserts, which allowed propane gas to escape into the house.

Smirking as he left the house, Greg thought about Jessie. Because of her rejection of him, she deserved what she was getting. She'd led him on and then found someone else. *Nobody* did that to him! Now they all had to pay! He retraced his steps to his car.

Jessie was glad that she'd ridden The Rebellion *before* lunch. As it was by the time the Hansons and she were ready to eat, her stomach and her legs were back to normal. However, she was certain that she didn't want to ride anything else that went very high or very fast.

Once they'd finished lunch, they decided to stroll around awhile before attempting any more rides. During their stroll, they came across some rides that were neither too scary for the little girls nor too tame for Bret and Becca. Jessie proposed that their dad should accompany them this time, a suggestion that Mara and Maggie didn't like at all. They wanted Jessie with them, too. So for the next couple of hours, they rode the less thrilling rides, which suited Jessie just fine.

At about four o'clock, they left for the water park. After paying the price of admission, Jessie accompanied the girls to the women's locker room, and Ray went with Bret.

Jessie was somewhat nervous about wearing a swimsuit in public, something she hadn't done since she was a teenager. More important was the fact that Ray would see her. Fortunately, it was a very modest suit, or so she thought. She failed to realize how stunning she was in the green one-piece with the sheer wrap knotted around her waist, or how it accentuated her curves and showed off her legs. Once the girls had finished changing, they stowed their clothes in the locker they had rented, but expecting that she would not be in the water that much, Jessie carried her purse with her for safekeeping.

Becca also wore a one-piece swimsuit, and she looked just beautiful. Jessie was sure that she would be a big hit with any young men present at the park. As the four of them made their way out to Ray and Bret, Jessie saw that Becca was already causing a lot of masculine heads to turn. She never for a second thought they might be looking at her, too.

Ray watched her approach, allowing his gaze to travel the entire length of her body. He felt his pulse race at the sight of her and knew that she was totally unaware of the effect she was having on him and every other male present. He could sense that she was nervous about being in public like that and was trying to appear nonchalant.

Jessie was just as affected by the sight of Ray in his swimsuit. His lithe, muscular body was magnificent in the blue trunks that he wore. She hadn't thought that she could be any more attracted to him than she was, but she apparently had been wrong.

Maggie interrupted their thoughts. "Daddy, can we go to the giant water slide first?"

"Sure, Pumpkin," he replied, a little distracted as the six of them headed in that direction.

When they got close to the slide, Jessie spied a nice shady area with several vacant chairs from which to watch their antics. "I'm going to sit here and watch y'all. I think I've had as many thrills as I can stand today," she bowed out with a smile. "Just leave your towels with me." Earlier, Ray had given her his wallet to keep in her purse, so she was left in charge of everything.

She watched as they climbed the stairs to the top of the slide. Since it was late afternoon, the line was not very long, so they had just a short wait for their first trip down the slide. The first one down was Mara, followed closely by Bret and Becca, all screaming for effect and making huge splashes in the pool at the bottom. Since Maggie was so little, she and Ray came down together, at least on the first run. They were all laughing and having a great time.

Jessie was enjoying herself just watching their enjoyment in each other. After they'd made several runs down the slide, they came out of the pool, and the kids wanted to go to the wave pool for a while. This also was something Jessie preferred to watch.

"Aren't you going to even get wet?" Ray asked her.

"Maybe we can go to the swimming pool when we finish here. That's more my speed," she replied wryly.

"We'll do that then," he agreed with her.

When the Hansons had ridden enough waves, they came back to Jessie and took her to the swimming pool.

"You swim while I watch our things, Jessie," Ray offered.

Accepting the offer, she went to the deep end and dove expertly from the side. Since the pool was not very crowded, she swam several laps and then splashed around with the kids. Smiling at her antics with his children, Ray watched Jessie the entire time she was in the pool.

Feeling a little waterlogged, Jessie went to the ladder and climbed out. When she walked over to the table where Ray was sitting, he stood up and draped a towel around her shoulders.

"Thanks," she responded to his gallantry.

They sat down, and Ray remarked, "You're quite a good swimmer."

"I used to swim a good bit, although it's been a while."

"Don't tell me. Not since you were a little girl," he proposed, with a smile.

"It hasn't been *that* long," she denied.

Mara and Maggie came to get their daddy. They wanted him to come play, so he obliged them.

While she watched the five of them having so much fun, Jessie found a comb in her purse and began untangling her hair. In the heat of the early summer evening, her swimsuit and hair were soon dry.

Ray pulled himself out onto the side of the pool and, at Mara and Maggie's request began tossing them into the pool. When Becca came to stand beside him, he grabbed her and tossed her in, too.

Wanting to get in on the fun, Bret tried to push his dad into the water. Instead, he missed, and Ray grabbed him and threw him in. Jessie just looked on and smiled.

Ray called Becca over. Climbing out of the pool, she went and listened intently as he whispered to her. Then she came over and sat down beside Jessie.

As Jessie eyed her, Becca favored her with an innocent grin.

"What's up?" Jessie asked suspiciously.

"You are!" Ray announced, as he reached and grabbed her up into his arms.

Surprised, Jessie screamed in alarm. Then realizing his intentions, she began struggling.

"Ray! Don't! I'm almost dry!" she pleaded with him.

Dangling her over the side of the pool, he just smiled at her as he held her in his arms.

Because his closeness had deeply affected her, Jessie could barely breathe. With her hand pressed against his bare chest, she begged quietly, "Ray, please."

"Please, what?" he queried with a devilish gleam in his eyes.

"Don't throw me in."

Gazing into her eyes, he promised, "All right. I won't."

Then, still holding her in his arms, he jumped into the pool.

When the pair hit the water, they made a huge splash, which caused Ray to release his hold on her.

Jessie sank to the bottom of the pool and then kicked her way to the surface. As she pushed her hair out of her eyes, she took in great gulps of air. Ray appeared beside her. "You promised you wouldn't!" she sputtered.

"I promised not to *throw* you in, and I didn't."

"You're splitting hairs. The result is the same because I'm still wet." She tried to maintain a stern expression with him, but when she started laughing, it sort of ruined the effect.

Laughing at the adult antics, the kids gathered around them. "That was funny, Daddy! Do it again!" Maggie demanded.

"Oh, no, you don't!" Jessie replied as she made to swim away from them to the side of the pool.

Since Ray was the stronger swimmer, he easily beat her and hauled himself out of the pool. He reached down to help her out, but distrusting his intentions, Jessie just eyed him.

He assured her, "Come on, Jessie. You can trust me."

Still hesitant, she reached up and took his hand. Then she gave it a sudden, strong tug that sent him somersaulting into the water.

The kids were delighted by this kind of aquatic horseplay.

Ray resurfaced in front of Jessie. Wiping the water from his eyes, he grinned at her and remarked appreciatively, "*Touche*."

This time when he got out of the pool and offered her his hand, she took it, and he pulled her up out of the water to stand beside him.

She went back to the table to get her towel and cast an accusing glance at Becca. "Traitor! You were in on that!"

Becca laughed, "Admit it. You had fun."

Jessie smiled at her and confessed that she had, in fact, enjoyed splashing around with the Hansons. Realizing the main reason for her enjoyment, she thought it prudent not to tell Becca that it had more to do with being held by her dad than anything else.

After Ray had fished the rest of his children out of the pool, they all came over to get their towels and dry off. Mara complained, "I'm hungry!" Her complaint was met by unanimous agreement.

"Let's get changed and go eat then," Ray suggested.

Everyone approved and headed for the locker rooms. Jessie dressed quickly and helped the little girls to comb out their hair. When the four girls were ready, they went to join Ray and Bret.

With everyone settled in the car, Ray turned and inquired, "Where to?"

"MacDonald's!" the kids chorused.

"Now how did I know that?" Ray asked with a wry smile. "Is that okay with you, Jessie?" He sent her a questioning look.

"That's fine by me. I don't think we're overdressed for it," she said in response and directed him to the nearest MacDonald's.

Once they had gotten their food, they found a booth large enough for six people and sat down to enjoy the last part of their fun day together. Maggie wanted to say the blessing this time and asked everyone to hold hands as she prayed. Since Ray and Jessie were both on the ends, he reached across the table and indicated that she should place her hand in his.

"Lord, thank you for the day you gave me with my family, including Jessie, and thank you for this food. Amen." As Maggie prayed, Ray had idly rubbed the back of Jessie's hand with his thumb. She didn't know if it was an unconscious act or not; she just knew that it was wreaking havoc on her senses.

When Maggie had finished her blessing, Ray reluctantly let go of Jessie's hand so that he could start eating his food. It took Jessie a moment to pull herself together before she could begin her meal. She really had to exercise more control. How could she allow a simple, innocent touch like that to affect her so much?

As they ate their meal, the kids chatted about the fun they'd had that day. Bret was especially enthralled with The Rebellion.

"It was fun, wasn't it, Jessie?" He looked to her for confirmation.

"It *was* thrilling! But I promised the Lord that if I lived through it I would never get on it again."

"You don't sound exactly enthusiastic," Ray noted, apparently enjoying teasing her.

"There's a reason for that—I'm not," she answered plainly.

"It took a lot of guts to ride it – more than I had," he admitted with a lazy smile.

They finished their meal and decided that it was time to go home.

"Who needs the restroom?" Jessie asked.

Of course, they all did.

After their restroom break, they headed back to Jessie's house. As usual, Jessie sat between Mara and Maggie, but being tired out from their big day they soon fell asleep, one little girl against each shoulder. Bret was stretched out on the back seat, while Jessie stayed awake by eavesdropping on the conversation between Ray and Becca. Once in a while, Ray would glance in the rearview mirror and direct a comment to her just to keep her awake.

Pulling up to the gate, Ray noticed something move in the glare of the headlights.

"What *is* that?" he asked uncertain about what he was seeing.

Jessie peered at the gate and saw a yellow dog, barking excitedly at them.

"It's Sanson! But how did he get out? I know he was on the couch when we left!" Jessie clarified.

Ray pushed the remote, which would open the gate and allow Sanson to come to them. As the gate began to swing open, Becca opened her door and started to call the dog.

At that very second, a loud noise that sounded like a huge bomb exploding nearly burst their eardrums and violently shook the car. The noise woke the three younger children, and Sanson started howling and bounded into the car. He crawled to the back seat, where Bret was.

"How did he get here?" Bret wanted to know.

"What was that noise, Daddy?" Mara cried.

"I don't know, Pumpkin. Shut your door, Becca, and let's get up to the house and see if we can find out," Ray ordered.

After pulling through, he reached to push the remote to close gate, but nothing happened.

"That's odd. The battery must be dead," Jessie guessed. "I'll put a new one in and close the gate later."

Unperturbed, Ray continued down the drive, but when the car rounded the curve, they were met by a terrible sight. Jessie's home – what was left of it – was engulfed in flames. The explosion had been at her house.

A horrified little cry escaped her lips. "Oh!" was all she could manage. She was too dumbstruck to say anything else.

"Daddy, what happened to Jessie's house?" Maggie asked fearfully. Jessie put an arm around both little girls, as much for her own comfort as theirs.

"I don't know, Sweetheart. We need to get to a phone, Jessie," he told her, as he turned to study her stunned expression.

"Jessie?" he said again, trying to bring her out of her daze.

She snapped out of it and told him to hit the emergency button on her Onstar panel. That would connect him to 911.

When he got the operator, he reported the emergency and asked for the fire department and the sheriff to be sent to Jessie's address. He realized that not much of Jessie's beautiful home could be saved, but they still needed to report the explosion.

Ray pulled as far off the driveway as he could to make room for emergency vehicles and left the lights on so that the car could be seen. Then he opened his door and started to get out.

"Ray! Where are you going?" Jessie gasped.

"I'm just going to see if I can save anything," he replied.

"Daddy! Don't!" Becca pleaded.

Jessie added her protests. "No! There's nothing in there that's worth your life! What if there's another explosion or something falls on you? Your kids have lost enough!"

He considered what she had said and decided that she was right yet again.

Shutting the door, Ray reached over to put an arm around Becca, who had begun to shake uncontrollably.

He thought to himself, "*This is no accident. Whoever did this was at least considerate enough—or careless enough—to let the dog out before it blew up. Who could hate Jessie this much?* Suddenly it dawned on him! Greg! He was psychotic, and Jessie's rejection of him could well have sent him over the edge."

He looked at her in the rearview mirror as she held his children in her arms. Tears were streaming down her cheeks.

"Jessie, I'm so sorry," he murmured, as he turned to place his hand on her blue jean-clad knee.

When she saw the concern in his eyes, she swallowed the sob that had risen in her throat.

"I'll be okay. I think we're all in shock," she admitted tearfully.

Sirens announced the arrival of the sheriff, followed closely by the volunteer fire department. The fire fighters began immediately to try to knock down the flames, but it was a losing battle since the fire was too far advanced to bring under control. Unfortunately, all they could do was keep it from spreading to the trees and just let it burn itself out.

The sheriff came over to the car to talk to Jessie. He could tell that she was upset, but he needed to know if she had any ideas about what had happened.

She glanced at Ray and told the sheriff, "I need to talk to you in private." Then she disengaged herself from Mara and Maggie and opening the door, climbed out of the car. She followed the sheriff to his patrol car and got into the front seat to talk with him.

"Talk to me, Jessie," he invited once they were settled. "What happened here?"

"I have no proof, so I really hate to make any accusations for the record."

"But you think you know who did this?" he guessed.

"I believe it was Greg Robertson. I went out with him exactly one time. Before that, we talked a few times at Chuck's health spa in town, and I met him in Memphis for a Dutch treat meal. Then when he persisted, I invited him here to tell him I couldn't see him any more, because his behavior and attitude really bothered me. That didn't go over too well, and he attacked me. If Ray Hanson hadn't been here with his children, he would have…well probably raped me. I found out later that it wouldn't be the first time he's done something like this."

"Go on," the sheriff prompted.

"I'd promised Ray's kids that we would go to LibertyLand and the water park, and we were gone all day, which would have given him enough time to rig the house. I think he did something to the gas lines in the house so that when we tried to enter we would all have been blown up with the house. He didn't know that using the gate remote causes two short warning buzzes inside the house, which evidently triggered a premature explosion and saved our lives."

Even though she'd been upset, Jessie had figured all this out while waiting for the emergency personnel to arrive. She'd always hated that buzzer, but tonight it had saved their lives. She felt that God had been at work for a long time orchestrating events to save Ray, his children, and her, something for which she would always be grateful.

As much as she had loved her home, it was just stuff. Most of it could be replaced. What had brought her to tears was the thought that Ray and his children could have been hurt or worse. Even now, it caused a chill to run down her spine.

"Do you want to press charges against him?" the sheriff asked, bringing her out of her reverie.

"I have no proof, just a feeling. I also believe that when he discovers he failed he'll come after us again. Even if you arrested him on suspicion of arson, his father would get him out in no time."

"I could put you in protective custody," he offered.

"For how long – a day, a week, a year? I don't think so, Sheriff. We'll come up with something." Jessie already had plans for what they should do, but she needed to talk to Ray first.

"Well, maybe the fire marshal can come up with enough evidence to make an arrest," the sheriff said hopefully.

Jessie doubted it but said nonetheless, "Maybe."

They talked for a few minutes more, and then she went back to the car. When she had settled back into her seat, Ray sent her a questioning glance, but she just shook her head.

In a little while, the fire had burned to a low enough level that Ray suggested that he and Jessie should go talk to the fire fighters. Asking Becca to watch the other children and admonishing them all to stay in the car, they walked over to what used to be the front of Jessie's house.

The heat from the still flaming logs was so intense that Ray and Jessie had to back away several feet. One of the fire fighters came over to answer Jessie's questions. No. They hadn't been able to save any of her belongings. It would probably be at least tomorrow, maybe longer, until the fire marshal would be able to conduct his investigation. She and her guests might as well go and find some place to stay the night. Cautioning her to contact the fire department sometime the next day, he extended his condolences and went back to work.

Ray took Jessie's arm and led her away from the fire. About halfway back to the car, she stopped and buried her face in her hands. All of a sudden, she was extremely tired. As she wondered how much more she could bear that night, Ray put his arms around her and drew her close.

Saying nothing, he appeared to sense her fatigue and just held her while she tried to get herself together.

After a while, he asked gently, "What do you want to do now, Jessie?"

She'd considered what they should do next so she answered, gazing steadily into his eyes, "I want us to go back to Memphis and stop at the Super Center on the way to get necessities. Then I want us to go to a five-star hotel, where they allow dogs and security is much tighter."

Somehow she knew what had happened here! Ray was always amazed by Jessie's intuition and her ability to pick up on a situation.

"Sounds like a plan to me," he agreed.

They went to the car and headed back to Memphis.

Chapter 16

By the time they'd finished at the Super Center, Jessie had bought enough pajamas, extra clothes, underwear, and toiletries, including an electric shaver for Ray, to last the Hansons and herself until they could take a proper shopping trip the next day. She even bought a leash and food for the dog. Though Ray tried to argue with her, she insisted on paying for everything. This time, she got the last word.

When they arrived in Memphis, she directed Ray to a five-star hotel. They were able to get a three-room suite, including two bedrooms with king sized beds and a sitting room. Also Ray was able to charm the female concierge into allowing them to take the dog into their suite after paying a cleaning deposit. Even with all that had happened that night, Jessie could still smile at Ray's ability to charm the women.

Conscious of the fact that they were still in danger, Jessie kept glancing around as they went to the elevator to go to the fourteenth floor. She just could not shake the feeling that they were being watched. Once they were in their suite with all the doors locked and the night latches on, she felt a little safer.

Since it was so late, Ray suggested that they get the kids ready for bed. All the girls could have one room, and the guys, including Sanson, could have the other one. Everyone had to have a bath, so Mara and

Maggie went first. While Ray and Jessie were getting them into bed, Becca took her bath. Not wanting Jessie out of her sight, Maggie refused to go to sleep unless she was in the room.

Knowing how upset and frightened the child must be over what had happened that evening, Jessie offered, "All right, Sweetie. I'll just lie down beside you right here until you go to sleep. Okay?"

"Okay," she replied, already close to falling asleep.

When Becca came out of the bathroom, Ray turned out all the lights except for one small one that acted as a nightlight. Then he told them that he was going to get ready for bed.

"When she's asleep, I'll do the same. Goodnight, Ray."

He studied her as she lay there on the edge of the bed, her arm draped protectively over Maggie. With everything that she'd been through tonight, she was still considerate of his daughter's fears. She had to be exhausted, but she put others first.

He smiled at her and said, "Thanks, Jessie. Goodnight."

Jessie lay there until she could hear Maggie's even breathing. Then she carefully got off the bed, picked up her new nightgown and robe, and went into the bathroom. Hoping that it would help her to relax, she took a long leisurely soak in the tub.

When she felt that she would shrivel up if she soaked another minute, she finally got out and dressed for bed. Though she was tired, she did not feel sleepy, so leaving the door slightly ajar, she went into the sitting room and sat with the moonlight streaming in from the window the only illumination.

As she sat there and thought about what could have happened *and* what still could happen, suddenly she was so overcome with fear for Ray and his children that she got down on her knees in front of the chair in which she'd been sitting and simply poured her heart out to God. Tears were streaming down her face because she realized that they were going to have to go home to California and, for the kids' safety, leave her behind. Somehow in the past few weeks, the Hansons had become her family, and letting them go was going to break her heart. But it was something she knew she had to do.

The door to the other bedroom opened, and Ray came into the room.

Seeing her there on the floor, he went over and knelt beside her.

"Jessie, what's wrong?" he asked tenderly.

"Ray, you have to go," she whispered to him.

"I'm sorry. I didn't mean to intrude." He started to rise.

Placing her hand on his arm, she cried in a hushed voice, "No! I didn't mean now! I meant that you have to take the kids back to California."

He studied her tear-stained face in the moonlight. Then he replied, "You're right, of course, but you'll come with us."

"I can't!" she wailed. "You know that Greg is behind this, don't you? He'll try again. I'm sure of it, but maybe if I stay behind, he'll leave y'all alone and come after me. I'm the one he's trying to hurt."

"Please, Jessie, I can't leave you here like this," he groaned.

"You don't have a choice, Ray. Your family comes first. Tonight was too close a call. I couldn't bear it if something were to happen to any of you!" Her voice shook with emotion as she tried to make him see her point.

"But…"

She got up and said, "No, Ray. I'm going to have the last word on this for your kids' sakes, as well as yours." Before he could argue further, she slipped into the girls' room and went to bed.

Ray sat in the chair and covered his face with his hands. She was right again. Keeping his children safe from Greg was his top priority. But how could he leave Jessie behind to face the danger alone?

With that terrible question weighing on his mind, Ray had trouble going to sleep that night. He lay in bed, the thought echoing through his mind.

Things didn't seem any brighter for the adults in the morning. Jessie insisted on calling the airline and booking five seats on an afternoon flight to Los Angeles. Ray couldn't argue with her any more because he knew that the longer they were in Memphis, the greater the chance that his family would be in danger. Resigning himself to the inevitable, he allowed Jessie to make the phone call.

After a quick continental breakfast, they went to the mall so that they could get clothes for their trip back home. When all the Hansons had complete outfits, Jessie had some other places to take them.

She went to the same jewelry store where she'd bought Becca's watch, which had been lost in the fire, and got her another one just like it. Then she went to the toy store and bought the younger kids the same toys that they had lost.

When Ray tried to protest, she just looked at him, her eyes filled with sadness, and replied, "Please, Ray. Let me do this one last thing for them."

It was as if she didn't expect to survive Greg's attacks. "Jessie," he moaned. Nevertheless, he gave in to her wishes.

They went back to the hotel to change into their new clothes and to pack their other belongings in the suitcase that Ray had bought. After lunch, Jessie drove them to the airport in time to get their bag and Sanson checked and go through security before their three o'clock flight.

"Aren't you coming with us, Jessie?" a tearful Maggie asked.

Jessie knelt in front of her and explained, "No, I have too much to do here about fire departments and insurance and things. So y'all will have to go on without me."

"But I don't want to leave you!" the little girl cried.

Jessie put her arms around Maggie and gave her a big hug and kissed her cheek. "I know, Sweetheart. But it'll be okay. I love you," she said, resting her forehead against Maggie's.

She got up off her knees and went to the other children, hugging each one and kissing them on the cheek. "I couldn't love y'all more if you were my own children," she told them with a smile, gallantly holding back the tears. The kids, from the youngest to the oldest, weren't even trying not to cry.

Then, still trying to maintain her smile, she turned to Ray. "Goodbye, Ray. I'm sorry about all this. I didn't mean for it to turn out this way."

"None of this was your fault, Jessie. Remember that, and don't blame yourself," he instructed her.

"I'll remember," she promised.

He smiled at her and prompted, "Don't I get a hug and a kiss?"

"Sure," she responded a little breathlessly as she reached up to place her arms around him and to give him a peck on the cheek.

As she made to pull away from him, Ray put his hands around her waist and drew her back against him. "Jessie?" he whispered.

When she looked up into his eyes, he lowered his head and kissed her tenderly on the lips.

Without another word, he released her and turned to his children. "We'd better go, Kids."

Taking Mara and Maggie by the hand, he led them through the gate and down the concourse, with Becca and Bret following reluctantly behind. He turned back to glance at Jessie, who stood there with her fingertips pressed against her mouth and a look of sheer anguish in her eyes.

Ray had to force himself to keep moving toward the boarding area. With his entire being, he wanted to rush back to Jessie and make her come with them, but he knew that was impossible. Knowing that he might never see her again, he just kept walking.

As wave after wave of sorrow washed over her, Jessie just stood there. Ray's kiss had been bittersweet, because so many times she'd wanted nothing more than to feel the touch of his lips on hers. But now that she knew that she might never see him again, it was almost more than she could bear.

When the Hansons had disappeared from sight, she turned to leave the terminal. Catching a glimpse of movement out of the corner of her eye, she glanced over and looked directly into the gloating eyes of Greg Robertson.

At first, she had to fight back the terror that rose up in her chest. Then anger and a courage she hadn't known she possessed took over. It could only have come from God. She glared defiantly at him and said, "Yes, you've hurt me, but let me tell you that God is still in control. You can't do anything to me that doesn't pass through His hands first." With that, she turned and strode from the terminal without so much as a backward glance.

Ray got his children settled in their seats. For their sakes as well as his own, he hated the suddenness of their departure. There had been no time to ease them into the separation from Jessie. It must seem to them the same kind of loss that they'd felt over their mother. If he would face the truth, he, too, felt a sense of loss.

As the plane taxied to the runway for takeoff, he thought about the reason for his feelings of loss, and suddenly it became excruciatingly clear to him. He was in love with Jessie! Somehow in the past few weeks, being in such close proximity to her and seeing her lovely face, her sweet, generous spirit, and her love for his children, he had fallen in love with her! And he had left her to face God-knows-what alone!

Placing his hands over his face, he let out a low groan. What was he going to do? This was tearing him apart!

Once they were in the air and the all clear had been given, Becca came over to her Dad and said for his ears alone, "It's *him*, isn't it? Greg is behind all this. And Jessie is sending us away to protect us, because he's not going to stop."

He was amazed at his daughter's powers of perception and decided to be honest with her. "Yes. That's what Jessie believes, and I think she's right."

"What are you going to do about it then?" she asked with a worried frown. "We can't just leave her to face him alone."

"I don't know yet," he admitted. "Let me think about it for a while."

"All right," she concurred and went back to her seat.

Thinking furiously, Ray considered his options. After some time, he came up with a plan that he hoped would work. He decided to call the kids' grandmother – Helen's mother – and take them to stay with her. Then he would pack a bag and catch a flight back to Memphis to be with Jessie. Having elicited a promise from her that she would remain in the hotel and get a smaller suite, he would take a cab there.

Motioning to Becca to come sit with the younger kids, he left his seat in first class and went to the public telephone to call his mother-in-law, Lorraine. He was able to get through to her, and after explaining the situation to her, they agreed that he would take the kids by his house to pack some clothes and then bring them to her.

Once those arrangements were made, he called the airport and booked a return flight later that evening. Finally, he returned to his seat to tell his children about his plans. Though they were unhappy about the prospect of their father's leaving them, they were glad that he was going back for Jessie's sake. She had seemed so sad and alone.

When they landed at LAX, they hurried to collect the luggage and the dog and then made their way to the parking lot to pick up the car. After a nerve-wracking trip on the freeway, at last they arrived at home. While he packed his own bag, Ray sent the kids to their rooms to get ready for an extended stay at their grandmother's house. Finishing up, he went to check on their progress.

As he entered her room last, Becca looked up at him and grinned. "I'm glad you're going back to help Jessie, Daddy, but I'm just wondering why you're really doing it."

"She's alone and in danger, and she's my friend. Why else would I be going?" he warily asked his daughter.

"Oh, I don't know. Could it be that you're in love with her?" she dared to inquire.

He sat down on her bed and reprimanded, "You're being nosey, young lady, but as long as we're on the subject, what would you kids think of that *if* it were true?"

Becca sat beside her dad and, putting her arms around him, confided, "I'm old enough to understand that you've been lonely without Mom and that you're beginning to need companionship. Also I've noticed the way you are with Jessie – friendly, protective, playful, tender. But to answer your question, we all love Jessie. She's been so kind and loving to us that we really began to heal during our visit with her. She even taught us to appreciate our old dad. I think she would be a wonderful step-mother."

"Hey! I think you may be jumping the gun a little. Even though I realize she cares about us, I don't know that she has any deeper feelings for me. I'm not sure she would have me," he admitted honestly.

Becca gave him a secretive little smile and told him, "I believe she would have you, but that's just my woman's intuition talking. Maybe you ought to find out the next time you see her."

"Maybe I will. But for now, it's time to get you kids to your grandmother so I can make my flight." He kissed her on the cheek and went to round up his children and the dog.

At last, after tearful goodbyes and traffic and security delays, Ray was headed back to Memphis. The urgency he felt to get back to Jessie was really wearing on his nerves. Up there in the sky, he felt so helpless. It was times like this that he wished he had a faith like Jessie's. Helen had come to that kind of faith, and he hadn't understood it any more then than he did now. Since Jessie had been able to explain it to Helen, maybe she could explain it to him sometime.

The plane landed, and by ten o'clock he had cleared the airport. Out front, he hailed a taxi, which took him to Jessie's hotel. He knew from experience that, as a security precaution, the concierge would not give him her room number. It just so happened that the same woman from last night was on duty.

After explaining the situation to her, he asked if she would call Jessie and then allow him to speak to her. Of course, he was assuming Jessie had done as she had promised him and had remained in the hotel. Apparently she had, because the woman agreed to call her suite.

When someone answered the phone, the young woman replied, "One moment, please," and handed the phone to Ray.

"Jessie?" he began.

"Ray! How are you? Are the kids okay?" He could detect the concern in her voice.

"Everybody's fine. How about you?"

"I'm okay, but I feel better knowing that y'all are safe now," she responded.

"Jessie, I'm calling from downstairs. I need your room number so that I can come up. You'll be glad to know that the concierge won't give out your location," he remarked, trying to head off the protest he knew was coming.

He was right. "Ray, why?" she moaned. "You were safe in California! Why did you come back here?"

183

He smiled to himself. He was beginning to know her so well. "Jessie...your room number, please?"

She hesitated before supplying it. "914," was all she said.

"I'll be right there." He hung up and, giving the young woman a charming smile and his thanks, grabbed his bag, and headed to the elevators. When the elevator arrived, he glanced around to make certain that he wasn't being watched. Only then, did he enter and punch the ninth floor button.

Jessie wasn't sure how to react to the news that Ray was back. On the one hand, she was terrified for his life, since he was in as much danger as before. On the other hand, she would get to see him again, something she had doubted just a few hours ago. She went to the bedroom to get her robe and make herself presentable.

There was a knock at the door, and after checking, Jessie opened it to Ray.

"Hi, Jessie," he said, as she stood there gazing up at him.

When she didn't respond, he prompted, "Aren't you going to invite me in?"

She stepped aside and held the door open for him.

After he had entered the sitting room, he turned around to face her. They eyed each other a little uncertainly, and then Ray asked, a tender smile on his handsome face, "Are you really angry with me for coming back here?"

"Not angry, just concerned for your safety," she admitted as she sat down on the couch, inviting him to do the same. "Greg was at the airport earlier today."

"You're sure? You actually saw him?" was his horrified reaction.

"Yes, I even talked to him." Then she told him exactly what she had said to Greg.

He marveled again at the faith that she had. Sensing that the time was right, he asked her about it.

"Jessie, so much has happened in your life – things that would make the average person doubt the existence of a caring God – especially

184

losing your home like you did yesterday. How can you still have faith in him?"

"How can I *not*?" came the simple reply.

"I don't get it," he admitted.

"I mean that He's blessed me over and over again, so why should His allowing some bad things, which He uses to teach me to be a better Christian, make me doubt Him?"

"I guess that I'll never understand why God makes Christians like you and Helen suffer," he told her.

"Oh, Ray," she said gently, "He doesn't *make* us suffer. He *allows* the suffering, but he's not the author of suffering. We don't understand either why he allows such things. We just accept it as His will and trust Him anyway. Helen is the one who understands right now. I can picture her, sitting at the feet of Jesus and happily asking all kinds of questions."

"But how do you know that's where she is right now? How were you able to assure my children that she's in Heaven?" he agonized.

Sending up a silent prayer for guidance, she reached over and took his hand in both of hers. "I know it because she accepted Christ as her Savior. As the Bible says, she believed on Him and was saved. We knelt in my great room and prayed the sinner's prayer together. She admitted that she was a sinner and confessed her sin. Then she believed that Jesus was able to save her from her sin. Finally, she made Jesus the Lord of her life and tried to live for Him. That's how I *know* beyond the shadow of a doubt where Helen is right now, Ray."

He shook his head. "It seems too simple. I'm a man who's used to being around other powerful men – the movers and shakers of this world. We work hard for what we've achieved. And for you to say that all I have to do to get to Heaven is believe is anathema to me. I don't know that I can accept that, Jessie."

"Wouldn't you like to know that when you die you'll be where Helen is?" she pressed him.

"Yes," he answered simply.

"Then will you pray the sinner's prayer with me now?" she asked.

He put her off, "I need to think about this some more. You don't hate me for that, do you?"

"I could never hate you, Ray. It's just that I don't want you to wait until it's too late. I want what's best for you. I always have, you know," she reminded him, still holding his hand.

"I know." Ray wanted so badly to take Jessie into his arms right that moment, but he knew that was not a good idea. She seemed so vulnerable, and at this point, he was not sure that he would be able to control himself if he *were* to have her in his arms. Since he had no idea about how she felt about him other than as a friend, he didn't want to scare her off.

So he asked for time to consider the things that she'd told him.

Not wanting to push him, she said, "Sure. We can talk about it later if it's all right with you."

He agreed to that. After talking for a while longer, they decided that it was time for them to get some sleep. Though Jessie offered Ray the bedroom, he refused, telling her that the couch would be fine. Since it made up into a king sized bed, he would be comfortable. Also there was a second bathroom adjacent to the kitchenette.

Jessie brought him an extra pillow and a blanket from the cupboard in the bedroom. Bidding him goodnight, she went to bed. For some time, she lay there listening to his movements in the next room. Even though his proximity made her feel safer, knowing that he was just a few feet away and that they were alone in the suite caused her heart to beat faster and a warm, flushed feeling to spread over her body. At last, she fell asleep.

Chapter 17

The next morning Jessie was up and dressed when there was a tentative knock at the bedroom door, as if Ray was afraid that she might not be awake yet.

"Coming!" she called. Then going to the door, she opened it with a warm, welcoming smile.

"Good morning, Jessie," Ray said, as he gazed down at her beautiful, smiling face. Sunshine. That's what her smile reminded him of – heartwarming, energizing, inviting sunshine.

"Good morning, Ray," she returned his greeting.

"I came to see if you wanted to venture out of the suite for breakfast this morning," he suggested.

After considering his suggestion, she responded, "To tell you the truth, I do. I haven't been out of these rooms since I switched yesterday, and I'm a little tired of letting Greg set our agenda. We can't hide in here forever, can we?"

"That's the spirit!" he told her. "Are you ready to go?"

"As soon as I get my purse." She went to the desk and picked up her purse. Then they left the suite and headed downstairs to the dining room. Opting for the buffet, they were soon sitting at a table, which allowed them a view of the entrance, and enjoying a leisurely breakfast.

Realizing that they hadn't had a meal alone together since she first met him over three and a half years ago, Jessie remarked on that fact to Ray.

"Has it been *that* long?" He seemed to be thinking back to that time. A lot had changed since then, most especially his feelings for the woman sitting across from him. Back then, she had been a good friend who had bullied him into being the kind of person he needed to be, and now... Well, actually she was still doing that. The only difference was that now he was in love with her, though he was no closer to discovering how she felt about him.

When they had finished their meal, they decided to take a stroll around the mezzanine, overlooking the lobby. Making their way up the stairs, Jessie kept turning around to look behind them.

Once they had reached the mezzanine, Jessie rubbed her arms as if she was suppressing a shudder.

"Cold?" Ray inquired.

Jessie shook her head. "No, it's just that I have the feeling that he's here somewhere watching us. It's making my skin crawl."

"I know what you mean," he admitted, as he glanced around the lobby below them.

"I wish there was some way to bring him out into the open," she sighed.

"There is only one way I can think of, but you'll have to play along with me. Are you game?" he challenged her.

She eyed him uncertainly and asked, "What did you have in mind?"

"Just follow my lead," was his answer.

Then taking her arm, he pulled her over to the rail, where they could easily be seen, and put his arms around her waist.

"Put your arms around my neck," he instructed, smiling into her startled eyes.

When she had complied, he lowered his head and sought her mouth with his. Jessie's breath caught in her throat, and momentarily she thought about resisting. But that thought quickly left her mind as the warm pressure of his lips awakened the desire for him that she had kept hidden for so long. With mounting passion, she returned his kiss.

Ray broke the kiss to gaze into her eyes. Wanting more, with her hands pressed against his neck, Jessie pulled his head back down to hers and abandoned herself to the touch of his lips and the sheer pleasure of being in his arms.

"Get your hands off her!" the voice growled threateningly.

The sound was like a bucket of cold water, causing them to spring apart and stare at the angry man confronting them.

Jessie gasped at the sight of the gun in Greg's hand. This was a possibility she had never considered. "Greg, don't do this!" she implored.

Greg moved in closer, menacingly waving the gun at them.

He shouted at Ray, "I told you that she's mine! If I can't have her, no one will!"

At the same moment that Greg aimed the gun at Jessie's head, Ray moved to stand in front of her, shielding her from the blast as Greg pulled the trigger.

Amidst screams coming from bystanders in the lobby, Jessie cried out Ray's name as he started falling to the floor. When she reached out to try to break his fall, Greg yelled at her, "This is all your fault, Jessie!" This time, he aimed the gun at Ray as if he would finish the job.

Reacting in a way that she had seen so many times on her favorite television show, she spun around on one foot and kicked the gun out of Greg's hand. It clattered harmlessly onto the lobby floor. Then as Greg took a mad lunge at her, Jessie dodged him at the last possible moment.

In horror, she watched him fall over the rail to the lobby below, clutching wildly for a handhold.

The sound of shattering glass brought her to the rail to see Greg's still, lifeless form sprawled on top of the remains of a glass-top table.

Bending over him, a man was checking for a pulse.

"Is he...?" Jessie couldn't complete the question. When the man sadly shook his head, she choked back a sob and requested shakily, "Would you please call 911? Someone's been shot up here!"

Immediately the man did as she had asked. Afraid of what she would find, she rushed back to Ray's side. Blood covered his right shoulder. Was he unconscious or...worse? Jessie reached to feel for a pulse in his neck and then breathed a sigh of relief. He was alive! Though he was bleeding profusely, he was still breathing! Sending up a quick prayer of thanksgiving, she sat down beside him and lifted his head onto her lap. To staunch the flow of blood, she firmly placed one hand over the wound. With the other hand, she gently caressed his face, while she frantically prayed for God to save his life.

After what seemed like an eternity though it was actually only a matter of minutes, two ambulances finally arrived on the scene. One group of paramedics checked on Greg, while the others were directed to the mezzanine for the shooting victim. On the heels of the paramedics, the police made their way in to secure the scene and to question witnesses.

With Jessie still applying pressure to the wound, the paramedics began checking Ray. A worried frown marring her face, she lamented, "I'm sorry. I didn't know what to do for him."

"You did fine, Ma'am," one of them replied. "You probably kept him from bleeding to death."

"Is he going to be okay?" she asked fearfully.

"It's not that critical a wound. He looks as if he's in good physical condition, and his vitals are pretty good for someone who's just been shot," he tried to reassure her.

After they had stabilized him, the paramedics placed Ray on the stretcher and prepared to take him to the lobby via the elevator. Jessie grabbed her purse and followed them downstairs. Intending to ride in the ambulance to the hospital, she was forestalled by the police.

"What's your name, Ma'am?" one of the officers inquired.

"Jessica Martin," she replied matter-of-factly.

He whistled appreciatively. "The famous author?" he wanted to know.

"I guess so. Yes."

They needed to ask her some questions before they allowed her to leave the scene.

"But what if he comes to and I'm not there? He doesn't have anybody else here in Memphis," she explained.

The officers talked among themselves and decided that Jessie could go with the victim and an officer would follow her there to take her statement.

"Thank you so much," she responded gratefully and hurried after the paramedics.

Since she wasn't a family member, the paramedics would only permit her to ride up front with the driver. When they arrived at the emergency room, Ray was whisked away to an examining room, where Jessie was allowed to wait with him until a doctor could see him.

After washing the blood off her hands in the lavatory, Jessie pulled a chair close to the gurney and took Ray's hand in hers. That action elicited a soft moan from his pale lips. Standing up, she bent over him and placed her lips against his forehead. He moaned again.

"Ray? Can you hear me? It's Jessie," she whispered close to his ear, hoping for more than a moan.

"Jessie?" he said softly without opening his eyes. "What happened?"

She breathed a sigh of relief. "Oh, Ray! It's okay! Greg shot you, and you're in the hospital."

"What about you?" he mumbled.

"I'm fine. Don't worry about me," she assured him.

"Greg?"

This was something that Jessie had not wanted to think about. It wasn't that she thought she was responsible for Greg's death. If she hadn't dodged him, he would have killed her and been happy about it. She just hated that it had happened because he'd been such a sick, troubled man.

"He's d-dead," she gently informed him, trying to control her quivering voice.

"Dead? How?"

"He lunged at me, and I jumped out of his way. He f-fell over the rail and was k-killed instantly," she said as she began to cry.

"Don't cry, Jessie," he whispered and gave her hand a weak little squeeze.

An ER doctor, accompanied by a nurse, came into the room and, when he discovered that Jessie wasn't a relative, shooed her out.

After his examination, the doctor came out where Jessie was nervously waiting and informed her that Ray was being prepped for surgery to remove the bullet lodged in his shoulder. She collected his personal belongings and, going through his wallet, gave the receptionist as much information as she could. Then she was told to go to the waiting room until surgery was completed.

But first, the police officer that had followed her to the hospital needed to take her statement. Quickly Jessie explained the events that had led up to the shooting and Greg's tragic death. When he was satisfied that he had all the information that he needed, the officer let Jessie go on her way to the waiting room.

She thought about calling the kids to tell them about their father, but then she decided that it would be better to wait until surgery was over and she had more information about his prognosis. While she waited for word from the OR, she prayed. If Ray didn't come through the surgery all right, Jessie didn't think she could bear it. Loving him as she did, she felt that she wouldn't be able to go on, especially since she knew that he wasn't a Christian.

At last, she heard the page that brought her news about Ray. On the phone to the OR nurse, she was informed that he was in recovery and that he was doing well. In about an hour, he would be moved to a private room, and she could see him then.

All Jessie could say now was, "Thank you, God! Thank you, God!"

In a little over an hour, Jessie answered another page and was told that Ray was being taken to Room 456. She could go on up there now.

When she got to the room, several nurses were in attendance, hooking up monitors and IV's. She asked one of them, "Will I be able to stay with him?"

"Yes, Ma'am. It's always good for a family member or a friend to be on hand. While he will receive excellent care here, it's best for a loved one to be present. Right now, he'll feel better just knowing you're here," the nurse told her.

"Jessie?" she heard Ray call her name in a faint voice.

She walked over to the bed and, touching his face, replied, "I'm here, Ray."

"Good," was all he said before he went to sleep.

Sitting in a chair that she'd moved close to the bed, Jessie was able to watch Ray carefully. The nurses were in and out, but she was almost afraid to take her eyes off him. But finally, as emotionally drained as she was, she placed her head on her arms, which she'd rested on the bedside, and promptly fell into a fitful sleep.

When the nurse came in the next morning to change the dressing on Ray's wound, she woke Jessie up.

Rubbing her eyes, Jessie sat up to find Ray watching her.

"It's about time you woke up, Sleepyhead," he teased.

She bemoaned, "I didn't mean to go to sleep. I was supposed to be taking care of you. Some nurse I am!"

"Jessie. It's okay. You were exhausted," he consoled her.

"Have you been awake long?"

He admitted that he'd been awake for some time.

Jessie felt bad that she hadn't known. "I'm sorry. Why didn't you wake me?"

"I was enjoying listening to you snore," he replied, taking pleasure from her reaction.

"I do not snore!" she denied hotly.

"Relax. I'm teasing you." He gave her a charming smile.

Changing the subject, she asked, "How are you feeling this morning?"

"Hungry," he admitted.

"I'll check on what you can have to eat." She went out to the desk to ask the nurse.

Jessie found out that Ray could eat regular breakfast foods, so she placed two orders when the meals were brought around. Because of his shoulder, Ray had trouble handling a fork, so Jessie fed him scrambled eggs and put jelly on his toast. The rest he could do for himself.

After they'd finished eating, they waited for the doctor to make his rounds to find out when Ray would be dismissed.

By mid-morning, the doctor had been in to see Ray. When he had read the chart and examined the wound, he informed them that Ray should be released the next day and the day after that he could fly home to California.

Jessie decided that while Ray took a nap she needed to take a taxi back to the hotel to shower and change clothes and pick up some of his things. But first, she wanted to call his family and let them hear from their dad.

She dialed the number that Ray gave her and then handed the receiver to him. Becca answered on the other end.

"Hi, Becca. It's Daddy. I'm calling to let you know what's going on here," he told his daughter.

As his explanation unfolded, apparently Becca became quite upset.

"I'm okay, Sweetheart. I promise, and Jessie's fine, too. We'll be home in a couple of days. I love you. Bye." Then he handed the receiver back to Jessie.

"I take it that she was not happy," Jessie asked.

"Not exactly, but she calmed down when she heard we were okay."

Jessie worried about the impact such news would have on the kids, but she felt they did have a right to know what was going on with their dad and her and that they would soon be home.

Returning to the hotel gave Jessie an eerie feeling. When she went through the lobby to the elevators, she tried not to look at the place where Greg had fallen. Back in the suite, she stripped and took a quick shower. Then she donned clean underwear, jeans, and a T-shirt.

Emptying her bag of everything but a few necessities, she put in the things that Ray would need for the next day. With that accomplished, she headed back to the hospital.

The following afternoon, Ray was dismissed from the hospital. After the nurse had shown her how to change the sterile strip on Ray's wound, he dressed himself while Jessie waited in the corridor.

"Jessie!" he called.

When she stuck her head in the door, he told her that he needed help putting on his shirt.

Shyly Jessie walked over to him and lifted his wounded arm into the shirtsleeve. Then she pulled his good arm into the other sleeve and slipped the shirt over his head and down over his bare chest. She had never helped a man get dressed before and was feeling a little embarrassed.

"You did that like an expert," he said, smiling at her obvious embarrassment.

"Thanks," she replied, unable to look him in the eye as she put in place the sling that the hospital had provided.

After Ray had signed the dismissal forms and the nurse had given him a supply of sterile strips, he got into the wheelchair, and an orderly pushed him out to the car, where Jessie was waiting to pick him up.

When she finally got him up to the hotel suite, Ray was exhausted. Insisting that he would be much more comfortable in the bedroom, Jessie made him lie down on the bed. She began moving her things into the sitting room.

"I'm too tired to argue with you," he admitted.

"As if you had a choice," she came back smartly.

Ray just smiled and closed his eyes.

She left the bedroom door opened a crack so that she could hear him if he called and quietly puttered around for a while.

When he'd been asleep for a couple of hours, Jessie looked in on him to make sure he was all right. He was just waking up.

"Hi. Feeling okay?" she inquired.

"A little groggy, but otherwise, fine."

"I was just going to call room service. Are you hungry?"

"I'm ravenous. I'd like something with lots of fat and empty calories," he confessed.

Jessie smiled at his confession. "That sounds like an order for a burger and fries to me."

"That would be great."

Jessie picked up the phone and dialed Room Service to place their order.

Before too much time had elapsed, there was a knock at the door, announcing the arrival of their food.

Ray felt like getting out of bed and going to the small dining table in the kitchenette to eat his food. Then Jessie blessed the food, and they began their meal.

When they had finished eating, Ray decided that he would get ready for bed. Reminding him that she needed to change his bandage before he went to sleep, she asked him to call her when he was back in bed.

While he was in the bathroom, Jessie stacked their dishes on the tray and put it out in the hall.

Then she sat down and contemplated something that had been bothering her ever since the shooting – the fact that Ray had not made a profession of faith. She felt led to speak to him about it again.

In a few minutes, she heard Ray calling her name and got up to check on him. He was lying in bed with the covers pulled up to his bare chest. Jessie went over to the table where she had laid out the medical supplies that she would need for changing his dressing. Picking them up, she went and sat on the side of the bed.

Carefully and gently she removed the sterile strip from his wound. Then she doused a cotton swab with rubbing alcohol to clean the area.

She looked at him and warned, "This may sting a bit."

He merely smiled in response and then winced as she began swabbing the wound. Also the nurse had given her a salve to speed up the healing process, which she spread on the wound before using a fresh sterile strip. The dressing was complete.

The entire time that she had been working, Ray studied Jessie's face. Gently smoothing the bandage with her palm, she glanced up to see him watching her. Since she seemed to have his attention, she decided that now was the time to speak with him about Christ.

"Can I talk to you for a minute, Ray?" she asked, a tentative note in her voice.

"Sure," he replied.

As she began to speak, her eyes filled with tears. "The other day, my worst fears were almost realized – that you would die without Christ. And you would have died trying to save my life. I couldn't have borne it if that had happened, Ray!"

With the back of her hand, she wiped away the tears from her eyes and continued, "We all have to die the first death. I know that. I just don't want you to face the second one – the one that is the just penalty for our sins. That would be hell and eternal death. Helen doesn't have to face that one; I don't have to face it; no one who has accepted Christ as Savior has to face the second death, because Jesus faced it for us and overcame it. Do you understand that, Ray?"

"I think so," he said quietly. Then, "What was it you said the other night about being saved?"

Jessie thought back to that night. "I told you that Helen was saved because she believed on the Lord Jesus Christ. She was convinced that she was a sinner in need of a Savior. We all have to come to that realization, and then she trusted Christ to save her and take away the penalty for her sins. Once she did that, she made Him Lord of her life. I'm sure you noticed a change in her priorities, because she was following His will."

"I did notice, though she never once preached to me or tried to make me do something I didn't want to do. But she *was* different. I realize now that it was the same difference I see in you – your concern for others, your generosity, your sweetness, your faith. Jessie, I want that difference, too," he choked, with tears in his own eyes.

"Will you say that prayer with me now, Ray?"

"Yes, please," he whispered.

Jessie knelt beside the bed and, taking his hand in hers, asked him to repeat after her. She prayed, "Lord, I believe that I am a sinner. I confess my sin to You and trust You to save me. I make You Lord of my life. Amen."

When she raised her head, he asked, "What do I do now?"

"If you prayed that prayer from your heart, you are saved. All you have to do is wait for Him to tell you what to do? His Spirit is in you now, and He will begin to teach you and lead you in what He wants you to do," she told him.

"I *did* pray from my heart, Jessie. I meant it," he admitted to her.

"Oh, Ray! I'm so glad!" Still holding his hand in hers, her eyes glowed with pure joy.

"Thanks for caring so much," he responded.

Sensing that Ray was tired, Jessie smiled and let go of his hand. As she got up from her knees, she bent over him and kissed him on the cheek.

"Goodnight, Ray," was all she said.

"Goodnight," he returned, sleep not far away.

Jessie left the door opened a crack so that she could hear him if he called. Then, saying a prayer of thanksgiving, she went to bed. Since they had an eleven o'clock flight to Los Angeles, they would both need a good night's rest.

Chapter 18

When they arrived at the airport, Jessie insisted that she let Ray out at the terminal because she felt that the walk would be too much for him. Leaving their bags with him, she went to park the car.

He waited for her at the door to the terminal, and they entered the building together. Once they'd cleared security, they were finally able to board the plane. Jessie kept glancing at Ray to see if it was all too much for him. Ray knew what she was doing and told her that he was fine.

After takeoff, he smiled at her and said, "By the way, I've been meaning to ask you something about the shooting. You don't have to talk about it if you don't want to."

"I don't mind. If anybody has a right to ask questions, you do," she replied candidly.

Studying her face to gauge her reaction, he asked, "Why didn't Greg shoot you?"

She thought back to that awful morning and acknowledged, "He was taking aim at you, and all I could think of to stop him was a karate kick to his arm to dislodge the gun from his hand. Imagine my surprise when it worked! That's why he lunged at me and fell to his d-death." She still had a hard time dealing with that fact.

"You saved both our lives, Jessie!"

"You saved mine first," she responded with a smile.

Another thought occurred to him. "I didn't know that you knew the martial arts."

"I don't," she confessed.

"Then how...? Don't tell me. You got it from Dr. Laura," he guessed sarcastically.

"No. You think you're being funny, but Dr. Laura actually *does* have a black belt in karate," she informed him.

"So where *did* you get the move?" he pressed.

"Never mind. You'll just laugh at me," she refused to tell him.

"I won't laugh," Ray promised. "Tell me. Please."

Giving in to the inevitable, she remarked, "Oh, all right. I saw it on 'Walker, Texas Ranger' once or twice."

In an effort to keep his promise not to laugh, Ray bit his lower lip. But he couldn't seem to stop himself. He started to chuckle, and then he threw back his head and roared with laughter. Rather than being offended, Jessie joined him in laughing at her habit of picking up tidbits of information from her favorite celebrities. She thought what a beautiful sound his laughter was, and anything that made him produce that sound was well worth the effort!

As the stewardess passed by their seats, she noted with appreciation the handsome man and the lovely young woman laughing with such abandon. She thought that they made a very striking couple.

"Oh, Jessie! You're priceless!" he was finally able to say.

"Is that why you wanted me to come along? To provide entertainment?" she asked, still smiling.

He shook his head and replied cheekily, "No, your entertainment value is just a bonus."

They carried on an amiable conversation for a while, and since neither one wanted any lunch, Ray leaned his seat back and drifted off to sleep.

When the 'Fasten Seatbelts' light flashed on and the plane was ready to begin its approach to LAX, Jessie woke him.

He stretched and, fastening his seatbelt, apologized, "I'm sorry. I haven't been very good company, have I?"

"You're forgiven. Besides, I'd be surprised if you weren't tired. It's going to take some time for you to get over this," she excused him.

After the plane had landed and they had made their way to Ray's car, he informed her that she would have to drive.

"I just don't think I can handle it yet. I'm still a little woozy," he admitted.

"You want *me* to drive on the L. A. Freeway?" She was incredulous.

"Sure. You're an excellent driver, so I have no doubt that you can do it," he assured her.

With much trepidation, Jessie got into the driver's seat and held out a shaking hand for the keys. After adjusting the seat and the mirrors, she cranked the car and carefully eased her way out of the parking lot. Once the parking fee had been paid, she drove to the freeway and got on to the ramp that would take them into all that traffic on the way to pick up his kids.

Because it was not during rush hour, she found that it was really not much worse than driving in Memphis, and, following Ray's directions, got to his mother-in-law's house without incident.

When she turned in to the driveway and stopped, Jessie heaved a sigh of relief.

"Relax, Jessie. You did great!" he complimented her.

They got out of the car. Then he led her to the front door and rang the doorbell. The fleeting thought crossed Ray's mind about how the mother of the woman he had loved for so many years would react to the woman he loved now.

Lorraine answered the door and greeted him. Ray turned to introduce them, "Jessie, this is Helen's mother, Lorraine Davis. Lorraine, Jessica Martin."

She eyed Jessie a little coolly, but Jessie stepped forward to embrace Lorraine and declared with obvious sincerity and warmth, "Oh, Mrs. Davis! I'm so glad to finally meet you! I'd like to tell you how sorry I was to hear about Helen's death. She was without a doubt the most beautiful human being I've ever known."

Apparently, Lorraine was completely captivated by Jessie. Her coolness was replaced by a warm, welcoming smile as she returned the embrace. "Thank you, Dear. That's so kind of you. I can see now why my grandchildren have been singing your praises ever since they got here."

Lorraine led them inside through the foyer into the living room and called the children, who came running to greet their dad and Jessie. Sanson was there, too, ecstatically wagging his tail in greeting.

Maggie grabbed Jessie around the waist and squeezed her hard. Then she did the same to her daddy.

"I was so worried about you!" she cried.

Unable to pick her up, Ray squatted down beside her and told her, "I know, Pumpkin. I'm sorry that I worried you."

"That's okay, Daddy, but please, don't do it again!" she begged.

"I won't," he promised.

After visiting for a few moments longer, Ray decided that it was time to go home. As they were taking their leave, Jessie told Lorraine, "I hope I get to see you again before I leave, Mrs. Davis."

"Please, call me Lorraine," she invited.

She countered with, "And I'm Jessie."

Jessie was really nervous about driving Ray's kids to his house in the Malibu Beach area, but they arrived safely, nonetheless. Impressed by the Mediterranean style house with white stucco walls and red-tiled roof, Jessie turned into the driveway and opened the garage door. As she pulled into the garage, she remarked on the beauty of his home to Ray.

"Wait until you see the ocean view," he advised.

"I've never seen the Pacific Ocean before, so this has been a first for me."

Ray glanced at her and before he could stop himself, said, "Another virgin experience?"

Seeing her face flame at his remark, he repented immediately. "I'm sorry, Jessie. I shouldn't have said that." He sometimes forgot that they were not on intimate terms – *yet*. Though he was now a Christian, he could tell that he was going to have a battle with his tongue where she was concerned.

"That's all right. I forgive you."

Everyone grabbed a bag and headed to the door, which Ray unlocked. Once they were inside, the kids dragged Jessie out onto the deck. The house sat on a craggy cliff overlooking the ocean and miles of beautiful sandy beaches. Leading off the deck was a staircase that gave way to a lower deck and more steps down to the beach.

Jessie was duly appreciative of the fantastic view.

When they felt that she'd spent sufficient time outside on the deck, the kids showed Jessie the guestroom where she would be sleeping. Then they were anxious to show her their rooms. Even though she was tired, she made the effort to see the children's rooms and marvel over their stuff.

Finally she was able to sit on the couch in the family room. Coming into the room, Ray sat down beside her. With a lazy smile, he said, "You look tired."

"So do you," she returned.

"It *has* been a long day, hasn't it?" He studied her for a moment before he continued, "So how do you like California so far?"

"It's beautiful, but it seems so busy. Everybody seems in such a hurry. I think I'm just used to a slower pace," she supposed.

Ray thought about asking her if she could get used to California, but he decided that the time was not right. Besides, the children chose that moment to come in.

"What's for dinner?" Bret inquired.

"To tell the truth, I haven't even thought about it," he admitted, as he started to get up.

Jessie volunteered, "Let me help, Ray. You don't need to overdo things."

They both went to the kitchen and scrounged around for food in the freezer and the pantry. Since the Hansons had been gone several weeks, nothing in the refrigerator was fit for human consumption.

"I believe a visit to the grocery store would be in order," Jessie suggested.

"I'll put it on the list for tomorrow. I don't believe either of us is up to it this evening."

By this time, Ray was beginning to look pale, and Jessie made him sit at the island while she and the kids prepared the meal. Locating all the ingredients for spaghetti, they soon had the food simmering on the stove.

When Mara and Maggie had finished setting the table, the food was ready to eat. Of course Maggie wanted to say the blessing and had everyone hold hands. She prayed, "Lord, I thank you that Daddy and Jessie are safe and thank you for this food. Amen."

The meal turned out to be quite delicious and became a kind of celebration that they were all safe and together again. There was a lot of joking and laughter as if they were all one family – the same way it had been in Mississippi.

After the dishes had been cleared away, Jessie suggested that before Ray went to bed she needed to change his dressing again. All the children wanted to help her. Jessie knew that it was out of concern for what had happened to their dad and didn't think that it would do any harm. So when he had showered and gotten into bed, they all gathered in his room to help with the dressing.

She showed them how to gently pull the old bandage off without making their father scream in pain. Then she took out a cotton swab and let Becca clean the wound with alcohol. Mara offered to put on the salve, and Bret proved that he could put on the clean sterile strip. The whole time, Maggie held her daddy's hand to comfort him.

"There. That's all there is to it. Y'all did great!" she complimented her aides.

Ray teased, "I was getting so much professional attention that for a minute I thought I was back in the hospital."

For a change, the kids tucked in their dad and carefully hugged him goodnight. Turning the lights out as she left, Jessie told him, "Goodnight, Ray."

"Goodnight, Jessie." He lay there thinking how natural it was to have her in his home and how much she loved his children. Since he was not used to praying, he made what he felt was a crude attempt at talking to God.

"God, please make Jessie love me and be my wife and a mother to my children. Amen," he said as he drifted off to sleep.

Jessie had been so tired that after she had tucked in the children and showered, she had gone straight to bed and had not moved all night long. She awoke, feeling refreshed and ready for the day.

When she had dressed in blue jeans and a t-shirt, she headed down to the kitchen to see what she could fix for breakfast. Fortunately, she found biscuits, butter, and orange juice in the freezer. This time, that would have to suffice.

While the biscuits were baking, she went upstairs to get everyone up. As usual, the kids complained sleepily, but got up nevertheless.

She knocked on Ray's bedroom door and waited. When she heard his "come in," she stuck her head in and informed him that breakfast would be ready in a few minutes.

"Thanks, Jessie. I really appreciate the help, but you're the guest. I should be waiting on you," he lamented.

"I don't mind helping you. Besides, y'all waited on me for a while back home," she reminded him. For a moment, her face seemed to cloud over as she thought about her home that was no more, but she shook it off and told him she'd better check on the biscuits.

By the time they had all trudged to the table, Jessie had everything ready. After Mara's blessing, they enjoyed a leisurely breakfast and made plans for the day, which definitely included a trip to the grocery store.

About mid-morning, the doorbell rang, and since Jessie appeared to be the only one on the first floor, she went to answer it.

Looking out one of the windows adjacent to the door, she saw the most beautiful woman she had ever seen standing there on the stoop. Jessie's instincts told her that this blue-eyed, raven-haired beauty was Alissa.

She opened the door and smiled at the stranger. "May I help you?" she inquired politely.

Alissa's smile had faded when Jessie opened the door.

"*Who* are *you?*" she asked rudely.

Jessie was able to keep her smile pinned to her face and replied, "I'm

Jessica Martin, a friend of the family. How can I help you?"

"I'd like to see Ray. I believe he's expecting me. I'm Alissa Dubois, a *very* good friend of Ray's," she said suggestively.

Jessie had been right about the woman's identity, and the fact that Ray had gotten in touch with her immediately upon his return cut through her heart like a knife. Her innate politeness kept her from slamming the door in Alissa's face. Opening the door wide, she invited her inside. She led Alissa into the living room and told her that she would go inform Ray of her presence.

When she started upstairs to find Ray, he started down. She felt as if she could burst into tears at any moment, but she valiantly controlled herself. As he pulled even with her, he got a good look at her face and said, "Jessie, what's wrong?"

"Your girlfriend is here," she accused. Then she turned to go.

Grabbing her arm, he asked in confusion, "What are you talking about?"

"Alissa's waiting for you in the living room," she informed him. Shaking off his hold on her arm, she turned and ran out to the deck. By the time she reached the lower deck, she had to stop. Finding a spot at a table with an umbrella where she felt she would be pretty well hidden from the kids, she let the tears fall.

Jessie wasn't sure what she had expected from Ray, but it had seemed as if they were getting closer. Though she had little experience in judging such things, the times he had kissed her seemed to mean something to them both. Now he had brought Alissa back into his life, and Jessie could see that she could not possibly compete with her for Ray's affection.

When Jessie had told him that Alissa was in the living room, Ray had winced. *What's she doing here?* he wondered, irritated by the unwelcome interruption to his life. He could tell that Jessie was upset with him. Although his instinct was to go after her, he knew that he had to handle the problem in the living room first.

As he entered the room, he saw the same beautiful woman with whom he had been so infatuated only a few short years ago. Looking at her now, he was totally unaffected by her beauty.

"Why are you here, Alissa?" he greeted her.

She pouted and whined like a little girl, "Ray! Aren't you glad to see me?"

"Not particularly. *Why* are you here?" he repeated.

"I talked to your assistant, and he said you were home and that you had been shot by some lunatic," she defended herself.

Ray reminded himself to have a talk with his assistant about giving out private information.

"That's all true, but I'll ask the question one more time – Why are you here?" Beginning to lose patience with her, he wondered what he had ever seen in her.

"I just wanted to see how you were and find out if you were still interested in a relationship," she replied. While he had been gone, she had recalled the attraction she'd always felt for him. She'd realized how much she still wanted him.

Ray took a deep breath and tried to send up a quick prayer for guidance. How should a Christian handle such a situation?

He told her gently, but firmly, "I'm not that person anymore, Alissa. I've turned to faith in Christ. So the kind of relationship you're talking about is out of the question. There's only one person with whom I'm interested in having any relationship, and that's Jessie Martin. I'm going to ask her to marry me."

"That milk toast? Ray, you've got to be kidding!" she gasped.

"Jessie's *not* milk toast. Cinnamon toast, maybe, but definitely not milk toast," he defended Jessie with a tender smile.

Alissa was completely disgusted and told him, "You'll be sorry, Ray Hanson! I'm through! I've given you more chances than I would ever give any other man because I thought you were worth it. Apparently I was wrong!" With that, she stormed out of the house, slamming the door behind her.

As soon as she was gone, Ray went in search of Jessie. Venturing out onto the deck, he scanned the beach for her. When he didn't see her, he began to get worried. He knew she had come out here, but where could she be? He started down the steps to the lower deck.

Before he could continue down to the beach, he heard someone crying. Then he saw her at the table with her head resting on her arms.

He went over to the table and pulled up a chair to sit beside her. He placed his hand on her shoulder and asked tenderly, "Jessie, what's wrong?"

"Nothing," she denied as she shrank from his touch.

"Something is bothering you. Please tell me," he begged.

"You couldn't wait to call Alissa!" she accused him.

He clarified with a broad grin, "This is all about Alissa's coming here?"

She ignored the question. "She's beautiful. I understand why you're in love with her," she mumbled her response and got up from the table to go stand by the deck rail. As she gazed out over the ocean, Ray came to stand behind her.

Sliding his arm around her waist, he pulled her back against his chest and whispered in her ear, "In the first place, I *didn't* call Alissa. She called my assistant, and he told her I was back home. In the second place, I'm not in love with her." He paused and then continued, "How could I be when I'm in love with you?"

"With *me*?" she echoed, her tone one of disbelief.

"With you," he breathed against her neck as he began to nuzzle the softness of her skin.

"Oh, Ray," she moaned. She turned in his arms and raised her lips to meet his in a passionate kiss.

When he finally broke their kiss, he demanded, "Say it!"

She didn't even pretend not to know what he meant. "I love you," she admitted, her tears turning to tears of joy.

He teased her lips over and over again with short, warm kisses. Finally overcome with passion, she put her hands behind his neck and kissed him until they both had to come up for air.

"Oh, Ray! This makes me happy and sad at the same time!"

"Why are you sad?" he asked, smiling into her eyes.

"When I think of what you and Helen and the kids had to lose for me to obtain my happiness, it makes me sad," she confessed.

JESSIE'S WAY: THE LAST WORD

That was Jessie! Always concerned about others! It was one of the things that he loved most about her. "I believe that Helen is smiling down on us now, because she knows we love each other and you love her children as if they were your own," he told her.

"She knew about me, you know," she remarked shyly.

"Knew what?" he asked, curious about her statement.

Jessie sighed and revealed the secret that she'd kept hidden from him for so long. "That I was in love with you."

"What are you talking about? How could she possibly know about this?" he eyed her skeptically.

She held his gaze, as she declared, "I started falling in love with you when I first talked to you on the phone. By the time I had met you, I was completely in love with you. When filming of 'The Sixth Commandment' wrapped and you kissed me goodbye, Helen guessed my feelings from the expression on my face. No matter how I tried to fight it, my love for you has never faded. It's just gotten stronger."

"But, Jessie...You did everything you could to save my marriage! Why would you do that?" he breathed in confusion.

"I wanted the Hansons to be happy – the kids and Helen, but especially you. I've seen so many families torn up by divorce. Everyone suffers. You would have gotten to see your children a couple of times a month. They needed their daddy, and their daddy needed them. Besides, you weren't ever going to be interested in the old Jessie."

He rested his forehead against hers, and whispered huskily, "I loved you back then, but as a friend. Since you came back into my life, I've come to love you with all my heart. You've given so much to my family and lost so much in your life. After we're married, I want us to rebuild your house in Mississippi."

"Married?" Jessie managed breathlessly.

"Of course. It's the right thing to do," he responded.

"Now *you* sound like Dr. Laura," she smiled up at him.

He pulled her closer, and they kissed one more time. When Ray lifted his head, Jessie noticed movement on the deck steps. She grinned at him and said, "I think we're being watched."

Ray turned around to see five pairs of eyes, including the dog, watching their every move.

Jessie wondered aloud, "What will the kids think of all this?"

"Let's go find out. But I know already that they love you. I believe they will love having you for a step-mother," he assured her.

He led her over to the steps, where they sat down. The children gathered around with Maggie sitting between Jessie and her daddy. Becca wore a knowing smile of approval, but the other kids looked a bit confused.

"Daddy, why were you kissing Jessie?" Mara began the questions.

"Because I'm in love with her and she's in love with me," he explained simply.

Bret wanted to know, "Are you guys gonna get married?"

"If you kids are okay with that, then, yes, we are?"

Everyone except Maggie chimed in with responses like *Wow!* and *Great!*

Finally, Maggie asked somewhat hesitantly, "Jessie, are you going to make babies with my daddy?"

Placing her arms around the child, Jessie replied gently, "No, Sweetheart. I can't make babies."

A cloud seemed to lift from Maggie's face as she squeezed her tightly and offered with a child's directness, "I'll be your baby, Jessie!"

With tears in her eyes, Jessie glanced at Ray, who seemed to be a little teary-eyed himself. Neither one was able to say anything. This time, Maggie had the last word.

Printed in the United States
42645LVS00007B/115

9 781424 111633